SNATCH & CATCH

SNATCH & CATCH

JOHN F. GORMAN

GMS Publishing

*Copyright © 2024 by GMS Publishing
All Rights Reserved.
Manuscript formatted by Kevin Theis, Fort Raphael Publishing Co.
Front Cover Artwork and Graphics by Paul Stroili,
Touchstone Graphic Design, Chicago*

The story, all names, characters, and incidents portrayed in this book are fictitious. No identification with actual persons (living or deceased), places, buildings, and products is intended or should be inferred.

PART ONE

The Snatch

CHAPTER 1

As Sylvia Ortiz opened the Jan. 10, 2011, edition of the Chicago Sun-Times, she knew in an instant how her day would go.

"Mom slashed, twin toddlers snatched, cops scratch," the S-T headline blared.

As the Chief of Detectives for the Chicago Police Department, Ortiz recognized a heater case when she saw one, especially with the mayoral election just a month away. It was just 6:05 a.m.

She was only in the fourth graf when she realized just how hot this case would be. The "mom" was the wife of Ald. Tom Byrnes, chairman of the City Council Finance Committee and first-term Mayor Edwina Borowski's most loyal supporter.

Just then, her cell vibrated and belched out a loud ring, the old-fashioned kind. It was her boss, the Superintendent of Police.

"Yes, Superintendent, I'm just reading it. Yes, sir. 8 a.m., your office. I'll be there," she said.

Heater cases were nothing new for Ortiz. As a young detective, she and her partner, Mike Halloran, had worked on the ultimate heater case--the murder of the State's Attorney's daughter. When they solved that case, it had turbo-charged her career. At just 40 years old, she'd made Chief of D's after a string of hard-earned promotions.

But a series of carjackings in tony Streeterville, Lincoln Park and her own Gold Coast neighborhood had the city on edge. Ortiz knew that the Chief of Patrol would take most of the heat today, but she was in the eye of the storm with the job of tracking down and arresting these thugs, who pulled up in stolen cars and hijacked luxury cars at gunpoint in broad daylight. Some of the armed carjackers had been as young as 12.

Moments after she disconnected from the supe, her husband, Joe Ortiz, a successful personal injury attorney and former prosecutor, grabbed the coffee pot, then spotted the blaring headline and the worried look on his wife's face.

"Jeez, looks awful. Who's on the phone so early?" he asked. "The boss, Superintendent Wallace himself. Ordered me to his office at 8 a.m. Can you get Elly off to school?" Ortiz asked, gazing out the front window to the accumulating snow on Dearborn Parkway. "The snow's getting too deep to walk to school."

The couple had graduated from their comfortable Tudor in Edgebrook to a vintage three-flat in the Gold Coast just a baseball throw from Restoration Hardware to the south and two good baseball tosses to the Cardinal's mansion on State Street at North Avenue. Most importantly, they were now just a block and a half from the Latin School, an indulgence they made for the kids' sake shortly after Joe won a historic $25.8 million verdict in a double amputation case.

Now looking sharp in her dress blues, Ortiz shouted, "Good luck on your geometry test" to her daughter, Elly, through a partially closed bathroom door.

"Bye, mom. Love ya," yelled Elly, a 15-year-old sophomore at the elite school at the corner of North Avenue and Clark Street.

Now outside, Ortiz popped the trunk on the black Crown Vic that her rank got her and grabbed the scraper and brush. She only slightly resented the sole slot going to Joe's slick Mercedes Class M SUV in the one-car garage that came with the vintage home, built at the turn of the 19th Century.

As she finished sweeping the snow off her windshield, she noticed a young Latina doing the same to the side windows of a beat-up gray Dodge van across the street.

"Probably a Molly's Maid," she thought. Then caught herself.

"Don't be such a smug, second-generation bitch," Ortiz whispered to herself before jumping in and heading to the Outer Drive.

Despite the falling snow and partially plowed roads, she pulled into the lot at police headquarters at 35th Street and Michigan Avenue by 7:30. She waved to the patrolman at the gate and slipped into her slot marked "C of D." Before leaving the car, she called her assistant, Sgt. Allen Thompson, and told him to summon the First and Third Area commanders to her fourth-floor conference room for a 4:30 p.m. meeting.

"And tell them to bring some fresh ideas to catch these gun-toting punks in the act," Ortiz barked.

Alone in the elevator on the way to her office, right beneath the supe's fifth-floor sprawl, Ortiz made her mental checklist: Get the incident report; talk to the dicks handling the alderman's wife's case; get last year's carjack stats through December versus this year's; ask about possible videos.

As she entered her office, she told Thompson her laundry list of needs, ending with the videos.

"I'm on it, boss," he responded and started typing furiously at his computer.

After quickly scrolling through her email, she walked up a flight to the supe's office. The Chief of Patrol, Edward Kassos, was slumped comfortably on a couch outside the supe's office, waiting to be beckoned. He and Ortiz nodded to each other. The less said outside the supe's office, the better. Dubbed "Easy Ed" by the troops and his peers, Kassos was six months from full retirement and would make no sudden moves that would derail his dreams of a cushy retirement to his two-bedroom, oceanfront condo in Fort Myers.

"He'll see you now," the Superintendent's secretary announced, then pushed the door open for Ortiz and Kassos, who let the Chief of Detectives enter first, perhaps to be the first to catch the boss's wrath. Perhaps Kassos, a savvy Southeast Side product, also thought the boss would be easier on a woman.

Not so.

"Ortiz, what in the holy hell are your dicks doing out there? The city is besieged by roving gangs of carjackers, and where are the arrests?"

bellowed Rudy Wallace, a wiry African-American in his early 60s and recently hired away from Cincinnati to replace a Latino superintendent who was found to have family ties to Mexican organized crime. Wallace remained seated as he let the two junior bosses stand, both with their hands folded in front.

"And Kassos, are your guys just sitting in their cars munching donuts, sipping lattes and smoking cigarettes. I mean, what the fuck is going on that an alderman's wife in a so-called safe neighborhood gets slashed and jacked in broad daylight, with two kids in the car? And don't start whining about staff shortages. That's my problem and the mayor's. And speaking of the mayor, she's all up my ass this morning at 5:15 a.m., screaming with a full head of caffeine-infused wrath. No matter the punks spotted the twins in the back after two blocks and abandoned the car."

"Sit," he finally ordered, glaring at two of his top operatives.

"This will not be a Q & A. I want you two to get the word out to the troops. Bust these guys, the peewees, teens, young bangers. All of them. If they look suspicious in a beat-up car, curb 'em. Ask 'em where they're going. If they hesitate, order them out at gunpoint and frisk 'em.

"Fuck the ACLU! We need boots on the ground, in the cars and in the faces of these punks. Tell 'em to pretend they're pulling over a suspected cop killer. I mean business even if it gets messy. I'll take the heat, and it'll be less than the incendiary tongue-lashing I got this ayem from Her Honor.

"Got it? Dismissed!"

Wordlessly, Ortiz and Kassos rose and filed out and continued mute to the elevator. The fifth floor was not a place for idle chatter or questioning the boss's orders. Once the elevator door closed and they were alone, Ortiz broke the silence.

"Jesus F Christ. I've never seen him so pissed. But it sounded like he was busting your ass more than mine," Ortiz said. "You're Patrol, but I'm gonna have to ratchet up my guys, too, to make them hypervigilant as they tool around town investigating even a retail theft."

"Yeah, that's my read too. First time I heard a supe say 'Fuck the ACLU' but perhaps the thousandth time I've heard a cop say it," Kassos smiled and winked at Ortiz.

As the elevator doors opened on Four, a half dozen captains, lieutenants and sergeants stood ready to board.

Capt. Ed Riley eyed Ortiz, and asked, "Chief, you got a minute?"

"Not this morning, Ed. Call me later," she said as she hustled to her office. For the rest of the day, she read "urgent" reports, answered her emails, compared notes with Kassos via cell phone and squeezed in a quick chat about the kids with Joe.

At 4:31, she headed to her conference room but stopped in her tracks when Thompson told her Area 1 Commander Rocco Roy was running 10 minutes late due to a double homicide of twin sisters in Washington Park that had just come in.

"Tell him we'll bring him in by teleconference," Ortiz instructed. Just then, Area 3 Commander Sheila Wrenn got off the elevator and greeted her boss.

"Chief. Long day?" asked Wrenn, a sturdy redhead in her mid-50s carrying a thick file of incident reports and supplemental reports her dicks had filed.

Inside her conference room, Ortiz asked Wrenn what her plans were to help curb the avalanche of carjackings, shootings and knifings.

"Well, boss, as I'm guessing you'd agree, it seems like the solution rests mostly with Patrol, but you wanted my ideas, and I have a few for the dicks in my Area," Wrenn said. Sitting at the head of a long walnut conference table, Ortiz nodded and waited.

Wrenn said she would lean on the dicks with their Black gang informants to pressure gangbangers awaiting trial for info on who was behind the jackings and would tell all the sergeants to make their troops extra alert as they rode around the city on their investigations. Black, she stressed, because that was the description of the jackers in 95 percent of the assaults and robberies. Not racism: fact, Wrenn said. Ortiz nodded.

Ortiz cleared her throat, then began her suggestions. Just then Thompson walked in to inform his boss that Roy was on line 2.

"Hi Boss, very sorry I'm late, but two bodies needed my attention. Young sisters—just 13," Roy said. Ortiz said okay and asked Wrenn to repeat her suggestions.

"All good ideas, and I'll steal them," said Roy, a hardworking boss.

"Those are fine first steps. But let's also start digging through the old files to find shitheads who've done this in the past five, 10 years. They may be out of the joint and the ones launching the peewees. And check with the Auto Theft guys to see if they have a likely chop shop where the gangs may be bringing in the Benzes and BMWs and Jags for a strip job," Ortiz said.

"I've met with a very unhappy superintendent who earlier this morning had a new asshole cut for him by the mayor, who, you may be aware, is running for reelection. The onus is on Patrol, but I want to make sure the dicks are on high alert and make major contributions to solving this shitstorm..." Ortiz continued until interrupted by a text message from her Elly.

Very strange, Ortiz thought as she grasped her cell and clicked on the text. Elly knows not to bother her at work.

She raised her right index finger to Wrenn as she opened the text to see a photo attached to a message.

"We have your daughter and she not be harmed if you follow instructions I send from a burner phone tomorrow morning. You no wanna call the FBI."

Wide-eyed and mute, Ortiz opened the photo and saw Elly, her mouth and ankles duct taped in the back of a cluttered van, her youngest child's eyes terrified and filled with tears.

"Family emergency. Meeting's over. Carry on," Ortiz said as she rushed to her office, past Thompson but not before telling Thompson to pass the Byrnes case and hijackings problem to Kassos.

She slid behind her desk and grabbed her cell to hit the second speed dial button to Elly's godfather and the best cop she'd ever known.

CHAPTER 2

Just a half hour after finishing basketball practice at the Latin School, Elly was trudging through a half foot of freshly fallen snow and checking her cell for texts as she turned east on Schiller Street off Clark.

As she crossed the alley between Clark and Dearborn Streets, she was suddenly lifted off her feet at the same time a strong hand clamped down on her mouth.

"Don't scream or struggle and you no get hurt," the man whispered as he shoved a black semi-automatic pistol in front of her face.

In that terrifying instant, she recalled the sage advice doled out repeatedly over the years by her parents--one a cop, the other a former prosecutor: If it's a strong-armed assault, kick him in the balls or go for the eyes; if it's a knife, try to run; if it's a gun, you comply.

She stopped struggling and lifted her right hand to signal "Okay."

In a swift move, the gunman dragged her to an open van's sliding door and pulled her backward onto the carpeted rear.

Inside, the gunman leaned back and tightened his grip on her throat as he pulled her back further into the van in the darkened alley. Once secure with the door closed, he whispered to the driver: "Come back here and tape her hands, then her ankles, and then start driving."

Her brown eyes equally terrified beneath her ski mask, the young Latina driver took the gray duct tape from the front seat, climbed back into the rear and began taping Elly's wrists, then ankles.

Back at the wheel, the driver quickly turned right onto Schiller, heading east till she hit the Inner Drive and turned left till she reached the Outer Drive's northbound entrance at LaSalle Drive. The gunman had planned carefully to time his abduction after a large snowfall, so his license plates were covered with snow. The weather also gave cover to wearing his ski mask; nothing too strange about wearing one in a Chicago winter.

"I going to relax my hold on your throat so I can put a piece of tape across your mouth. If you scream, I will slice your face and then you be real ugly for rest of yo' life. You no want that. Do you?" Elly shook her head no. She was beginning to think clearly now about her situation and making mental notes. After taping her mouth, the gunman slipped a ski mask over her head with the eyeholes taped shut.

The gunman passed Elly's phone to the driver and told her to pull off briefly at the Fullerton Avenue exit to toss the phone. By this time, the weather had turned as a south wind had brought heavy rain.

Scared but not paralyzed in terror, Elly gathered her thoughts.

"Okay, turned right out of the alley and then left off Schiller, then obviously we are on the Drive headed north. Let's keep track. Remember Mom always lectured the 'devil's in the details.' Yeah, but the devil's also in this van."

So, Elly started counting the time on the Drive. Her mom had told her years ago when she was timing her running, that if she counted one-one hundred up to 76-one-hundred, that would make a minute. At 75-one hundred, the van slowed almost to a stop. She heard the driver's window open and shut before the van started moving again.

At 532-one hundred, the van slowed almost to a stop, and turned right.

We must have hit the end of the Drive--at Hollywood? She reasoned.

After the van had turned a hard right, it stopped after a count of 38-one hundred. Then again, the same length of time before another stop. Then a longer stretch of about 55-one-hundreds and a stop followed by a left turn. Two more stops (stop signs?) and she heard what sounded like an L train passing over, then another stop. For about a minute.

Stop light, she figured. Two more stop signs, a left turn after three seconds, and another right turn and eight seconds of slow driving till they slowed to turn left as they arrived and stopped at their destination after rolling over some gravel or broken asphalt. But where?

CHAPTER 3

When Mary Beth O'Malley's body parts were found in two 55-gallon drums in Montrose Harbor in the fading days of September of 1978, Mike Halloran had been in the Police Academy.

But Mary Beth was a St. Scholastica's girl, a St. Margaret Mary's grad, the kind of girl that Halloran dated as a North Side Catholic and a St. Gertrude's alum. He didn't know her or her family, but he knew many like her.

As the details leaked out in the Tribune and the Sun-Times, the city was shocked at the same level as it had been by Richard Speck's butchery of the eight student nurses on the South Side a dozen years earlier.

Mary Beth's head and torso had been found in one barrel, her arms and legs in the other barrel. The killer had apparently used a chisel and hammer to cut slats 8 inches deep in the sides of the barrels, and then bent them inward to seal the body parts inside.

Mary Beth, a 16-year-old junior, had last been seen after she finished her 3-10 shift at the Candlelight restaurant on Western Avenue and was headed to her home at 2548 W. Fargo Ave.

The case had been sensational and exhaustively investigated for months, then years, but no one had ever been charged. Mike Halloran's new partner, Area 3 Detective Jane Thoma, a six-year vet, read the reports and the news clips, so knew this cold case was huge, but ancient and would be nearly impossible to solve.

In this joint federal/CPD Cold Case squad, Halloran put the O'Malley murder on the top of his to-do list. Now as he stood in the massive warehouse on Damen Avenue on the near West Side sifting through the mountains of evidence from the O'Malley case, his muted cell went off as he examined one of the barrels. He ignored the call, then it went off again, and again, seconds apart. He picked it up finally and connected when he saw it was his old partner, Sylvia Ortiz, now his boss as Chief of D's and not someone to ignore, even if you were working on a joint federal task force.

"Syl, you must be missing my sharp Irish wit pretty bad, eh?" Halloran opened.

"Mike, someone snatched Elly. I need you. Now! Can you get to 35th Street post haste?" Ortiz pleaded.

"Ten minutes."

Halloran wasn't about to waste Ortiz's time with questions about where his goddaughter had been taken. He dropped everything and ran to his Jeep, yelling to Thoma and his new fed partner, FBI Special Agent Juan Ochoa, "Emergency. I'll call." Ochoa thumbed up. Thoma did the same. They shrugged at each other.

Eight minutes of weaving in and out of late rush hour traffic headed east past Sox park, he hoisted his star to security at police headquarters, parked in handicapped (at 5:45 p.m., he figured it was okay) and ran inside the building he usually tried to avoid and rushed past the exiting officers into the elevator to get to Ortiz's office.

Ortiz rose from her desk and brushed past a phalanx of commanders and other brass to embrace her old partner.

"Mike, Thank God you're here."

"Whattya got, Syl," Halloran said after dislodging himself from Ortiz's grasp.

"Here, Mike, look for yourself," Ortiz said, holding her phone up for Halloran to see. "It ain't much. And it's Elly's phone that we traced to a snowbank at Fullerton and the Drive where they tossed it after they sent the message."

"So, we can figure they're probably heading north and knew enough about you and Elly and the family routine, right" Halloran asked. Ortiz nodded.

"What's your game plan so far?" Halloran asked.

"Well, I was waiting for you and Joe..." Ortiz stopped, as Joe Ortiz rushed in and embraced his wife, tears welled up in his eyes. Theirs was a strong marriage, a highly successful professional one. But this was her domain even though Joe was a former prosecutor and an experienced litigator.

"Honey, what are we gonna..." Joe stopped, spotted Mike, and extended his hand, then hugged the long-time family friend. "Glad you're here."

"Okay. Joe, take a seat, please. Mike, I put together a quick plan I want to implement immediately and want your strong input and guidance," the Chief of D's said.

On the CPD side, the Patrol division was already out canvassing the neighborhood in newly falling rain two blocks either side of the Latin School at North and Clark, and two blocks either side of the Ortiz home, knocking on doors, looking for video cameras. Because it was a kidnapping, the FBI had been called in, which made it easy to slip Halloran in seamlessly with his cross-designation on the Cold Case Task Force.

The recovered phone was taken to the Illinois State Police lab on the near West Side to be examined for prints and DNA and to see what other calls may have been made before or after the kidnapper's call. Simultaneously, Ortiz had dispatched a detective to her home to grab her daughter's toothbrush to bring to the lab to extract a DNA sample for comparison.

"What else, Mike?" Ortiz said, turning to her longtime partner and the most experienced detective in the room. But his rank was just Detective and the room was now filled with CPD's top brass.

That didn't faze Halloran.

First, he looked again at Ortiz's phone and the photo of Elly with her hands and ankles taped and a ski mask over her head, the eye slots taped over.

"Great start, Syl. But we want to look at motive, too. Money and revenge. You have put a lot of assholes away, and Joe, you, too, as a prosecutor before you went into private practice. So, who threatened you? Who got out of the joint recently that did? Or even got out in the last year or so? Any letters, calls, emails, shouts in court as they were being led away in cuffs? Think back."

Halloran knew he had Ortiz's blessing and backing, so he plowed on.

"And Joe, I don't want to guilt you up, but you got a great settlement on the double amputee case a couple of years back, and that huge multimillion prize made the papers. Some of the bad guys can actually read," Halloran said.

"Yeah, Mike, I know, but I think it just made the Chicago Daily Law Bulletin," Joe said.

Halloran nodded and continued on a different track, but he knew the inmates had access to the law library and kept up with cases, and the "jailhouse lawyers" read the Law Bulletin voraciously.

"Let's assume these guys staked out the school and the home long enough to know a pattern of Elly's movements, and of both parents. So, let's make sure the uniforms check out the apartments in the morning too, when the residents may be home getting ready for work and the shift changes at the Potash Brothers on State where Elly would walk by every day. Did they see anyone parked out front every day? Did the apartment folks see any new people move in recently? What about the landlords?

"Right now, we have a heavy shoe-leather case. Agreed?" Halloran turned to Ortiz

"Thanks, Mike. And now FBI Special Agent in Charge of the Chicago office John Macel will give us the federal rundown."

CHAPTER 4

With just a slight nod, Ortiz got Halloran's attention, and they eased their way out of the office and down the hall to the empty conference room.

Ortiz closed the door behind her.

"Anytime the feds enter, you know, Mike, they think they're in charge. That will not be the case now, not with my daughter," Ortiz spat out, brown eyes flashing. "You and I are in charge. But we will take all the help in manpower, technology and science the feds can give us, right?"

The door was closed; the blinds were shut. Halloran moved in to grab his diminutive, longtime friend and partner in a quick bear hug. He stepped back and saw the tears welled up in this tough cop's eyes.

"We—you and I—will bring Elly home safe. You have my word," Halloran said, "but you're right, we can use all the help the feds can give us as long as they don't start bigfooting and fucking things up. But don't forget that with kidnapping, the feds got great resources and experience. But this will be delicate, Syl."

"Right, so here's how I see things for the next 12-24 hours," Ortiz said.

She then told Halloran to stop her if he disagreed as she outlined her plan: Let the uniforms do the canvass and file the reports, then wade through them—with Halloran as the point man sifting through the significant hits; Ortiz would personally interview Elly's friends in the next few hours, figuring they would be more comfortable with, but also more frightened of, her than just another cop; the sweep of the area for cameras and videos would be a priority, and that would be funneled back to the feds with their superior tech skills and equipment.

"Maybe one of the Outer Drive cameras caught the phone being tossed, unlikely but maybe," Halloran added. "And going against us is the six inches of snow that could cover up the license plate number, can't forget that even though that rain may now have melted it."

"Your rank is still Detective, but I'll let Chief of Patrol Kassos know that you are the acting deputy Chief of D's and all the incident reports are to flow through you, especially anything that jumps out in the next few hours or days, or God forbid, week. Check?" Ortiz said.

"Check."

Halloran thought of saying "mate" or asking if this meant a corner office and more money but knew that even with someone who knew his wicked and strange Irish sense of humor so well, this was not the time to crack wise.

"Right now, I'll talk to her friends, and you can check with Patrol, and then we wait for the call in the morning. Okay?" Ortiz asked.

"Will do, Syl. You'll worry, I know. But we know she's a smart and strong girl, and we will get her back. I swear."

* * * * *

Cold, scared, hungry and thirsty, Elly had dozed off but woke up in total darkness and tried to figure out her situation. She was fairly sure she was somewhere on the North Side. She knew she was in a basement apartment because she went down two steps into the apartment. She could hear distant sounds of a washer going through its cycle and the hum of a dryer or dryers. She knew her mom and Uncle Mike were on their way. She just had to do her part and remember everything she could to catch these two scumbags.

Just then the door opened, a light went on overhead, and the man entered.

"I gonna pull your gag down so you can drink and take a bite of this samich. You try bite me, and I hit you. Understand? Nod, if you do."

Elly nodded.

Jesus Martinez-Gomez pulled up Elly's ski mask slightly and roughly pulled off the tape from her mouth.

"Drink first," he said and thrust the water bottle into her mouth. Then he let her take a bite of a ham and cheese sandwich, chew, and then another swallow of water, another bite and a final drink of water. As he did this, Elly could see through the bottom of the tape a tattoo on his right hand of what looked like a snake's neck, maybe a cobra hood. But it was just part of a tat, she thought.

"Bastante," he growled, and took the food and drink away, retaping her mouth and pulling the ski mask back down. As he did, he began to slowly rub her right shoulder and then his hand crept down toward her breasts.

"Non la molestes," shouted Gomez's girlfriend, Leticia "Letty" Diaz, a 20-year-old waitress unfortunate enough to have hooked up with Gomez several months prior, as she entered the room and spotted Gomez's action.

"What you say, puta?" Gomez yelled and slapped Letty hard enough to throw her back through the open door.

Gomez followed her out and slapped her again; Elly heard her cry before he turned off the lights. Then total blackness again.

"Now, I go make the call. I be 30-40 minutes, maybe. Depend on traffic. Entiendes, puta mia?" Gomez barked, switching between English and his poor Spanish, referring to her as his whore.

"Si, si, mi amor," Letty responded, placating Gomez, fearing another slap or fist, or worse. He had backhanded her more than once since they met when she was waitressing at Nuevo Laredo the night he got out of Stateville Penitentiary at the end of his 12-year-sentence for drug trafficking and aggravated battery to a peace officer.

Gomez had dreamed of a good meal at Chicago's premier Mexican eatery almost as often as he had dreamed of evening the score with Joe Ortiz, the Assistant State's Attorney who had vigorously prosecuted him and asked for the stiff sentence because Gomez had pulled a knife and slashed an undercover narcotics officer.

"You gonna get yours and I gonna get your money too, muthuh-fuckuh'" Gomez said to himself as he drove to Belmont and Ashland to make the call to Ortiz. Gomez knew the feds would be involved and would be pinging the call to find its location.

He pulled up in front of the Whole Foods store on Ashland, facing north, and texted Ortiz's number at 9:19 a.m. Tuesday on one of the "burner" phones he'd bought at Target.

"You have till Friday noon to get $60,000 in cash, half 50s and half 100s, not sequence numbers, and $250,000 in diamonds in one- and two-carat sizes—top quality, flawless-- if you don't want me to start showing photos of severed parts of you daughter as attachments in a text Friday afternoon. When you send me photos of the cash and diamonds, I send you further instructions Friday morning."

That night Halloran gazed north down the Drive as the first huge snowflakes of what would be a 13-inch blizzard began obscuring his 12th floor view from his home at the Edgewater Beach Apartments.

Maybe this will slow him down if we spot him, Halloran thought.

"Yeah, right," he said to himself before retiring for another fitful night.

CHAPTER 5

In prison, Gomez had been a regular in the law library, looking for a way to appeal his conviction, but along the way he also found a story in the Chicago Daily Law Bulletin detailing the windfall his prosecutor, Joe Ortiz, had received in a personal injury case several years after he left the Cook County State's Attorney's Office.

Once Gomez discovered that, he had constantly Googled the family and seen how they had moved to a posh mansion on the Gold Coast and how their daughter Elly was a star athlete at Latin School, according to the neighborhood rag.

Next, he started plotting how much he could squeeze out of the family and the best way to do it, and in what denominations. He figured that the cash would weigh less than 2 pounds and the diamonds maybe another pound. Easy to transport and carry. Then he knew he would have to stake out the family and the girl's movements so he could easily snatch her without getting caught.

So, he coerced Letty into applying for a rental apartment at a four-plus-one apartment building just across the street from the Ortiz home and down a few places. With his prison and gang tats on his neck and hands, he knew he'd have a tough time renting in that neighborhood, but pretty Letty was pristine and could be persuaded to apply, by force if necessary.

She'd seen him pistol-whip one of the drug runners just for being 15 minutes late for a drop. She was scared to death of Gomez but couldn't figure out how to break away from him.

Gomez had had plenty of time to plot his revenge as he researched kidnappings on the Internet. He found few were successful because the money was usually bugged with a tracking device or easily traced. He read of a New York City plot where the bad guy bribed a homeless man to pick the bag of money up and drop it off a highway bridge where a motorcyclist waited below to grab it and disappear into the Lincoln Tunnel during rush hour. Didn't work as the cops were waiting at the other end of the tunnel, but not a bad idea, Gomez thought.

His plan would be similar but different. As a teen, he had helped clean up the subterranean tunnels that wound underneath the Loop that most Chicagoans never knew about until the big flood of 1992, when the Chicago River poured into tunnels after a construction mishap. He knew he was too smart for the cops. The tunnels were a maze that would be his edge.

* * * * *

All the smart cops and feds were gathered around Ortiz's cell phone after the text came in.

"Any luck getting a fix on it?" Ortiz asked Special Agent Macel, who hovered over his own techies, holding his hand up.

"Close, close," Macel said, but they all knew it took a few minutes to get a fix, and they also knew they didn't know what exactly they were looking for unless the kidnapper was stupid enough to stay in the same place after he texted. Which he was not and did not.

"Belmont and Ashland," Macel announced a few minutes later and Ortiz repeated to her team. The beat cars and all the dicks and agents in the vicinity raced to the intersection; Gomez smiled as he approached Lake View High School at Irving Park and Ashland before turning east to head to the Drive as squad cars raced by, sirens blaring and lights flashing.

The gathered brass were mostly silent as they waited to hear from the scene. Then they got the word. Nothing there.

"Okay, let's get all the cameras from there. There's bound to be something," Ortiz ordered. Macel and Kassos repeated it to the underlings.

They all knew it wasn't an exact science and that the kidnapper probably wrote the text elsewhere and sent it from the six-way intersection of Lincoln, Belmont, and Ashland. Tons of cars and scores of cameras.

Halloran caught Syl's eye and tipped his head toward the conference room.

Once inside, he closed the door. "Syl, not much I can add in there, so I'm going to start wading through all the canvassing reports and see what pops. It's gotta be done, huh? I'm not holding my breath on the cameras at the site of the ping, are you?"

"Well, no, but hoping for something, anything," Ortiz said, her voice choking up. Just then, Joe Ortiz popped in.

"So, whattya think? Anything?" Joe asked, looking first to his wife, then Halloran.

Halloran shrugged, deferring to his boss.

"Joe, Mike and I aren't too hopeful we'll get too much from the ping site. Too busy, too many cars, and people, and cameras. Mike's gonna look through the canvasses and see if anything jumps," Syl said, grabbing Joe's hand.

"I understand, I understand," Joe said, tearing up. "Our baby..."

Halloran slipped out and found the room with the printouts of the canvass reports. There were more than 200. He took off his jacket, put on his reading glasses and shut the door.

Before she went to bed, Syl filed a brief report about Elly's best friends and a few teammates, but Halloran learned none had seen or heard anything suspicious. Most of the reports were of businesses that were still open and of neighbors that responded to bell rings. That would have to be repeated to make sure no one was missed.

One report caught Halloran's eye, though, because it was about a salesclerk at the Potash Bros. store on State directly along the route that Elly would likely take each day. The clerk said that on several days prior to the kidnapping he had seen a gray minivan parked outside, sometimes across the street in front of the Germania Club or by the Tiparo's Thai restaurant, with a man smoking inside the van.

The clerk said the van would show up about 2 p.m., before school let out and would stay till 5 or 6 some days. The man, a Latino, would occasionally come in to buy a pack of Marlboros. The clerk said he noticed because the van was old and a "bit beat up" for the upscale Gold Coast, and the driver "looked a little shaky."

No license plate. No further description. But worth revisiting, Halloran thought. Besides he knew most convicts smoked like chimneys. Nothing? Something? We'll see.

* * * * *

Five hours later and thousands of words and scores of phone calls later, Ortiz asked the large crowd of cops and agents in her office:

"Can Special Agent in Charge Macel, my husband and I have my office for 15 minutes please?" The CPD brass and FBI agents and techies all filed out wordlessly.

Ortiz spoke first.

"Look, time is critical. This guy seems to have a plan, and we're just trying to hatch one. I want a Plan A and B. Joe, you're going to be in charge of Plan B, and that's to gather the money and start to buy up those diamonds. Maybe the place to start with that is that place in Villa Park where you bought my engagement ring—that will be the tough part..."

"Chief Ortiz, I don't think that's a smart play..." Macel began.

Ortiz raised her palm and her voice at the same time.

"John, I said Plan B. You and your team are going to be charting Plan A. You're the experts, but this is our daughter, and we want to give them what they want if it means getting her back safe. And, John, this is not a PLAY to me or Joe. You understand? I will step on your toes and stomp on the feet of the U.S. Attorney if I have to, and the Superintendent and the Mayor will back me."

"Chief—Sylvia—poor choice of words. Sorry. We'll follow your lead, but I'm glad you realize we have vast experience in these situations," Macel said.

"Understood," Syl said. "Joe, you can get started immediately. I don't know how hard it will be to gather those rocks, but the sooner you start, the better. Right?"

"I'll have my cell on at all times," Joe said, and leaned in to hug his wife, and kiss her forehead.

After Joe left, Ortiz turned to Macel and said: "I'm going to take a jump here that I wouldn't say publicly but I will say privately—from what I heard in that first recording, our guy sounds like an immigrant Mexican with his use of the language and his accent.

"Mike Halloran is here because he's my former partner and the smartest dick I have, the most intuitive and the most relentless—on any case. But he also held my daughter, my Elly, in his arms at the baptismal font, and so he is the godfather, too. So, Mike will be leading this for me with only the rank of detective and that may rankle—will piss off—some of my captains and commanders. Tough shit. I hope it won't be a problem with any of the agents?"

"My people are pros, and Mike's reputation precedes him—mostly good," Macel smiled. "It won't be a problem." A vague reference to Halloran's Size 13s stomping on an errant agent in joint schemes past.

"Good," Ortiz said, "I'll bring him in for a minute, just the three of us." A quick text from Ortiz and Halloran materialized, all 6'5" and 250 pounds of him.

"Close the door, Mike. This is Special Agent in Charge John Macel. Detective Mike Halloran." The two shook hands. Halloran gave it a little extra squeeze, as he often did with a fed or a suspect, just a slight alpha male signal.

Ortiz noticed the prolonged grip.

"Mike, I just explained to SAC Macel our understanding of your relationship in this investigation and our own unique relationship. He understands. There're a lot of egos here, a lot of guns, ranks and testosterone and ideas about how to handle this. But Agent Macel and I--and you-- will work seamlessly till we get Elly back. Right?" Ortiz said.

"Syl--Chief—the only thing that counts for me is to get Elly back-now—unharmed. Second place is to get this scumbag, or scumbags most probably, and make them pay. I have danced with the feds before successfully and will not step on their toes. You have my word on that, Syl. You too, Agent Macel," Halloran vowed.

Macel nodded.

"Now, I've got something that needs a follow, I think, and I'd like to do it myself immediately," Halloran said, and laid out the report of the Potash clerk's suspicion. "It will take me 15-20 minutes to get there once I phone the store to make sure this kid's there."

"You done with the rest of the reports?" Ortiz asked.

"Done."

"Then go."

Halloran nodded and disappeared on his way to the parking lot.

"Quite a grip on your old partner," said Macel, an ex-Green Beret.

"Played tight end at Illinois till he banged up his knee against Purdue his junior year. Never saw him play, but I hear he took no prisoners," Ortiz quipped.

"I hear he still doesn't," Macel replied.

"Only guilty ones," Ortiz responded.

CHAPTER 6

Arnold Wambach had driven a taxi, bartended at Mother's gin mill on Division Street, and delivered pizza for Rosati's before taking the job at Potash. The pay at Potash was comparable, and it was just a few blocks from his studio apartment on Eugenie Street.

It was easy duty, and he found himself people-watching a lot during the down time between customers. So, it wasn't unusual for him to take notice of the van parked day after day across the street, with the man chain-smoking just down the street from the Latin School. Several times, the guy came in to buy smokes at Potash, Wambach told Halloran.

"He just didn't quite look like he belonged in this neighborhood," the slightly built Wambach told Halloran moments after the detective displayed his star and walked him back to a rear office. "That teardrop tattoo under his eye looked so odd. Neck tat also."

Not odd to Halloran. He knew it was the sign of a kill for a Latin Cobra, one of the city's oldest and most notorious Latino street gangs.

"Right eye or left?"

"Uh, left."

"How old, how tall, heavyset, skinny, medium build, light-skinned, dark?"

"Maybe 45. Average to short—maybe 5'8-5'9". Light-skinned. Looked even in winter clothes like he was in pretty good shape."

Halloran asked a question he knew would probably draw blanks.

"Get a license plate number?"

"Naw. No reason to," Wambach said.

"See any other tats?" Halloran asked.

"Didn't notice, but he was bundled up pretty good against the cold," Wambach said.

"Would you be able to pick him out of a photo lineup if I brought one by," Halloran asked, knowing it was a bit premature since he had no name to go with, but he felt in his gut he was getting warm.

"Yeah, I guess," Wambach said, shrugging.

"Good, I'll get back to you. Here's my card. If you think of anything else, call me," Halloran told Wambach. Halloran already knew the patrol guys had checked the block for cameras and came up with nothing useful. They found a fuzzy video from across the street in the alley east of 88 W. Schiller that showed Elly being snatched and pulled into a gray van by a guy in a ski mask, but the snow blocked the license plate.

As he got back into the squad, Halloran's cell went off. Caller ID--Ortiz.

"Hal, get anything more? I may have something. But you first."

"Yeah, the guy in the van, a gray van, probably a Dodge, the Potash guy thinks, has a teardrop tattoo under his left eye. Latin Cobra. Right? Getting closer. Now you?"

Ortiz almost shouted.

"Monday morning, I'm getting into my squad parked in front after brushing off the snow, and I notice a young Latina sweeping off her rear windshield, and I'm thinking Molly Maids, and then I'm admonishing myself for stereotyping a young Hispanic girl in my neighborhood for being there only to clean up after us rich folks. But, Mike, it's not yet 9 a.m. and she's cleaning the snow off. She lives in the neighborhood. And she's cleaning the snow off a gray Dodge van."

Halloran slammed his right palm into the steering wheel.

"Hot shit, Syl. We're getting close. We gotta put the full court press on that area to try to find that girl, right?" Halloran asked.

"Abso-fucking-lutely. I'm getting Wrenn and Roy to get the troops to go building by building, block by block, landlord by landlord, tenant by tenant till we find that girl," Syl said.

"Great," Halloran said. "I'm a block away but this has to be organized so I'll stay out of their way while I make my way back. Maybe you can get Al to search for a Latin Cobra recently released, say in the last year, with a tear drop, left side, that was put away either by you or Joe?" Halloran asked.

"Good thinking. Can't hurt. Better than him looking all forlorn at me every time I walk by," Ortiz said. "And Mike, on your way back, drive by that four-plus-one across the street from my place. I'm liking that better than a lot of the other higher-priced places around me."

"Will do."

Halloran pulled onto southbound Clark and turned left immediately at Schiller, basically tracing what would probably have been Elly's route before she was grabbed. He drove slowly looking for cameras and spotted only one, on the outside of the Sandburg high-rise at 88 W. Schiller, alley side. Looking back south, he saw a few above garage doors but knew the patrol guys had already covered that ground.

So, he hung a right at Dearborn and drove slowly up to Ortiz's place at 1345 N. Dearborn and stopped. Across the street and a bit south was a four-plus-one newer structure of what looked like one-bedrooms and studio apartments with a ground-floor entrance, a foyer, panel list and a buzzer entry system. A guy behind him honked a few times, and Halloran held his star out the window and waved the guy on, who turned out to be a woman. She gave him a dirty look and a dismissive wave as she passed.

"More assholes on the road than there are assholes," Halloran muttered, as he further took in the block. As he sat there, a couple of detective cars rolled up from either direction, undoubtedly to carry out Ortiz's and their immediate bosses' orders. Halloran waved to the first dick before he took off for the Drive.

He called Ortiz again as he headed past the Drake Hotel.

"So, let's run this out with what little we got, Okay? Shithead is a Cobra gangbanger and he's staking out the school, watching Elly's movements. Smart enough to do that. But to do the snatch right, he needs a driver. And to rent in that neighborhood, and looking like he does, he needs a beard, right? So, he gets little Miss Molly Maid to rent? Make sense so far?"

"It plays for me. Keep going," Ortiz replied.

"So, you see Molly cleaning off her car getting ready to go to work, presumably, at 9. Meanwhile, shithead is still sleeping or maybe he gets up to watch you leave and Elly set off for school, and then waiting to begin his early afternoon stakeout. Now I gotta believe this is a guy you or Joe put away, and he has plotted this out for years, right?"

"Makes a lot of sense. But where was he?" Ortiz wondered.

"Well, maybe Al's research can turn that up, but meanwhile the dicks are swarming your 'hood right now and asking a lot of good questions. So, for now, we work your neighborhood and wait, but hopefully not for long. How are the feds doing?" Halloran asked.

"They're very organized and ready to spring into action. But we'll see what that action will be, won't we?" Ortiz asked.

"To be determined," Halloran said, and reluctantly headed home to his high-rise co-op apartment at the stately sunset-pink stucco Edgewater Beach Apartments at 5555 N. Sheridan Road as it was now nearly midnight.

CHAPTER 7

As luck would have it for the Ortiz family, the manager/landlord of the four-plus across the street from their home lived in the building but was at his day job bartending at a Rush Street joint when the dicks came calling.

After one of the tenants gave up his cell number to Detective Sharon Blakley, the manager, Andy Albers, left his post at Butch McGuire's bar posthaste, as the detective ordered, and returned home.

"Yeah, I know the young lady you're talking about, Leticia Diaz, nice girl, just enough English, but she's taking classes at the Loop college," Albers said as he pulled her application from his file and handed it to Blakley.

Blakley and her partner, Frank Schell, looked at the last employer's address, which was in Puerto Vallarta, Mexico, and the current employer, which was Nuevo Laredo, one of Chicago's most popular Mexican restaurants in Pilsen.

"You verify her employment?" Schell asked.

"Yep, always do. But she'd only been there for a month, so I kinda took a chance. Didn't call Mexico, though, given my poor Spanish. The apartment had been open for a few months and the renting season was slipping by," Albers said.

"You got a key to the apartment?" Schell asked.

"Sure, but I don't know if she's home," Albers said.

"We'll find out," Schell said.

In a minute they were all at Apartment 304, with Albers ringing the buzzer and then knocking, to no response. Schell wasn't waiting.

"Police, Miss Diaz. Open up. We have some questions for you."

Silence.

They waited another 30 seconds before Blakley said, "Use your key."

"You got a warrant?" Albers asked hesitantly.

"Yeah, fuckface. I got exigent circumstances," Schell said, and pulled out his Smith & Wesson snub-nosed .38 revolver.

Albers spoke not, and quickly used his key.

Inside, it was dark and empty. After turning the lights on, the two detectives found a pizza box with a few crusts and a four-day-old receipt. There were no toiletries in the bathroom but white stains on the sink indicating toothbrushes had recently been used. In a corner of the studio apartment was a pair of men's dirty boxer shorts and in the closet a few women's blouses. Two coffee cups with dried coffee in the bottom stood by the kitchen sink.

"Let's bag those cups and call this in," Blakley said. "Did you know there was a man living here?"

"I'd seen a boyfriend, a man really, come and go a few times, but living here, I don't ask as long as the rent comes in."

"How did she pay?" Northern asked.

"Cash," the manager said. "She's a waitress."

Schell called Roy's cell and reported what they'd found. Roy called Halloran.

"Nice work. Let's get the tech guys over there and get those coffee cups to forensics for possible DNA hits. And have your guys babysit that building round the clock just in case they come back. Okay, Commander?"

"Roger that, Mike," Roy said. He knew Halloran spoke for Roy's boss.

But Halloran knew that if this pair had used the apartment to stake out the Ortiz family, it was unlikely they would return once they grabbed the girl.

So where did they go? Wondered Halloran. North, somewhere. Best pursue that after we chat with the folks at Nuevo Laredo.

Halloran dialed Ortiz. She picked up halfway through the first ring.

"Yeah, Hal?"

"Syl, the dicks searching across the street from your home found an empty apartment rented to a young Latina we gotta like a bit right now. Could be the Molly you saw. She said in her application she worked at Nuevo Laredo. I wanna pick up my partner, Jane, and head over there immediately to see what we can see. She's on call today with me reassigned. She lives in the South Loop, so I'll swing by and pick her up on the way," Halloran said.

"Let me know how it goes," Ortiz said and disconnected as Macel entered her office.

Thoma's phone rang six times before it went to voicemail and Halloran left an abrupt message: "Jane, call me ASAP. It's important." Then he texted her an identical curt demand.

Minutes later, Thoma emerged from the shower after her workout and checked her phone. With her head in a towel turban, she called Halloran back.

"Mike, what's up?"

"We need to go to Nuevo Laredo for an interview. Can you be ready in 10 minutes?" Halloran asked.

"Can do. But don't expect the next Bachelorette."

Twenty minutes later, they barged into Nuevo Laredo and asked the receptionist for the manager. It was dinner time, and the place was jammed, with a waiting line stretching out to the street entrance.

"She very busy. Can I take your card and have her to call you later?" the receptionist asked.

"You cannot have my card, and if she's not in front of me in one minute, one minute, I'm marching into your kitchen, waving my star, and announcing we're from ICE (Immigration and Customs Enforcement). You want that?" Halloran asked.

"One minute, one minute, por favor," the receptionist said, and scurried off to the rear of the restaurant.

In 30 seconds, manager Roberta Ruiz, appeared, smiling, but obviously shaken.

"Officers, what can I do for you?"

"Let's go to your office--now," Halloran said, then followed Ruiz to a small office at the rear of the restaurant, Thoma a few steps behind.

Inside, Halloran got straight to the point after introducing Thoma.

"We have an emergency situation, and we need to talk to your employee Leticia Diaz immediately. Is she working today, or do you have her cell or know where we can find her?" Halloran asked, standing in the small office along with Thoma.

"She's not here today, but let me get her application," Ruiz said, her hands slightly shaking as she dug through a file door.

"Here's what I have," she said, handing a one-page application with a small photo attached.

Halloran looked it over and saw the PV restaurant named La Dolce Pizzeria, but no contact info, and her last known address at 1922 S. Hermitage Ave., not on Dearborn, and her reference was a "Karine Hernandez" on Hermitage. He handed the application to Thoma and told her to take a photo of the photo with her cell and send it to Ortiz's team.

"One reference, no phone number and no provable work history. Pretty thin to get a waitressing gig at a high-volume joint like this. How come you hired her?" Halloran demanded, still hovering over the tiny manager.

"Karine is my aunt and Letty was a distant cousin just arrived and living with her. She had experience as a waitress in PV and Karine felt sorry for her. Her English was okay, but I had her wait mostly on the Spanish speakers," Ruiz said. "Is she in trouble?"

"You got a number for Karine?" Thoma asked.

"I do, but it's a land line. She's in her late 70s, speaks broken English and hasn't figured out cellphones," Ruiz said. She jotted down a 708 number and handed it to Thoma. Ruiz dialed it from the phone on her desk, put the call on speaker but got a message in Spanish.

"It says to leave a message and she'll call you back, but I wouldn't hold my breath. She's a widow and afraid of strangers—especially gringos who might be ICE," Ruiz said.

"When was the last time you saw Letty?" Thoma asked.

"Last Thursday. She was supposed to work yesterday and tonight. I left messages but only got Karine's answering machine."

"Okay. Thanks. If Letty shows, call us immediately but don't let her know. Understand?" Halloran said, sliding his card toward Ruiz.

"Yes, sir."

Outside, Halloran hopped in the squad and announced. "House call. We're three minutes away. Won't need backup on an old lady, right?"

"I'm with you."

After pulling into a spot in front of a fire hydrant on the snow-clogged street, the two dicks advanced as one to the address.

Karine Hernandez lived on the first floor of a two-flat that she and her late husband, a Streets and Sanitation laborer, had bought in the late 1980s. They paid off the mortgage a year before he died, leaving her with a nice pension and a debt-free home. She rented out the second floor and the basement apartment (illegally), which she advertised in the Spanish-speaking media as a "Jardin (garden)" apartment.

Halloran rang the bell. Nothing. Again. Nothing. Thoma went around to the rear door and knocked repeatedly. There were no lights on in either of the other two apartments and no response to her knocks.

They then went door to door down the street but found no adults who spoke English. So, Halloran called Ortiz and asked for a Spanish-speaking detective, then headed back to Area 3 with Thoma after explaining over the phone to the Spanish-speaking dick what they needed.

After hanging up, Halloran vented his frustration. It was 8 p.m. and Elly was still with some violent asshole—scared, alone, miserable, wondering where Uncle Mike was.

"Fuck," Halloran yelled, and slammed his hands into the steering wheel.

"Amen, partner. But we're getting close," Thoma said.

Ten minutes later, he dropped Thoma off at home and then checked in with Ortiz for any progress.

"Joe's got the cash and the diamonds, but the feds aren't happy about that. Tough shit. I wanna be ready. Nice work getting the photo, and the dicks got some cups from the apartment that we sent to the State Police lab for DNA testing. So, we're getting close," Ortiz said.

"Not close enough, and the clock's ticking," Halloran said as he pulled off the Drive and headed to Ranalli's in Old Town, for a quick pint, frustrated with nothing else to do this night.

CHAPTER 8

Inside Ranalli's, the joint was deserted but for a few young guys in suits at a side table and a couple of flight attendants still in their navy-blue uniforms, chatting over drinks at the L-shaped bar.

Halloran slipped onto a stool at the end of the bar.

"How about a pint of Guinness?" Halloran asked the redhead with the nametag "Irene" who approached from behind the bar with a green hand towel in one hand and a Goose Island beer coaster in the other. She slid the coaster in front of Halloran.

"Of course, love," Irene said, with a trace of a brogue.

"Ah, then, you'd be knowing that; a pint of the Guinness it is," Halloran said, throwing his best Barry Fitzgerald imitation back at her.

"Now don't you have a bit of the gab in ya? Pick that up watching old Victor McLaglen reruns or have you actually been to my fair island?" Irene smiled up at Halloran as she poured the black beer slowly down the inside of a pint glass.

"Both. Been to both the south and the north. Connemara and Donegal are my favorites. My grandmother came from a tiny village not far from Clifton. And yes, I have most of 'The Quiet Man' memorized."

"I'm a Galway gal myself. Came here when I was 12, but the accent lingers. And what wee town would that be that Grandma had come from?" Irene said, placing the pint on the coaster, then hands on hips, blue eyes flashing.

A bit of a flirt, Halloran thought.

"And how long ago was that?" Halloran said.

"Just a few years ago," Irene laughed. "Now was that your clumsy Yank way of asking how old I am?"

Halloran laughed and shrugged. One of the most skillful interrogators on the police force, Halloran had just been making small talk. He'd never married, but at near pension age he found himself less in the hunt for the future Mrs. Halloran than 20, 25 years ago. Now a good book was mostly what he coveted when he hit the hay. He threw his hands up.

"Guilty. Bet it's been a hard life for an immigrant to our city." Halloran eyed the 42-year-old moonlighting schoolteacher and returned her smile.

"So, it shows, does it? Well, aren't you the smooth-talker, and now what about answering my question?"

"What question?"

"What village your grandma came from?" Irene asked.

"Lettermore Island, Glastrana," Halloran replied. "Hard to find."

"Maybe for a Yank. And don't I know it well? I, spending the years leading to puberty just a good pub crawl from Lettermore."

"Can I buy the hired help a drink?"

"Well, I'd be a liar if I said anything but the truth." She leaned over the bar and whispered. "You pop for a shot of Jameson's and I throw the five bucks in that nearly naked tip jar. I drink for free, a perk of the job."

"Pour one for us both, then, Irene." Halloran pushed a double sawbuck across the bar.

As Irene walked to the other end of the bar, one of the young men at the nearby table, about 28, approached the blonde flight attendant and started talking, pointing over to his friend. Halloran could just catch snippets of the conversation, but the young guy obviously had a snootful.

Halloran could tell by looking at the blonde that she had a decade on her would-be suitor and had heard better lines while serving peanuts on a 737.

"Well, I'm really not sure what it is you're talking about or what you want, but I'm just interested in having a drink and some quiet conversation with my friend," she said, then turned back to her friend.

"What I want," the suitor said, raising his voice so his friends could hear "is to get into your pants tonight."

"Yeah, well that would make two assholes in there," she said, barely glancing over her shoulder.

The guy's friends erupted in laughter. The suitor turned red. The blonde's friend smiled; she'd never heard the line before but liked it.

"Who the fuck do ya think you are?" the suitor said.

"Can you please leave us alone?" the other flight attendant said.

"Fuck you, too," suitor said.

Halloran had heard enough.

"Son, why don't you leave the ladies alone. They're obviously not interested." Halloran hadn't moved and was simply eyeing the young man through the mirror.

"And fuck you, too," the suitor said.

Halloran stood. He turned and pulled out his star from his back pocket. As he did, his sport coat opened, exposing briefly the shoulder holster holding his 9 mm Browning semi-automatic.

"I'm sure you don't want to spend the night in the lockup. You've made a small mistake; don't make a big one. Now run along." By now, he was at full height as he stepped forward, towering over the 5'8" suitor, 80 pounds out of his weight class.

"Oh, sorry," suitor said to Halloran. "Sorry, sorry," he repeated as he turned to the women at the bar. Suitor left in a hurry, his pals quickly joining him.

"Thanks. He had a bit too much to drink," the blonde said, smiling at Halloran.

"I've been there. He's young and stupid." Halloran turned and went back to his stool at the end of the bar.

Irene was waiting with the shots.

"A cop. I should've known. Murphy, O'Brien, Sullivan?"

"Halloran. And it's Irene what?" Halloran hoisted his shot to clink glasses with the barmaid.

"It's Irene 'Happily Married With Three Kids' I am." Irene clinked, winked, then threw down the Jameson's and was off to freshen the flight attendants' drinks.

Halloran finished the Guinness and the shot in silence, pushed an extra fin across the bar for Irene, nodded to the two ladies at the other end of the bar and left.

As he entered the Drive at North on his way home, he whispered to the dashboard.

"I'm coming, honey. You'll be safe at home soon."

But when, he wondered as he eased into his garage.

Inside, he went directly to the pool locker room and slipped into his swimming pool. The pool was nearly empty at this hour, but for a gray-haired lady just finishing her last lap.

Halloran swam kitty corner for half an hour as hard as he could, alternating backstroke and freestyle.

Back in his apartment, he drank a Sierra Nevada Pale Ale as he heated up some Chicken Lemon Grass from Pho 888 on Argyle and gazed into the darkness of the Edgewater neighborhood where he lived and had grown up.

You dirty fuck. I'm gonna get you and if you so much as mussed Elly's hair, I'm gonna break every bone in your hand before I drop kick you in the balls into a holding cell.

CHAPTER 9

At 5:35 a.m., Halloran woke with a start. His dream was murky, but vaguely he remembered Elly calling his name for help and his trying to run to her, but his legs wouldn't work.

He rolled over, grabbed his phone and began texting Ortiz.

"Gotta get the dicks or the uniforms, or both, back early to that apartment building opposite you and get the rest of the residents talking before they're off for work. Did they ever see her in a car? With a guy? Last time? I'll grab Thoma and go back to that building where our girl Leticia once lived, then circle back to you and be in by 8. Okay?"

Ortiz was up--of course. And texted back in a few seconds.

"Change of plans. We're meeting at the U.S. Attorney's office at 9 for a couple hours to coordinate before we get the drop info from Leticia and her pal. Makes sense, Hal. State's Attorney Dunne and First Assistant Egan are invited," Ortiz said.

"Gotcha. I know how to play ball with the feds. No fouls," he texted back.

He then texted Thoma that he'd pick her up in a half hour. She replied all caps "OKAY."

Halloran showered, put on a blue button-down shirt, a blue and red striped tie, brown slacks, his brown-tweed wool sport coat he'd bought in Donegal, his black wingtips, clipped his Browning to his hip, checked his phone and headed to his garage.

"Morning, Harry," Halloran greeted the garage attendant who kept his 5-year-old Black Grand Cherokee clean and close to the exit door.

"Morning, Officer Halloran," Harry responded with a wave. That Franklin in a Christmas card each December made Harry happy, guaranteed another year of fine service and made Halloran feel good, too.

Who's your guy, Letty? I know we're gonna know him. How'd you find him? Or how'd he find you? Halloran mused as he headed south on the Drive through early rush-hour traffic as he passed the Fullerton exit.

Thoma's hair was still wet when she jumped into the shotgun seat.

"So..." Halloran asked.

"Well, jeez, Mike, I was just thinkin' last night...how does it feel ordering all the brass around, ya know? We're just—you're just a dick..." Thoma said.

"For beginners, Detective Thoma and young partner of mine, I never took the sergeants' exam or any of the other promotional tests just for that reason. I like being a dick and not ordering anyone around. But Syl--Chief Ortiz to you," he said grinning, "and I go way back, and she's made it clear all the way up and down from the supe to the patrol guys that someone has to be in charge of this shitstorm, and Mike Halloran is Sgt. Shitstorm."

"So, is that an official title I can call you from now on? Sgt. Shitstorm?" Thoma asked, smiling to her left.

"Sure, but not in public, and don't even think about shortening it to just Shitstorm," he winked. "This morning let's go door to door on the whole block banging on doors. We got her photo and I got this little speech written down in Spanish with my card to use. And a copy for you. I know it's a long shot, but we got an hour to go before we go to 219 and learn how to do our jobs from the Mensa mopes in their $500 suits," Halloran said. He added that the Spanish-speaking dick had gotten zip from Karine.

As expected, his prepared Spanish speech and the photo produced nothing in a largely Mexican immigrant neighborhood wary of authorities. But that base was at least covered as they drove north on State to the federal building on the south end of the Loop.

The 30-story black, austere Dirksen Federal Building designed by Ludwig Mies van der Rohe intimidates all who enter there. Almost as if that minimalist Teutonic architect wanted it that way and the FBI and federal prosecutors all said: "You betcha. We like it" and moved in.

Halloran was used to it. He'd testified there many times and been in meetings with the various federal agencies, FBI, DEA, ATF, but gratefully not the IRS, and often with the U.S. Attorney's office when their jurisdictional reach and the federal laws better served the evidence in a case he'd worked up. That was what this meeting would be about, so far. Since the investigation was continuing, or "ongoing" as the feds loved to say, it was too early to call.

For Thoma, a 30-year-old officer, it was her first experience. She entered the elevators wide-eyed.

"Don't let 'em scare you, Jane. Ortiz will do all the talking. We're just window dressing," Halloran said before the elevator hit the fifth floor, and they had to go through the ritual of signing in before they entered the inner sanctum of the U.S. Attorney's Office. Fortunately, there was a line and they stepped in right behind Superintendent Wallace.

"Boss," Halloran said, nodding, when Wallace half turned.

"Ready for the big guns?" Wallace whispered, smiling.

"Right," Halloran returned the grin. Thoma hid behind her partner.

In a few minutes they were led into a huge conference room overlooking the Kluczynski Federal Plaza. Already seated and speaking in muted tones were U.S. Attorney Manfred Price and Cook County State's Attorney Richard Dunne. Next to Dunne was First Assistant State's Attorney Mary Catherine Egan, who paused in her conversation with a federal prosecutor, to smile and say, "Hey, Mike."

* * * * *

Theirs had been a long-standing relationship of convenience. Halloran hadn't seen Egan since they met last year in Puerto Vallarta to stay in a two-bedroom condo her parents bought at the Grand Venetian complex overlooking the Pacific and just a 10-minute, $14-taxi ride from the airport.

Egan's mother, Bridget, now in her upper 80s had not been back to PV since her husband, the Honorable Thomas V. Egan, died just shy of his 85th birthday. The widow Egan let her two children, Mary Kay and brother, Joe, and his family use it, and both figured they could sell it after she died.

Halloran and Egan first worked together on the infamous Hit Squad trial of two dirty cops accused and convicted of killing drug dealers but really forged their personal and professional relationship when they successfully investigated and prosecuted the scumbag who killed the daughter of Egan's boss, then State's Attorney's Thomas Cavaretta, just a football field stretch from Ranalli's in Old Town.

That had been a long investigation, and a tough trial, that ended sensationally when Cavaretta pulled out a .45 after the jury refused to render a death penalty verdict and imposed his own death penalty-- instanter. Cavaretta later pleaded out; Egan got a huge promotion; and Halloran got assigned to cold case with a tacit nod from the then-supe that he had a ticket to ride into retirement in whatever role he wanted.

While their careers were secure, Egan and Halloran were as much in love with their jobs as they were with each other. Marriage was discussed but remained under advisement, like a pair of equivocating judges. But the two had great chemistry and history, so at their mutual convenience they went away together about twice a year and had great fun.

This Dirksen meeting would not qualify as great fun.

* * * * *

"Folks, if I could have your attention, please," Price said, standing at the head of the long table, around which 24 cops, agents and prosecutors had gathered and now were rendered mute.

"Clearly, if this turns out to be a straight out kidnapping with a ransom demand, it will be federal. But if in the process of catching this suspect, he gets shot or shoots some cop, or is involved in what is clearly a state crime, the law can get murky. We all know that, and will compare notes, and the law, to see who can get the heaviest whack," Price said, nodding toward Dunne, then Ortiz.

Then he continued: "But such speculation is just that right now. I'm going to turn it over to SAC Macel to detail his team's preparations," said Price, the African-American Harvard Law grad and Obama appointment.

Macel explained how the feds would have 10 mobile units equipped with sophisticated tracking devices that could pinpoint within a 50-yard radius where a call was being made, and that could be accomplished in less than a minute.

"The problem, as you all can guess, is that he may have multiple burner phones. So, he can make a call to Chief Ortiz, make a demand, then toss the phone and make another move. We're hoping he's not that smart, but we can't count on it, so we have to be ready. And we don't know if it's just one guy yet," Macel told the group.

For the next hour and 45 minutes, police, prosecutors and agents brainstormed various scenarios, but they were all depending on what the kidnapper's, or kidnappers' plural, play would be—and they all knew it.

As the meeting was running out of gas and opinions, Price stood up again and turned to Wallace.

"Superintendent, since you have the most boots on the ground, maybe you should have the last word here?"

"Thanks. Our best move till we get the call tomorrow is to concentrate all of our efforts to find Letty Diaz. We got a photo of her, a description of her car, and a BOLO (Be on the Lookout for) on her. If we can find her, I think we find Elly and the thug who grabbed Chief Ortiz's daughter. So, let's do just that."

On that note, the group all stood and began filing out of the conference room, Halloran and Thoma among the first to exit. Halloran glanced back at Ortiz and held thumb and little finger to ear and cheek. She nodded slightly to affirm the phone call plan as she continued talking to Macel.

CHAPTER 10

Felipe "Flip" Lupo and Jesus Gomez joined the Latin Cobras about a month apart, Gomez from Pilsen and Lupo from Little Village a bit west on the Southwest Side.

Lupo never made it higher in the gang than a street peddler and occasional collector, hawking junk on the corner, while Gomez's street smarts and willingness to kiss ass at the high end of the gang and kick ass below him gave him a quick rise to collector. That also earned him a nice car to make the rounds.

Very early on Gomez provoked a fight with Lupo and established himself as the alpha male by grabbing Lupo by the balls, bringing him to his knees, then choking him out, till he lost consciousness. Though a few inches shorter, Gomez was as solid as an NFL safety and as vicious as a pit bull. Lupo was more like a substitute goalie in 6th grade soccer, soft as a burrito and as vicious as a hamster.

"Flip da flop," Gomez labeled his friend, and taunted him with it often. Still, they remained buddies, though on Gomez's terms

At the end of the day, Gomez would gather and count the cash from Lupo, and then they would often grab a few beers and some tacos. That flashy silver BMW SUV and that cash collection also earned Gomez the attention of the cops and the feds.

When Gomez finished his prison sentence, his pal Lupo was still working the corner and still living at home with his parents in Little Village. In the last year, a distant cousin, Leticia Diaz, had arrived from Jalisco state with a few hundred dollars and an equal number of English words but a willingness to work and learn.

She was only 20, a shapely raven-haired beauty, but "muy joven" (very young) for Flip, his parents warned. That didn't really matter since the comely Letty took one look at the slow-moving and -talking 41-year-old street-hustling dope dealer and stayed in her room while searching Craigslist for a job and a place of her own.

Before she found either, though, the recently released Gomez regained his status with the Cobras and spotted Letty when he reunited with his pal Lupo. With money, easy bullshit and a fancy car, Gomez impressed the jejune jewel from Jalisco. He knew all the best restaurants where her experience waitressing in Puerto Vallarta would be valued, he told her one night over a few beers at a local cerveceria.

"No Ingles. No problema, mi amor, pero puedo ensenarte rapidamente las palabras clave," he counseled, bragging that he could teach her the key words in a jiffy. But equally important, he continued, he knew the night manager of the best restaurant in Pilsen, Nuevo Laredo, because he supplied him with primo coke.

In early August of 2010, a month after she had been escorted across the border by a "coyote" near Ciudad Juarez, Gomez introduced Letty to the night manager at the same time he dropped off a weekend's supply of coke for him and some of the wait staff. She took the menu home and started memorizing it in English and Spanish.

Jesus Gomez had bigger plans than waitressing for young Letty, she would soon learn.

* * * * *

Elly heard the door click and could see some light filter through the duct tape over her eyes under the ski mask.

"Is Okay. Is Okay," Letty said. "No hurt you. Yust eat."

As soon as the tape was off, Elly said, "Thank you. Gracias. Please let me go."

"She no speaka da Ingles so good, so save that shit, little Elly. We gettin' close. Tomorrow morning, if you parents smart," Gomez said, standing in the doorway watching and sneering at the interaction between the two.

Elly ate three pieces of Home Run Inn pepperoni pizza and sipped a Dr. Pepper, as Gomez watched silently.

"I have to go to the bathroom," Elly said.

"Allight. She take you. Don't do stupid thing," Gomez said.

Letty took Elly into the bathroom and waited for her. Like the mother of a toddler, Letty cleaned Elly up after she finished. And helped her dress.

"Thank you," Elly whispered. "De nada," Letty whispered back.

A few minutes later, Elly was back in total darkness, her mouth retaped. It was 8 p.m. Thursday evening.

The clock was ticking.

CHAPTER 11

It was early for lunch but not too early for a late coffee at Cavanaugh's at the Monadnock Building kitty-corner from the Dirksen Building. It was empty when Ortiz, Halloran and Thoma grabbed a rear booth.

Ortiz spoke first.

"I'm gonna take a quick ride to Nuevo Laredo and have a chat with the owner and find out all I can about why they hired this girl for a premier spot. The dicks who went back today say the building manager wasn't too impressed with her English. I can't just sit on my ass in my office. I can't. It's my baby..." Ortiz said, looking away for a moment to hide the tears welling up.

"Good idea, Syl," Halloran picked up on his old partner's embarrassment, needless as it was. Thoma excused herself to the john. "And maybe there's a fellow waitress who can shed some more light on our Letty. You will scare the shit out of them."

Ortiz choked out a laugh.

"Hope so."

"I'm in a bit of a holding pattern till the uniforms file some more reports, so, for the next couple hours, I'm gonna take Thoma back over to that warehouse to check a few things out on that cold case before we head back to the Area, or do you want us back at headquarters?" Halloran asked.

"We both hate waiting, but we gotta find something to fill the time profitably till tomorrow, yeah? So, your plan sounds good. I'll reach out if I need you," Ortiz said. "I'm outta here."

As Ortiz cleared the doorway, Halloran finished his coffee, and turned to Thoma as she eased back into the booth.

"We got a few hours and we're 10 minutes away from that warehouse with the O'Malley evidence. Let's make a quick run," Halloran said. Thoma nodded.

Fifteen minutes later, they were signed into the massive evidence warehouse and once again sifting through the piles of evidence and files amassed during the investigation into the gruesome murder of the teenage girl.

"Jane, I want you to start going through all these files like they were written yesterday. Fresh eyes, right? Anything unusual jumps—flag it. I'm going to use this hacksaw to cut off one of these flaps off this barrel to see if we can raise some DNA off of it," Halloran said, holding the saw he just pulled from his duffel bag of tools.

"Whattya looking for, Mike?" Thoma asked.

"Well, first off, we don't know if anyone in the last 10 or 20 years has used the new technology available to raise DNA profiles, and then we also don't know if anyone has run that through the CODIS (Combined DNA Index System). Lots of 'don't knows' in these old cases, right?"

Halloran decided to take a sample slat from each oil drum, so that took him more than an hour of sawing, then placing the slats in evidence bags and marking them, getting the co-signature from Thoma, with a date and time and place.

There were mountains of clothes marked as being Mary Beth's, then her diaries, a hairbrush, photos, old yearbooks. Much of it was mildewed and yellowed by age. Halloran didn't know what he was looking for, but he was looking. He told Thoma he'd take the hairbrush with its few reddish blond strands to the lab to get a DNA profile to make sure they had a match with the bloody slats.

Three hours into it, Thoma announced she'd found something unusual in the files.

"Take a look at this file, Mike, from a retired lieutenant named Charles Fitzsimmons," Thoma said, handing Halloran a 2-inch-thick file.

"Fitzsimmons. He was a legend. They called him 'The Indian,' presumably because he effectively tracked the bad guys, not because of his ethnicity; but back in the day, who knows? He might have had a bit of Cherokee or Comanche in him," Halloran grinned.

Halloran sat down and read the letter from Fitz "The Indian" to detectives in Pasadena, Texas, homicide division.

Dated June 2, 1985. It read:

"Attention Pasadena Detective Division: There is a serial killer in your jurisdiction recently paroled from the Illinois Department of Corrections. His name is Larry Lynch. He was convicted of attempted rape in eight separate cases in Chicago and did 8 years but was acquitted in an infamous case called the Spyglass Murder by the press, all in the mid- to late- 70s. He was also my main suspect in the grisly 1978 murder of Mary Beth O'Malley. He received permission recently from the Illinois Parole Board to live with his parents at 1343 Olive in Pasadena. He is now 48 and will kill again, I assure you. I am retired but I am available to discuss this monster who has slipped off the scales of justice. My number is 312 743 5921. The Area 3 detective division and the Cook County State's Attorney's office have more details on this dangerous man. Enclosed are copies of some of the case files and notes I took with me into retirement. I had 38 years as a Chicago cop, 33 as a detective, and this is the guy who got away. He still haunts me."

Halloran closed the file and handed it to Thoma.

"Did you read this?" he asked.

"Not all of it, but the letter, yeah, and some of these old newspaper clips in the file. Pretty awful," she said.

In one of the supps Thoma found, a detective had noted that a neighbor of Lynch's reported she heard loud bangs coming from the basement the night Mary Beth disappeared. That same neighbor reported seeing Lynch building a large barbecue pit a few days later. She said it was seldom used after it was built.

"Banging could have been him slotting the drums," Halloran speculated.

"And maybe he dug that foundation for the pit and then dumped his bloody clothes and hers into the hole before he topped it off with the pit?" Thoma responded.

Then she held up an 8x11 yellowed card with a newspaper clip taped onto it. It was the death notice that ran in the Tribune, noting services at St. Margaret Mary's church and burial at All Saints Cemetery in Des Plaines.

"The Indian didn't miss much," Thoma quipped. "She had a younger brother, Donald, says in the death notice. Parents probably dead."

Just then, Halloran's phone went off.

"Okay, we're on our way," Halloran said. "New incident reports to dig through. Gotta wrap this up. But pretty interesting stuff, eh?"

"I'd say," Thoma replied.

First, they dropped off the barrel slats at the crime lab before they returned to 35th Street to wade through the fresh reports collected by the uniforms. There was clearly no rush but they were in the neighborhood near the Illinois State Police Crime lab, so why not drop the slats and hairbrush to start the process, Halloran told Thoma.

Before he forgot, Halloran dropped a quick email to Karen Svenson, the lead DNA expert at the crime lab, advising her that they'd left the barrel slats and hairbrush at the lab. It was a huge case, he said, but they were on a more immediate case. He didn't want the samples misplaced.

CHAPTER 12

As they rode back to 35th Street, Halloran gave his young partner a crime history lesson of sorts.

"All this was before I became a cop and some of it was while I was traipsing around the world as a 20-something Peter Pan trying not to grow up," Halloran said, winking at Thoma, who wasn't even born when these crimes occurred.

"But I remember as a teenager my folks talking about this Larry Lynch being from the parish, though much older than me and living on Paulina west of Clark Street. When he got busted for the attempt rapes, there was a lot of talk," Halloran continued.

"Parish. What parish?" Thoma asked.

Halloran had mentioned his parish before but reminded her.

"St. Gertrude's, runs from Devon to Thorndale, the Lake to Ridge. Didn't you have parishes in Minneapolis?" Halloran asked.

"Yeah, but we didn't define ourselves by them like you guys do," Thoma responded.

"Your loss, but this is Chicago, and the main players in cops, fire and politics are still Catholic, though the Blacks certainly have established a formidable base," he continued.

"I digress...I think with the new technology we got a good chance with this O'Malley case. But this is so old, we got problems—like: Is our guy still alive? Has he ever been swabbed? Where the fuck is he now? If he's still alive and never been swabbed, how do we get him, and get him where? But... baby steps, right, partner?"

"Yeah, like the trail of a snail across your patio on a June morn," Thoma quipped.

"Dickinson? Shakespeare?" Halloran asked.

Thoma countered:

"You autodidact. Didn't they teach English Lit at Illinois?"

"Not to the dumb jocks. Especially to the ones who fucked up their knee, dropped out after four semesters and never looked back," Halloran laughed.

"How's that knee now, Mike?"

"Only hurts when I laugh, but as long as I swim and don't do anything too stupid, it doesn't bother me much," he said. "Here we are. Let's join the joint city/federal clusterfuck—that's the official name." Halloran laughed, but not so hard that his knee complained.

The door to Ortiz's office was closed, but Halloran could see Wrenn and Roy on the couch, listening to the boss, just as Thompson walked out.

"I think you can walk in, Mike, Detective Thoma," Thompson said.

"Good timing, Mike," Ortiz said. "Just telling the commanders here that Joe has put together the diamonds—and it wasn't easy. The cash wasn't easy either, but they're both done. Weighs less than 4 pounds. Can you believe it?"

"Yeah, I can. Gotta give shithead a little credit. He wants to be able to run with it, I think. Hope the feds have a fleet of helicopters ready to swoop down on him. Do they?" Halloran asked. "And let's remember to take a photo of the cash and diamonds to show asshole."

"Right. The feds have a pair of choppers and so do we. We got a fleet of motorcycle cops and bike patrol guys and five of our fastest runners—including Jesse "the Jet" Johnson. Remember when he ran the 40-yard in 4.37 in the Bears mini-camp before he tore his ACL?" Roy asked.

"I do," Halloran responded. Ortiz nodded before she ran through the feds' electronic plans with the microchip planted in the base of the duffle bag that would hold the cash and diamonds.

"I did not want to plant anything on the money or diamonds that could be easily detected that could queer the deal and end up costing my daughter her life. I don't need the money or the bad guys immediately—we will catch these fuckers. I guarantee it," Ortiz said, grim-faced, her right fist clenched around her gold Cross pen hovering over her to-do list.

"Anything to add, Hal," Ortiz looked up at her partner.

Halloran shrugged and turned to Jane.

"Uh, nothing right now, boss," Thoma said.

"Right now," Halloran jumped in, sensing his partner's discomfort talking to her chief, "we're going to check through those latest incident reports from the uniforms and the supps from the dicks to see if anything scares us. That okay with you?"

"Great, Mike. Stay close. I'm gonna need you...both," Ortiz said, adding the "both" lest she ignore Thoma.

"Get anything useful at Nuevo Laredo?" Halloran asked.

"Nada, but I don't think I'll eat there soon. A few of the wait staff I interrogated might spit in my burrito in the kitchen," Ortiz said, with a grimace rather than a grin. Nothing funny on Ortiz's mind.

"Gotcha, I'll be sifting through reports and charging this," Halloran said, holding up his cell before exiting the chief's office.

Safely down the hall and in the office with a pair of computers where they could peruse the latest reports, Halloran settled into a desk next to Thoma.

"Grunt work. But sometimes there's a few nuggets in this shit. So, let's do some prospecting till 9 and then cut out of here, eh?" Halloran said.

"10-4 on that," Thoma said, already pecking away.

At 8:45 p.m., Thoma lifted her head to catch Halloran's attention.

"One of the Spanish-speaking uniforms went back to that old address for Letty and caught the first landlady, just back from Mexico. The landlady didn't know much but said she heard Letty on the phone once talking about how she liked Gertrude's place, and the landlady thought Letty was gonna move," Thoma said.

"Maybe Gertrude is another waitress at Nuevo Laredo, a nail joint or a bar. Print that. May be worth a follow," Halloran said.

After grabbing the printout, Halloran pointed at the door for Thoma.

"It's gonna be a long day tomorrow. Let's get outta here," Halloran said.

"Amen," Thoma said.

And the partners called it a day. Tomorrow might be called a shitstorm for Sgt. Shitstorm and the small army of local cops and feds poised to spring.

CHAPTER 13

"How many times the pigs scooped you?" Gomez asked the scrawny 15-year-old, already tatted up his arms and his left calf.

"Oh, Jefe, how many time for you, man?" Victor Suarez countered.

Whack. Suddenly Victor was on the ground rubbing his left cheek where Gomez had slapped him, not punched him. He was going to use the punk.

"You see this teardrop, cabron? You no talk smack to a prince in the Cobras, kid. You been chosen to do a special job, but you may not be up to it if you stupid enough to speak like that. You smart or you estupido?" Gomez asked, hovering over Victor, who was still on the ground rubbing his cheek.

"Smart, smart. Sorry, sorry, man. Didn't mean nothin'. Jeez. Gimme a chance," Victor pleaded, using his hands and Jordans to slide backward away from Gomez.

"Okay, we see. You second-generation payasos (clowns) piss me off, you got things so easy," Gomez said, backing away. "Lupo tells me you are the fastest of the runners he uses. Is verdad?"

"I was the fastest guy in my 8th grade class and on the Park District track team," Victor bragged, now standing up but keeping a healthy distance from Gomez.

"Okay, I take you word. How many times you use that electric skateboard we buy you to lose the pigs?" Gomez asked about the Mippo electric skateboard Lupo bought his prized runners for their hard work shuttling drugs and cash.

"Dozens of times. Fully charged, that little guy go up to 28 miles an hour, and that's faster than Michael Vick. No pot-bellied narc has had a chance since I got this last year," Victor said, puffing up a bit.

"Bueno, bueno. Now we take a little trip downtown where you can make some nice money if you follow my orders, entiendes?" Gomez asked.

"Si," said Victor.

Forty minutes later, Lupo got off Lower Wacker Drive and parked his Ford Explorer on Post Place just north of Lake Street and put his hazard blinkers on. Gomez walked Victor over to Clark Street and a block south to the Daley Center. They took the escalators down to the lower level where most of the minor traffic offenses were heard.

"Right over there where we just got off the escalator is where sheriff's guys search people before they can get into the courts. Now we out here where the public can roam," Gomez said, taking the boy by the elbow.

"Now, see this small door there," Gomez said, walking Victor to the far northwest corner of the small hallway parallel to the security entrance. "This is where you're going to drop the bag. Got it. Once you drop it, you calmly walk toward the Blue Line station through this tunnel. See?" Gomez said, pointing east. As he did so, he checked his Apple watch and hit the compass. Gazed at it for a minute, then jotted down the location of the door on a notepad he kept in his back pocket. "327degrees NW, 41 degrees, 53.4" N. 87degrees, 37'49" W."

"Yeah, I know my way around the CTA, Jefe. I mean, thanks, I know," Victor said.

"Now we take another walk," Gomez said.

The Cobra Jefe walked Victor a bit east and then headed south down a long corridor leading to more Traffic Court entrances and a corridor that led to the Dunne Administration building but also to the CTA Blue Line station on Dearborn and a long tunnel that connected to the Red Line station. Multiple escape routes, Gomez knew. And at the end of that long corridor heading south were two escalators leading to and from the Dunne building lobby.

"You'll pick up a small bag there under the down escalator, and then calmly walk back to that small door near sheriff's security check where we yust came down, place it there, and walk away east toward the Blue Line and Red Line stations. Got it? If anyone stops you, you say stranger gave you $100 to move the bag. But better you use your speed and not get caught. Got it?"

"Got it, Jefe." Victor nodded.

Lots of exits to cover, but not the one Gomez would use.

"Tomorrow morning, you wait by the escalator, si? And someone, probably a gringo, will place a bag there and walk away. Your $100 job will be to calmly pick the bag up and walk back to the sheriff's station and drop it at the base of the small door and walk back toward the Blue Line station as we discuss now a minute ago, si?" Gomez repeated.

Victor nodded again. "I got it."

"Repeat it."

Victor repeated the plan almost word for word. It was simple, and Victor was not simple-minded. He saw this as a way to make a fast buck and an easy way to move up in the Cobras.

"Bueno, mi cabron pequeno," Gomez said. "If they try to stop you after the drop, you take off for the Blue Line with the speed you brag about."

Back in the car, Gomez jumped in shotgun, Lupo at the wheel, and turned to Victor in the back seat.

"You make sure to bring that skateboard tomorrow and make sure it fully charged, or you be in huge trouble. Pain trouble," Gomez warned.

"Si, si, for sure. Seguro," Victor assured the boss.

"And you, Flip, not Flop, make sure he has it and that it be charged. Entiendes?" Gomez asked his driver and lackey. "Now pull out onto Lake and head to Michigan Avenue, then right at Adams and park across from Art Institute. Just want a dry run."

When Lupo pulled over at the southwest corner of Adams and Michigan, Gomez got out, patted his back pocket to make sure his notepad and phone were there, and then disappeared into the Art Institute for 10 minutes. Inside, he jotted down the compass coordinates of a lower-level door near the men's room, a door very similar to the one at the Daley Center. Minutes later, satisfied, he returned to his co-conspirators.

"All still good. Perfecto," Gomez beamed. "Lez go, Flop."

Lupo fumed. Don't call me Flop. Asshole.

* * * * *

A week prior Gomez had walked through the plan by himself. After taking a Red Line train to Monroe, he'd entered the Art Institute 10 minutes before closing, clutching his tool bag, and then had hidden in the janitor's closet in the basement near the 3x4-foot metal door leading to the lower-level tunnels. After closing and an hour of silence, he crept out and heard the hum of a waxing machine coming from the second floor.

Satisfied he could get started, he slipped on a pair of blue surgical gloves and pried the hallway door open just enough to slip his hacksaw blade in behind the narrow lock. Putting on a pair of rawhide gloves over the blue gloves, he grasped the hacksaw blade and quickly started on the inch-wide, but thin, lock latch.

In 20 minutes, he'd cut through the latch and quickly grabbed a piece of putty from his bag to shove into the top opening of the door to keep it closed before he climbed down the 20 rungs of the ladder to the next level. There, he put on a hardhat with a flashlight attached and switched it on to illuminate the narrow path that was only dimly lit by an occasional 15-watt bulb.

From there he checked his compass, jotted down the reading and started walking north, then west to the Daley Center. It took him only 15 minutes, reading the sporadic wall signs and checking his watch/compass before he arrived at exit CC25, the CC standing for the Civic Center, the building's original name but changed to honor Mayor Richard J. Daley after he died in 1976. Gomez checked the compass; he was directly under the Daley Center lower-level sheriff's security station.

Gomez climbed up to the top of the rungs till he got to the door. There, he positioned himself and began slowly sawing through an identical lock. Once finished, he attached a bicycle chain and lock to the door handle and the top rung of the ladder, without locking it. Again, he shoved a piece of putty into the space between the door and the overhead jamb.

"Perfecto," he whispered to himself.

He was ready. He didn't bother explaining his plan to his co-conspirators on the way back.

CHAPTER 14

Up well before dawn, Halloran gazed out his 12th floor living room window as the eastern sky started to lighten over the horizon. Then in a matter of minutes, the giant orange orb slowly rose above the gray/blue waters of Lake Michigan. It was a sight he never tired of and one of the chief reasons he'd bought his two-bedroom apartment in the venerable monolith overlooking the north end of the Drive.

Once the sun had cleared the water, he spotted the first flakes of what would be a six-inch snowfall. Unfazed, he went down to begin his laps, alone in the pool, running dozens of scenarios through his mind before realizing he was on a fool's errand. This wouldn't be his play till shithead made his call, and even then, Sgt. Shitstorm would be a player but not Admiral or General Shitstorm.

After a quick shower and shave, Halloran got dressed and texted Thoma.

"Can you check the NCIC this morning to see if Lynch ever reoffended and what his LKA was?"

Halloran didn't want to forget his other case and wanted Thoma to know she needed to juggle assignments, no matter how time-sensitive—or not—they were. The NCIC (National Crime Information Center) kept incredible notes on the convictions, arrests, last known addresses (LKA), known associates, past prisons and jails, cellmates and much more.

In seconds, Halloran got a thumbs-up icon back from Thoma. And a "C U soon."

Halloran, like many older detectives, had resisted and resented the technology as it cascaded down on him. First, the manual Underwood typewriters gave way to the computers; then came those damn beepers—the first electronic leashes--then the cells and texts with the mixed blessings of the Internet. Thoma, however, grew up in it and could do amazing things in seconds on her phone even as she spoke on it to Halloran.

But she won't catch shithead with her phone today, he smirked as he eased into his Jeep Cherokee, after saluting Harry in the garage.

For logistical reasons, rather than a nod to Ortiz, the feds and the entire team set up for the call at 35th Street in Superintendent Wallace's spacious conference room and waited for the call.

At 9:04 a.m., Ortiz's cell buzzed, and the conference room filled with a score of federal agents and CPD brass fell silent.

"Ortiz here," the chief said.

"They said to say I'm okay..." Elly began, before the phone was snatched away.

"That's enough. You listen now. You bring the bag to Dunne Building, 69 W. Washington..." Gomez started.

But Letty burst in from the background. "Ella esta bien. Protejo. (She's fine. I protect.)"

"Shut up, puta (whore)," Gomez shouted, then resumed his instructions.

"You drop bag with cash and diamonds under the down escalator at noon and you see your daughter alive again. I drop phone now. You no find me. Once I get bag. I call and tell you where daughter is. Now you send photo of cash and rocks. Call later."

And he disconnected.

Ortiz looked to Macel, who was hovering over his tech coordinator, who held up his right palm.

"Somewhere near the Washington Library, within a few blocks," the tech said.

Kassos was on his phone immediately to launch the CPD patrol cars to look for the gray van, but they all knew the kidnappers might have switched cars. Indeed, Gomez and Lupo were in his Explorer with Victor in the back with his skateboard. The cops were chasing their tails; and the kidnappers knew it.

As ordered they texted the photo of the ransom. But there was no reply.

* * * * *

At Harrison and State, Gomez checked the photo, then tossed the burner to the curb before he broke out one of the new ones he'd bought at the Target at Roosevelt and Clark a few weeks earlier, just in case. At 11:50 a.m., near State and Randolph, Lupo turned left onto Randolph and left again at Clark and left again at Washington. There, Victor got out and headed for the Dunne Building escalator and waited.

Not long.

Victor got to the bottom of the escalator at 11:58 a.m., saw nothing beneath it, then circled around to the up escalator and went up. By the time he returned to the bottom of the down escalator, a white man dressed in a dark gray suit was walking away from a black gym bag lying beneath the escalator stairs.

Looking around furtively, Victor picked up the bag and began walking north through the long hallway, as planned. In the busy hallway no one seemed to notice the slightly built youth sauntering through the lower level, but there were scores of eyes on him with agents whispering into their phones as he passed.

Three minutes after picking up the bag, which weighed less than a half gallon of milk, Victor walked casually toward the small door near the sheriff's security check, glanced around briefly, and dropped the bag beneath the small door. He then walked a few dozen feet back to the main east-west corridor and began walking toward the Blue Line station.

None of the undercover cops or agents made an effort to grab him for a few moments until the small door near the bag swung open and a hand reached down and snatched the bag up and disappeared. The nearby cops and sheriff's deputies heard a metallic snap from behind the door.

"Grab the kid and stand by. We got the GPS tracker on the bag," ordered Macel, who was running the show. But as the agents approached Victor, he took off. Not at Michael Vick-speed but faster than the agents closest to him. And as bad luck would have it, Jesse "The Jet" had been assigned to the Dunne outpost.

Bobbing and weaving through the commuter foot traffic, Victor outran the agents and undercover cops and then two uniforms who were alerted on the radio to grab him. He jumped the gate at the Blue Line ticket counter, slid down the escalator, and jumped into a westbound train just before the doors closed.

Poof. He was gone.

"We're not getting a signal now," the tech told Macel. "The building's concrete and he's going down farther."

CHAPTER 15

The metallic sound the agents heard was the bike padlock being secured on the inside of the door where the arm had disappeared seconds before.

Gomez descended the ladder, then hopped on the electric skateboard, glanced at his compass and raced due east at 28 miles an hour, the scooter's top speed. In less than a minute, he stopped under the Cultural Center and examined the bag as the cops and agents yanked helplessly at the chained door. Gomez opened the gym bag and took out the money and a small red velour bag containing the diamonds. He checked the stacks of money for tracking devices but found none. But he spotted a small bulge at the bottom of the gym bag.

"So, you track me. You think?" Gomez whispered. Then, he pulled out a small navy-blue cloth bag with a drawstring and opened it wide. He poured the diamonds slowly into his hands a few dozen at a time, and then emptied them into his own bag. It took a few minutes, but he wanted to make sure there were no tracking devices attached to any of the rocks. In less than three minutes, the transfer was complete to his backpack.

Climbing back on the skateboard with his backpack on, he left the gym bag at the lower level beneath the Cultural Center and then headed south for a few blocks to beneath the Art Institute. Once there, he slowly, clumsily, ascended the ladder with skateboard and backpack. He pulled the putty out of the small metal door and peeked out into the corridor. A maintenance man was just passing by, talking on his cell. In seconds, no one was in the corridor.

Quickly and silently, Gomez exited the small metal door on the lower level, closing it quietly behind him, replacing the putty to jam the door shut. He walked quickly to the exit on Michigan and spotted Lupo across the street with the Explorer's blinkers on, facing west on Adams. He nodded his head, and Gomez walked casually toward the getaway car before tossing the bag and skateboard into the Explorer.

"Let's turn right onto State and then head toward Oak. Got it?" Gomez asked.

"Got it, Jefe. What we got in the bag?" Lupo asked.

"Too many questions, Loops. Entiendes?" Gomez said, his voice rising in a familiar threatening tone.

"Si, no problema," Lupo replied. "No problema."

At Walton Street, Gomez ordered Lupo to pull over to the curb and pop the rear door.

"You see how Victor's doing, and if he okay, bring him his skateboard back. I check with you later. I make it back from here," Gomez said. He pulled a $100 bill from his wallet and handed it to Lupo.

"This for Victor." Then he hesitated and pulled another $100 from his wallet, "and this for you, Loopy."

With that, Gomez grabbed his backpack, walked a block north and descended the stairs to get on a northbound L train at the Chicago Avenue subway station.

As he waited at the sparsely populated platform, Gomez dug out a burner phone from a side pocket of his backpack, looked around, then texted Letty two thumbs up emojis. Seconds later, she responded with three hearts.

"Treinta minutos, mi amor," Gomez answered.

As Lupo drove away, he swore at the windshield.

"One hundred for the chico and one hundred for me? Chenga tu madre, Jefe, you cheap fuck. What's in the bag?"

* * * * *

The GPS implanted in the bottom of the gym bag didn't move as the agents swooped down on the Cultural Center. They found a small door at the lower level and used a crowbar to easily open it. At the base of the ladder the lead agent found the empty bag, slipped it into a larger evidence bag and climbed back up to report back to Macel.

"The bag is empty. No sign of our guy. All we got now is the photo of the girl and a description of the van. Not much," Macel said, looking directly at Ortiz.

"Okay, I understand. He said he'd let her go, and the girl said they wouldn't harm her. We can still work the shit out of this. Lots of leather work till we get Elly back, and hope they release her," Ortiz said, before excusing herself. "Gotta call Joe."

For the next few hours, a swirl of activity enveloped the federal/CPD team. Halloran and Thoma sat in a nearby office awaiting orders, but the clock was ticking. It was past 3 p.m. when Halloran made a move. Per an earlier conversation with Ortiz, Halloran dialed the cell of bilingual Special Agent Juan Ochoa. He picked up immediately.

"Juan. It's Halloran. SAC Macel spoke to you earlier. You available now?"

"Sure am. What you need?" Ochoa asked.

"I need your Spanish for a couple interviews not far from you. You at Roosevelt Road now?" Halloran asked. Ochoa was indeed at his desk at the FBI West Side office, he told Halloran.

"Be outside in 10 minutes. I'll swing by in the Black Crown Vic with the M-plates beginning M190... Got it?" Halloran asked.

"Got it. See you soon," and Ochoa grabbed his Glock off his desk and slipped on his bulletproof vest, unsure what he was about to get into.

Halloran turned to Thoma.

"This is a two-person interview. Don't want to overwhelm these women. In the meantime, can you continue your search for our guy Lynch?"

"Sure, I'll catch an Uber back to Belmont," Thoma said.

Halloran wanted to drill down on both the former landlady and the Nuevo Laredo manager but needed an interpreter, at least with the landlady. He picked up Ochoa and headed to the landlady, Senora Hernandez, who was finishing her morning cleaning when Ochoa knocked on the door and announced "Policia."

In a minute, the front door cracked open an inch and Ochoa held up his shielfd and ID.

"Por favor, Senora, tenemos algunas preguntas sobre tu sobrina, Leticia Diaz."

"Si, si," the 79-year-old landlady said, swinging the door open wide.

Ochoa led the way into a dimly lit two-bedroom apartment on the first floor. Halloran followed the two into the living room, where widow Hernandez motioned to a couch as she sat in an aging, sagging brown La-Z-Boy.

"Habla ingles?" Halloran asked.

"No, senor. Lo siento," she said, looking beseechingly at Ochoa.

"No es una problema," Ochoa said, with a reassuring smile.

Ochoa asked a series of questions about Leticia, to which Hernandez answered, "I don't know" or "No se" in Spanish. Halloran listened patiently because they were the questions he wanted asked--the who, what, why, when, where and how.

But Ochoa was running out of questions and patience after 20 minutes of "No se's" and what a nice religious girl Letty was who went to mass at St. Pius V, like she does.

"Ask her if she ever overheard any phone conversations, even fragments. Tell her it's her duty to tell us, not a betrayal to Letty. She's in a lot of trouble and a young girl's life is at stake. Scare her," Halloran said.

He watched as the old lady's expression changed from curiosity to fear as Ocho turned up the heat.

Then she spoke rapidly in Spanish for a minute, looking at Ochoa. And then to Halloran, holding her hands up to Halloran.

"She says she once heard her say she wanted to go to Gertrude's," Ochoa said.

"Is that a friend or a beauty salon or a restaurant or what?" Halloran zeroed in.

Ochoa repeated Halloran's questions.

More "No se's."

Halloran turned to Ochoa.

"Ring a bell with you? Know some joint called Gertrude's. Maybe Gertrude's Grill?" Halloran asked.

"Nada," Ochoa said.

"Bastante," Halloran announced, nearly exhausting his Spanish vocabulary, and nodded to the landlady, "Gracias," before exiting.

"Nuevo Laredo," Halloran said.

"Great food." Ochoa responded.

"Yeah, but questionable hiring practices," Halloran responded.

Ten minutes later, just as the joint was emptying from the last luncheon crowd, the Crown Vic pulled up and parked in a loading zone in front of the restaurant on 18th Street.

"I've already braced the dayside manager, Roberta Ruiz, so I want you to barge your way into the kitchen, flashing your shield and start interrogating the waitresses, see what you can shake loose. I'll grab Ruiz and escort her back into her office again. Sound good?" Halloran asked.

"I'm on it," Ochoa said. Halloran hated "I'm on it" almost as much as "Roger that." But he kept his sarcasm to himself.

"Roberta Ruiz," Halloran said, flashing his star at the receptionist, looming over her and blocking her view as Ochoa slipped into the restaurant and headed for the kitchen.

In a minute, Ruiz appeared and walked Halloran back to her office.

"When I was here earlier this week, you told me Letty had worked in Puerto Vallarta before and you took your aunt's word for it. Did Letty or your aunt say which restaurant or restaurants she worked at? It's not on this application," Halloran asked. "Take a deeper dive into your files if you have to."

Halloran wanted the information if it was available, but more importantly, he wanted time for Ochoa to brace a few waitresses before Ruiz or another manager could interfere.

"Well, I'll look," Ruiz said.

"I like Puerto Vallarta," Halloran said, getting sweaty in the tiny office with his winter coat on over the bulletproof vest. "You been there?"

"I was born in Evanston, Detective, and I prefer Florida for vacation," Ruiz replied, the jaws getting tighter with each response. "I thought police wore uniforms."

"They let detectives wear their own clothes."

Her question didn't bother Halloran. He would plow on.

Ruiz had the file open again and was reading some handwriting on the side of the inside left of the manila folder.

"I wrote 'La Dolce' here, but I don't have any notes that I or the night manager actually verified her employment there in PV," she said.

Halloran kept asking questions about their hiring practices, including how they verified Social Security numbers and immigration status, just to make Ruiz nervous and keep her talking, equivocating.

In the meantime, Ochoa and his gold fed shield had quickly loosened the tongue of a young waitress.

"She real nervous her last day. She say she moving to 'hood. I ask her what 'hood. She say it's a street. It make no sense to me," the waitress told Ochoa in Spanish and English.

"What else did she say?" Ochoa asked in English.

"Nada. Nada, por favor," she pleaded.

Ochoa cornered a few other waitresses, but since the word had spread quickly of a fed, no one knew anything about anything, and it was as if Letty never existed at Nuevo Laredo.

Halloran had finished with Ruiz and joined Ochoa at the exit door.

Ochoa told Halloran about Letty moving to "hood." It was now 3:20 p.m.

"Good Jesus Christ. I get it. Hood. Gertrude's!"

He dialed Ortiz without explaining the connection to Ochoa.

CHAPTER 16

Ortiz's cell buzzed as she was sitting in the U.S. Attorney's office conference room with her boss, Wallace, Macel, and a roomful of agents from various federal agencies and her own phalanx of support staff. No one questioned the mother of the victim when she silently slipped out of the conference room as she raised her right index finger.

"Yeah, Mike. What's up?" Ortiz said, as she walked into the open and empty office of the First Assistant U.S. Attorney Steve Muller.

"Syl, I think I know what street he's on and it's not a long street. In my old neighborhood, and it would have been on his way north from where he tossed Elly's phone," Halloran rushed the words out, then slowed down.

He related the "hood" mention and the "Gertrude" reference and admitted he was making a leap but a logical one.

"Hood Avenue runs for about four blocks from Broadway to Clark, and St. Gertrude's Church is halfway through that stretch, a block north. She's a religious girl, the landlady says. So, we got her photo, and I say we send the troops out with the photo. First, I'll go to the rectory and then we'll go door to door, and there aren't that many apartment buildings on that stretch," Halloran said.

Ortiz heard the urgency, felt it, and knew her old partner was not one to go off half-cocked.

"So, the Rogers Park (24th District) station is closest. I'll get Kassos right on it and immediately get a BOLO out. Great work, Mike," Ortiz said, breaking off, and then bursting into the meeting to share the news and get the extra help she needed.

* * * * *

Gomez was eager to dump Elly but waited for dark before setting off for an area where he could get away seamlessly in an area he knew.

As a teenager fresh from Sinaloa, Gomez had vacationed with family friends in Indiana near St. John and swum in nearby Cedar Lake just off U.S. 41. Gomez learned to swim there and as an adult had returned to the area for weekend getaways with gangbanging friends, just a 75-minute drive from Chicago.

So, with three Subway sandwiches and Diet Cokes he'd bought on his way back to the basement apartment, Gomez was ready to pack up his hostage and head to a secluded drop-off point far from the feds and locals.

With her feet tied with duct tape but at a 15" spread to allow limited walking, Elly was uprighted and her hands were freed temporarily. The ski mask and the tape over her mouth remained intact.

"We taking you home, bitch. If you try something stupid, maybe I just slice you up now and dump you in the lake, entiendes?" Gomez asked. Elly nodded.

Leaving Letty and their hostage in the apartment, Gomez walked outside and slowly slid open the side door to the van, then looked down the alley in both directions. Nothing. No one lurking in the dark alley.

Back in the apartment, he grabbed Elly's right hand and walked her to the van, got in first and pulled her in behind him. Letty followed with a bag containing the sandwiches, pop, duct tape, a cell phone and the backpack with the loot.

Letty stayed in back with Elly as Gomez slid quickly into the driver's seat.

As he exited the alley at Lakewood, he glanced right and saw the rear of a black SUV heading west on Hood. Gomez turned left to Granville and right to head to Sheridan Road. From Sheridan, he entered the Outer Drive at Hollywood and headed to Indiana. In rush-hour traffic, he made it to the St. John area in less than two hours, taking I-294 to the U.S. 41 exit.

He maintained his speed at five miles over the limit and kept an eye on the rearview mirror. Just as they crossed the Indiana-Illinois border, Letty pulled down the tape and asked Elly if she wanted a sandwich and some pop.

"Yes, please," Elly said, "but first the pop. Very thirsty."

"Si, si, mi pequena amiga," Letty whispered, then held the diet cola to Elly's mouth like a bird feeding her baby chicks. Then Letty fed Elly the ham and Swiss cheese, bite by bite, to the starving teen, and washed it down with the rest of the Diet Coke.

"Thanks very much," Elly whispered.

"Over soon, over soon. I not let him hurt you," Letty promised.

After getting on U.S. 41 South in Indiana, he approached the Highway 231 exit. There, Gomez turned left and headed east. The road was unlit and deserted. After two miles, he turned right down a country road that led to a farmhouse about 1,000 yards south. He pulled over to the soft shoulder and stopped about 300 yards down the narrow road.

He pulled Elly from the rear and walked her a few minutes into the middle of a plowed corn field, then pulled a burner and dialed Ortiz's number after lifting the ski mask to her nose and pulling down the tape from Elly's mouth.

When Ortiz answered the call from the unknown caller, she heard Gomez's voice:

"Say hello to mommy."

"Mom. I'm okay. They're letting me go. They drove for two hours. I don't know where I am..."

Gomez grabbed the phone back.

"She smart girl. She make her way to safety. You no find me. Adios, chief," Gomez said and laughed, then disconnected.

"Now I loosen your hand tape a little. You get free in maybe 15 minute. You'll see house with lights on a few mile away. They help you. You tell mama we good to you. Hasta luego, nina rica (rich girl)" Gomez said.

With that, he slit the tape on her hands, then loosely rebound her hands but in a way that she could get free with some effort, he knew. He slid the cell under the front tire and crushed it as he pulled away.

* * * * *

Joe and Sylvia had gone home to be with their two other children, Joe Jr., 19, and Anita, 21, both still in college. The family stood in the living room, hugging, occasionally sobbing and waiting.

"It's gonna be okay," Syl Ortiz told her family. "We just gotta wait."

Just then, the land line went off and Joe Jr. swiftly picked it up and handed it to his mother, saying, "It's a 219 area code." Before she could speak, she heard Elly's voice.

"I'm okay, mom. I'm with a nice farmer here and his wife. He's going to drive me home, he says. I'll be home in a couple of hours," Elly said.

"Let me talk to him, honey," Ortiz answered.

After a brief conversation with the farmer, Elmer Covington, and hearing his offer to drive Elly home, Ortiz hung up.

"She'll be home soon. She's safe." A fresh round of tears and hugs broke out.

CHAPTER 17

Standing at the massive oak door entrance to St. Gertrude's rectory, Halloran was hit with a few flashbacks, some mildly unpleasant.

Monsignor Liam Kelly opened the door wide as Halloran held out his star, Ochoa his shield.

"I still recognize you, Mike. Even after all these years and all your growth," said the aging priest. "What brings you back to the parish and so late in the evening?"

"An urgent matter, Monsignor. This is Special Agent Ochoa of the FBI. We are looking for this girl," he said, holding up an 8x10 of Diaz. "We have reason to believe she frequents the church."

The priest pulled up his cheaters from his chest necklace and peered at the photo.

"Yes, I believe I've seen her recently, at the 9 on Sunday. What's she done?"

"She may be involved in a kidnapping. Do you know where she lives?" Ochoa asked.

"I'm sorry. I only saw her at the communion rail. Never outside church," Kelly responded.

"Thanks, Monsignor. That helps. We gotta go," Halloran said, and the two retreated to their cars. Ochoa had picked up his government car on the way to save time later. Halloran got in the shotgun of Ochoa's federal ride, a nondescript gray Chevy Impala. Halloran left the black Crown Vic on Glenwood in front of the gym.

"Okay, there's a nine-flat at about 1322 West. There are at least a couple two-flats between Glenwood and Broadway and I'm going to hit them, then hit the thirty-flat at the corner of Glenwood and Hood. You hit a couple of the two-flats west of Glenwood, and we'll meet at that big nine-flat," Halloran said.

"You need a translator—you call me. Right?" Ochoa said.

"Right."

Now there were other cops and agents arriving, but Halloran told Kassos their plan and asked that the uniforms knock on the doors of the single-family homes.

They all knew then that Elly was safe. So, the urgency was now to find Mr. and Ms. Shithead. And Halloran, as the designated Sgt. Shitstorm, smelled blood.

Just as Halloran was about to go to his car, his cell buzzed. A 219 area code. Curious, he connected.

"Uncle Mike, it's Elly. I memorized your number, but that's not all I memorized. I think I can help. I..." Elly said, before Halloran jumped in.

"Honey, are you okay. Where are you? You talked to your parents?"

"Uncle Mike. I need you to listen, please. Please. I memorized where they went after they grabbed me, the turns and stops. Can you listen? Take notes. I think I can help you find them," Elly pleaded.

Halloran knew Elly was a straight-A student and had obviously memorized his cell. So, he said:

"You talk. You're on speaker with me and FBI Agent Ochoa. We'll take notes. Go!"

"Okay. They grabbed me on Schiller at the alley between Clark and Dearborn and turned right out of the alley, going east on Schiller. Three stops to Inner Lake Shore Drive, then hang a left. A block slow, then at the light and a soft right to the Outer Drive. Then about three minutes and they slow to a momentary stop for about a minute and then speed up again. I figure they got on and off at Fullerton or Belmont, and rolled down the window for a few seconds. Then another five or six minutes till they make a slow left turn and then a hard right. They go about a block and stop for about a minute, figured a red light. Then another two minutes of steady traffic and come to a stop. Figure another stoplight. Then they hang another left. Ten-fifteen seconds and a stop. Then another 10-15 seconds and a stop. Then after a few seconds I can hear the L passing overhead. And then another full stop for maybe a minute. Figure a red light.

"We then drive for maybe 15 -20 seconds and come to a full stop, then turn left, then after five seconds a right. We drive down what I think is an alley and soon the sound of some crunching when we turn left and stop. Now it's raining hard. We wait there for maybe an hour and I can hear them talking a bit about waiting till dark. They got a ski mask over my head and tape over my eyes. Then they loosen the tape on my ankles. Next, he put a jacket over my head and shoulders and walked me about 15 feet and down two stairs to the basement apartment. When we left a few days later, I heard what sounded like cracked asphalt as we pulled out.

"Is that helpful?" Elly asks. "I'm with a nice farmer who's driving me home. Should be home in a couple hours."

"That's tremendous. Thanks, honey. Now get home and give your mom and dad a big hug and kisses," Halloran said, his voice cracking slightly before disconnecting.

He turned to Ochoa.

"This is my old neighborhood. I know exactly the building she's talking about. They took the Outer Drive to Hollywood, Sheridan to Granville, Granville to Lakewood, and then the alley between Hood and Granville to that nine-flat at 1322 Hood. Bingo. Let's get some undercovers in the front while you and I hit the back," Halloran said.

Ortiz had dispatched Wrenn to the Edgewater neighborhood to herd the dicks' end of the hunt. Halloran called Wrenn's cell with his plan. She wanted five minutes.

No problem, especially with a commander who might be his boss next week or month. Yes, ma'am.

They took Ochoa's less conspicuous Impala and parked it in the alley, behind 1343 Granville, half a block from the basement apartment, then walked on the south side of the alley slowly, guns out and down by their right sides. Halloran, his Browning; Ochoa, his Glock.

They entered the parking lot and slowly crept to the side of the building before inching their way east, Halloran in the lead. He'd hoped for some tire tracks but the rain had washed half the snow away even as a fresh round of huge snowflakes started falling.

When they got near to the gangway leading to the apartments, Halloran raised his left hand, then his index finger to his lips, and waited. Hearing nothing, the two crept up to the basement apartment, positioning on each side of the door, and again--listening.

"All ready?" Halloran whispered into his phone to Wrenn. She texted a thumbs up. "On the count of 10," Halloran whispered.

Then Halloran motioned his lead pointing to his chest. Ochoa nodded. And at 10, Halloran stepped back, and in a swift move, kicked open the six-panel door.

"Police. No one move!" Halloran yelled.

"FBI" Ochoa bellowed.

Not a sound.

Slowly, weapons raised, they searched the two-bedroom apartment in minutes. Quickly, they discovered the room where Elly had been stashed. There were Styrofoam cups, discarded strips of duct tape, fast-food wrappers and bags, and the slight smell of an unbathed body.

Halloran called Wrenn.

"We found it. No one here. But this is where they had her. Let's get the evidence guys in here and find out who this asshole is," Halloran said.

"Coming," Wrenn responded, bristling just slightly, but realizing that the command was really coming from Ortiz in a roundabout but faster way.

Halloran looked at Ochoa, hands on hips.

"Fuck. Just fuck."

"Amen, bro. Amen, but I guess I wouldn't say that to the monsignor," Ochoa said. And both of the fatigued, temporary partners laughed.

CHAPTER 18

"Now we celebrate," Gomez told Letty as he headed back to the city. "We go to Gibson's and eat first class."

"Que es Gibson's?" Letty asked.

"You see, mi amor. You see," Gomez said.

He got off the Kennedy Expressway at Ohio Street and headed east to turn north on State, then turned right at Walton, where he found a parking garage a block from Gibson's, the posh Rush Street eatery.

After parking on the second level, he climbed into the back seat and took three Franklins out of the hostage loot, then pushed the bag back under the front passenger seat, the gang's Mac-10 wrapped in a dark gray towel beside the bag.

"We eat good," Gomez said, then led Letty hand in hand down the fashionable strip to Gibson's.

The pair looked out of place as they weren't quite dressed like the usual clientele in their denims and beat-up down coats, but the hostess showed them to a remote booth anyway, where they ate and drank like millionaires, as they now thought of themselves.

After steak dinners, they roamed down Rush Street and decided to have a night cap, turning west on Division and settling on The Lodge. It was now almost midnight, and this gin mill was nearly empty as they ordered nightcaps—tequila straight up for Gomez and Sprite for Letty. As the pair of kidnappers relived the last hectic hours in hushed whispers, the place emptied but for the bartender.

For Letty, she was petrified but stimulated by the money, the diamonds, the dazzle of the Rush Street nightlife and the prospect of a new life with this crazy ex-con sitting across from her, gently holding her hand.

For Gomez, he'd hit the jackpot. He'd evened the score and then some with that "fucking prosecutor," outfoxed the cops, toyed with the feds and scored big-time. And had a beautiful girlfriend, albeit almost young enough to be his daughter.

At 1:10 a.m., he decided to return home to collect their things at the basement apartment before heading south to Mexico and a new life. He was aware the cops might have a photo of the van from the various video cameras but knew they had no license plate due to the snowfall covering the plate numbers before the rain hit. A cocky con, he felt safe going back to the Hood Avenue address but would be vigilant, he told Letty; so should she, he added.

* * * * *

Halloran and Ochoa sat in the agent's car at the west end of the alley on the apron of the garage behind 1343 W. Granville, drank coffee and discussed old cases. Halloran had more old cases, and Ochoa asked a lot of questions. By 1:30 a.m., Halloran called Wrenn's replacement and asked for relief in the alley for himself and Ochoa.

"Go home," came the lieutenant's immediate response. "We got it and Ortiz said to take the unmarked car home with you." As Halloran got out and walked through freshly fallen snow to the unmarked squad, Ochoa eased out of his spot.

Halloran took only five minutes before he pulled the Crown Vic into his garage at the classic pink stucco building at Sheridan and Bryn Mawr, the Edgewater Beach Apartments, which had been built as an adjunct to the north of the stately and elegant but long-gone Edgewater Beach Hotel.

Ochoa lived farther away. As he got to the end of the alley, he stopped for a few minutes and checked his messages. Spying nothing vital, he headed west to Broadway first, then north to Hollywood. But as he turned east on Hollywood, he spotted a gray Dodge van driven by a Latino heading west. Ochoa quickly turned into the alley just east of the L tracks, backed into the westbound traffic and looked for the van but saw nothing.

At the Broadway light, he looked north and spotted the van a block away. Unsure what he had, Ochoa followed the van to Glenlake, where it turned left, then right into the alley toward Hood. He was close enough now to see the outline of a woman riding shotgun. Ochoa picked up his phone and called Halloran.

"Mike, I think I spotted them," and then in frantic bursts, described what he'd seen, turning right to follow Gomez into the alley.

As Gomez reached Hood, he spotted several Crown Vics parked on Hood near his apartment, then spotted Ochoa's headlights in his rear-view as the Impala pulled into the alley behind him.

"Mutherfuckuh," Gomez yelled and yanked the wheel right, flooring the accelerator till he hit Broadway and headed north and blew through the red light at Granville—Ochoa now in hot pursuit.

"Mike, he's made me and is on the run. Heading north on Broadway—fast," Ochoa said.

Seconds before Ochoa's call Halloran had just given his keys to Harry but quickly grabbed them back and backed up through the garage onto Sheridan, tires screaming.

"I'm on my way," Halloran yelled into his phone. "Five minutes away. I'll call in your position for back-up. Don't try to take this fuck yourself. Help's on the way."

Gomez had the van floored and had hit 70 by the time he passed Hamilton's Lounge just south of Devon. He jammed on the brakes at Devon, fishtailed into a right turn onto Sheridan and quickly righted the van. In half a block, he spotted an alley, and slammed the van into the alley, hit a utility pole damaging the driver's side, but hoping the cop wouldn't see the turn.

Just as he turned onto Sheridan, Ochoa spotted the brake lights of the van as it disappeared into the alley. He pulled his Glock from his shoulder holster and placed it on the passenger-side front seat. In seconds, he pulled into the alley.

The alley quickly turned into a labyrinth. Eighty yards south, the alley had a 90-degree left turn, then after another 50 yards came another sharp 90-degree turn right. Gomez negotiated the first two turns sliding. As he made the last turn, right behind the rear of Hamilton's, he slid into a snowbank in the unplowed alley and got stuck after skidding for 20 yards, Ochoa right behind him. He quickly pulled the Mac-10 from under the seat where Letty sat petrified.

Ochoa still had Halloran on speaker.

"Mike, he's stuck in a snowbank. I'm passing him to block him going farther south. He's getting out of the car. He's got a gun…" Ochoa said, and Halloran could hear rapid gunfire. Halloran was still six blocks away, driving wildly, weaving into the southbound traffic and then back into northbound Broadway.

"I'm coming, partner. Don't engage. Repeat, don't engage." But then he heard more gunfire, some rapid, some sporadic and close to the speaker.

"Fuck," Halloran yelled in frustration and floored the Crown Vic, which fishtailed on the still slick streets.

As Halloran swore, Gomez had his Mac-10 trained on Ochoa and was spraying the open driver's side door with a barrage of bullets, as Ochoa crouched behind the open door and returned fire blindly over the top of the door. One Mac-10 round ricocheted off the bottom of the windshield and hit the top of Ochoa's vest, stunning him, and knocking him to the ground, his Glock flying out of reach beneath the car.

Gomez was firing from behind a dumpster, his arm extended but nothing else exposed. He yelled to Letty and continued firing. A second bullet struck Ochoa just above his vest, going through and through after ricocheting off his collarbone.

"Back the van into that loading zone and turn it around! The cop's blocking us!" Gomez screamed.

Letty slid over, slipped the van into reverse, spun the wheels for a minute, pushed it into drive, then back into reverse. After the van caught traction, she backed into a loading slot of a moving and storage company. Then, as Gomez watched, mouth agape, Letty put the van into drive and sped back to where they came from. Then the Mac-10 jammed.

"Motherfucker," Gomez swore, then turned his attention back to Ochoa, who had crawled between two dumpsters.

"I'm hit, Mike," Ochoa cried, hoping Halloran could still hear him with the phone on the driver's side floor of his Impala.

Uncertain if the cop was hurt and still armed but certain help was on the way, Gomez took off running south down the alley. As he made another 90-degree turn, he spotted headlights approaching the alley from Broadway and dove behind a huge dumpster. Seconds later, Halloran whizzed by, siren wailing and Mars light flashing.

Once the cop car passed him and made a hard right turn out of sight, Gomez leaped up, brushed snow off and crossed Rosemont into the alley east of Broadway. Then he continued running down the alley through more turns till he saw Broadway just shy of Granville. He looked around for a hiding spot but found none, so he just stuffed the jammed Mac-10 deep into a snowbank 50 yards shy of Broadway.

As CPD cars whizzed by, blue Mars lights flashing, sirens wailing, Gomez then walked calmly east on Granville to the L station, where he deftly vaulted the turnstile, raced up the steps and luckily caught a southbound train just before the doors closed. The car was deserted but for a homeless man, asleep and smelly near the far door.

He rode unmolested to Wilson. Hopped off, then called an Uber and rode to Lupo's to plot his next move, penniless, unarmed and pissed.

"Where you go, Letty? Perra, Puta. (Bitch. Whore.)"

* * * * *

Halloran slid to a stop behind Ochoa's car and spotted his partner with his right hand clutched to his shoulder, blood oozing through his fingers.

As he ran toward Ochoa, he grabbed the radio Velcroed to his shoulder and shouted: "Ten-one! Ten-one! Officer down! In the alley behind 6341 N. Broadway, approximately Hamilton's bar. Need an ambulance. Stat."

"Ten-4," came the static reply.

Halloran could soon hear other cops arriving in the alley from the other direction.

"I got you, partner. I think It's just a nick. How you doin'?"

Ochoa was up on his left elbow, grimacing, still clutching the wound.

"I'm gonna be okay. Not a direct hit, I don't think," Ochoa said. "How's it look?"

Halloran took a close look for the first time. Just below where Ochoa was holding his hand, Halloran spotted a second bullet lodged in the vest, 6 inches lower than the shoulder wound and precariously close to the heart.

"You look like you got hit just above the shoulder blade," Halloran said.

"The girl got away in the van headed to Sheridan," Ochoa said.

Just then the first paramedic swooped in and took over at about the same time squads raced into the alley from the north.

"How was he dressed, partner?" Halloran asked.

"'Didn't get a good look, but I saw it was a Latino and he had some kind of automatic machine pistol," Ochoa said before the paramedics loaded him onto a stretcher for a frantic ride to Northwestern's ER.

Halloran went back to his car, but by then there were 10 other squads piled in behind him.

"Fuck!" he yelled and took off running.

Figuring the guy was headed for the L, Halloran commandeered the last squad in line and told the startled young uniform cop to take him to the Argyle L station. It was pure guesswork. Halloran figured if shithead got on an L at Granville, he would've made it at most to Argyle.

At Argyle, he jumped the turnstile, charged up the stairs and waited for the next southbound L train, figuring the gunman was headed into the city. In a few minutes, a train pulled in. Halloran watched each car as the train pulled slowly into the station, seeing only a few passengers. Then he boarded.

Going car by car as fast as he could, his Browning in his right hand as he used his left to open each adjoining car door, he found only three sleeping homeless men and one drunken college kid in the whole train.

Halloran got off at Lawrence.

"God damn it!" Halloran yelled into the empty Uptown night. "Fuck!"

* * * * *

On the way to Northwestern, the paramedic examining Ochoa leaned over the wounded but not seriously injured agent.

"Ever hear the expression: 'Dodged a bullet?' The one that winged you went through and through right over the clavicle, but there's another bullet stuck in your vest, not where you'd want it to have hit without your vest on," the paramedic told Ochoa. "We'll get you patched up right away at the ER. Don't worry."

"Thanks," Ochoa mumbled at the end of a very long day.

* * * * *

Letty didn't pull off for gas till she hit the rest stop exit on I-55 just short of Edwardsville, about a four-hour drive south of Chicago. Along the way she'd turned the radio on and heard her name on WBBM-780 as wanted by the FBI and Chicago cops.

It was still predawn as she pulled into the rest stop's parking lot. She pulled next to an empty Camry and looked around and listened. Grabbing the tool kit from the glove compartment, she took out the two screwdrivers, a flathead and a Phillips.

Kneeling down in the snow, she used the Phillips to unscrew her rear plate and set it aside. Then she unfastened the rear Indiana plate of the Camry and replaced it with her plate. Next, she affixed the Camry's plate to the van. Before leaving, she removed her front plate and tossed it into a trash can.

If they're looking for that plate, I'll be okay, she thought, knowing Indiana did not mandate front plates. Heading home.

Ten miles later she pulled off the Interstate and into a Speedway gas station. After grabbing two cups of black coffee, she bought a small box of NoDoz pills, washed a couple down with the coffee and hit the road again after filling the tank.

Letty drove for 10 straight hours at just a few miles over the speed limit till she got to a rest stop outside Tulsa, exhausted. As she drove, her mind was spinning. It wasn't till she was in the far end of the rest stop parking lot that she parked, slid open the rear door and climbed in to take a nap.

She slept a fitful three hours and awakened groggy and disoriented. When she regained her bearings, she looked around, turned on the overhead light and spotted Gomez's backpack sticking out under the passenger seat of the van.

Though alone in the darkened van, she still hesitated before opening the backpack. Inside, she found the cash neatly wrapped in rubber bands and the velour bag containing the diamonds. She began shaking.

"Madre de Dios. Ayudame (Mother of God. Help me)," she whispered.

PART TWO

The Catch

CHAPTER 19

Empty L trains kept passing by in Halloran's scattered dreams. Then he'd wake up, curse his bad luck and try to go back to sleep.

By 5:45 a.m., he gave up and threw on some sweats to go to the locker room and changed into his swimming suit. While swimming, he planned his questions for Elly when he got to the Ortiz home by 9, as planned.

She's a smart and strong girl, but she's just been through hell, and her parents are going to be protective, especially Syl but also Joe, so I'll go slowly with Elly.

When Halloran rang the bell at 9:01 a.m., he was shocked to see a smiling Elly open the door, dressed in her basketball uniform.

"Uncle Mike," Elly shrieked before throwing her arms around her godfather. With his laptop in his left hand, Halloran swept Elly off her feet with his right arm and carried her into the foyer, where Joe and Syl stood, beaming.

"It's all good, Mike. She wanted to go to practice this morning, but we told her you'd have questions. So, come into the kitchen and have a cup of coffee while we debrief," Syl said, taking Halloran's right elbow and guiding him into their designer kitchen, all stainless-steel appliances and brilliant white cabinets.

As Halloran expected, Syl was both mom and boss as they sat down at the kitchen table.

"She never saw either of their faces, but she did see what we both know was part of a gang tat, looked like a snake head on the guy's hand. She was blindfolded with a ski mask and her mouth taped shut but for drinking and eating. She spotted the snake tat through a slit in the blindfold," Syl said. "His English was spotty and hers very sparse."

Halloran was nodding and taking notes.

When Syl hesitated, Halloran jumped in.

"What could you hear them talking about, if anything?"

"They kept the door closed and the washing machines were almost always going next door in what I guessed was the building's laundry. So, I couldn't hear much," Elly said.

"I understand, honey, but anything you did hear could be helpful," Halloran gently coaxed.

"Well, he was a real jerk to her. Heard him slap her, and her outcry. Called her his 'puta' you know, whore," Elly said, glancing at her mom. "When he left one day, I think to call you, mom, I could hear her talking to someone on the phone and mentioning 'puta mia.' I think she was quoting his bad Spanish, as he referred to her as his whore," Elly continued. "But she seemed nice and, judging by her voice and her hands, she seemed not much older than me."

"Could you see how she was dressed?" Halloran asked.

"All I could see was her blue jeans and the bottom of a red Nike sweatshirt. It was cold in that basement," Elly said.

"And him? How was he dressed?" Halloran asked.

"Pretty much the same. Levis and a black shirt was all I could see," Elly said.

"Okay, El. That was great, and your guidance to the stash apartment could not have been better," Halloran said, giving Elly a final hug. "Now we gotta catch this son of a bitch, and we will, thanks to you."

At that, Halloran turned to leave and nodded to Syl to follow him to the foyer.

"So, couple that slap Elly heard and the way he addressed her that we overheard on the phone, I think we can at least guess she was an unwilling accomplice," Halloran said, with his voice rising to indicate a question.

"She's young and vulnerable but no one wants to be treated like shit. So yeah, I'm thinking he sweet-talked her at first and then gradually intimidated her to the point she feared for her life," Syl said. "I'm guessing here, but I'm betting that our guy never let the stash of cash and sparklers out of his sight—until he jumped from the car and started shooting. Then she sees the opportunity to get away from this asshole and ditches him.

"But she doesn't go back to the apartment-- and stay with me here-- she soon realizes her guy has his hands full and now she can get away, so she keeps moving--but where?" Halloran said.

"I think your logic's sound. But now we have to coordinate with the feds to catch them both, fleeing separately, and the sooner the better," Ortiz said. She quickly dialed Thompson and told him to set up a meeting the feds.

"Gotta figure shithead is looking for her, too," Halloran said. "But is he also wondering where?"

CHAPTER 20

After a fitful nap, Letty drove steadily just 2 to 3 miles an hour over the speed limit, lost in thought and fear. She soon realized two horrible truths and one enticing possibility.

First, Gomez was going to try to find her and would probably kill her if he did. Second, a small army of police were looking for her, too. But she also realized she had a small fortune in her van and needed to get to Mexico as fast as possible, ahead of the cops and Gomez, neither of whom knew where she was headed.

Refreshed and resolved, Letty, with no American driver's license but her Mexican passport and a fortune in the backpack, began the long trek to El Paso, still another 11 hours away.

In El Paso, she parked in front of Sacred Heart Church, made the sign of the cross and prayed silently for a few seconds for safe passage. Then, she walked a few blocks to South El Paso Street and joined the procession of reverse commuters returning to Mexico.

At the Mexican side, she folded two $100 bills inside her passport and told the border guard that her driver's license had been stolen. Seamlessly, he switched hands as he glanced at her passport and then waved her through as he pocketed the bribe like a bent alderman.

An hour later, after changing $500 American into Mexican pesos, she found a cheap hotel and slept for 12 hours. When she awoke, she caught the last bus for a long overnight bus ride to Guadalajara, a booming town of more than a million and a perfect place to rest, hide and consider.

There, she changed another $200 and bought a burner phone at a Walmart, where she also picked up some new clothes. She knew that by now the cops, and maybe Gomez, had descended on Pia Karine, and she wanted her aunt to know she was safe. But that could wait.

* * * * *

By noon, Gomez started realizing Letty was not coming to Lupo's joint. His calls to her cell went to voicemail.

"Fucking bitch," Gomez said over his coffee in Lupo's kitchen. "Need you to take me to 27th Street house, ahora."

There, at the gang's stash/safe house in Little Village, he went to the basement storage locker and recovered more than $30,000 from the sizable stack of gang cash and his spare Glock and two full magazines from a safe.

"Now we gotta find her and my money," Gomez told Lupo.

"Yeah, Jefe, but where she at?"

"Text all our guys and tell them they get $1,000 if they spot Letty or the van."

Lupo quickly complied.

Before leaving, Gomez stopped by the first-floor sorting and cutting room, where a team of mask-clad ladies prepared Oxy and meth laced with small amounts of fentanyl under the watchful eyes of "Jefe de jefes," Proco Morel.

"Hey, boss man, I take 30k of mine from the safe, my piece and a couple clips. I catch the bitch and put it all back real quick. You see," Gomez said.

Sitting in the corner in his leather recliner with his AR-15 propped by the table near his schooner of Tecate, Morel barely moved but cast a threatening glare at his minion.

"Yeah, sure. But you know—you fail, you die," said the second-generation dealer with deep roots in Sinaloa.

"I be back in a week, two at most, with the money and the rocks," Gomez said. Morel grunted and waved Gomez out dismissively.

* * * * *

Macel began the early afternoon meeting, angry and clearly in charge.

"All hands are on deck. We have a fugitive who tried to kill a federal officer and kidnapped the Chief's daughter. We have clear jurisdiction, sentencing power and outrage on our side. The CPD has the outrage and the manpower. We will combine the best of both of our offices and catch this motherfucker—now," said the SAC in uncharacteristically profane terms. He nodded to Ortiz, who sat to his right side in the FBI's conference room in the Dirksen Building.

"We just got the prints from the Hood Avenue apartment, and they came back to Jesus Martinez-Gomez, a career criminal my husband sent away for a 12-year stretch," Ortiz said. "He's a mid-level Cobras operative with access to the gang's guns, drugs, cash and connections nationally, in Mexico and in Puerto Rico. I've got 12,000 cops looking for him, his girlfriend, Leticia Diaz, and the van.

"We can assume one of them has the ransom loot, because it wasn't in the apartment and we're betting it was in the van that Diaz drove away from the shoot. So, while we're looking for Gomez, we're betting that Gomez is looking for Diaz if she didn't circle back to pick him up somewhere," Ortiz told the throng of agents and cops.

She then turned to Halloran and nodded. He slowly stood and looked at Ortiz before speaking.

"Now that we know shithead's name, we can put together an extensive to-do list to track him down. I'm spit balling here but I think: First, we check his known associates; second, we check with the prison, probably Stateville or Menard, and find out who visited him; third, we check with the our VCD/Narcs to see what they know and turn the heat up on the Cobra jefes; fourth, we check with our Tac leaders in Pilsen to see if they know where he's been dealing—'cause we know he's…"

Ortiz jumped in and held an index finger to Halloran, then looked to Macel, who cleared his throat as Halloran sat down.

"Our DEA (Drug Enforcement Administration) guys got snitches in the Cobras that we will reach out to with threats and cash. We will touch base with the Marshal's office to let them know we may have two on the lam. And it may be premature, but I want to alert the Border Patrol and ICE that we are looking for Diaz, as well as Gomez," Macel said.

"We got photos; we got names. Now let's get this pair of fugitives," Macel said, rising and shaking hands with Ortiz, nodding to Halloran and leaving the room.

The various federal agents quickly followed, leaving the room to the CPD.

Ortiz stood slowly and looked around the still-crowded room of armed and anxious Chicago cops.

"Needless to say, I want these two badly. All of you go through Sgt. Thompson to make sure we're not stepping on each other's toes. I want reports filed on every contact with our pair's friends, relatives, associates, dealers, etc. And Mike Halloran--he is me, except in an emergency. Now let's find these two," Ortiz concluded, gathering up her notes and heading for the door.

Five minutes later, Halloran and Thoma found an empty office with a computer and a landline phone.

With just a few minutes of research, Thoma found out Gomez had spent his time at Menard Correctional Center, a six-hour drive from Chicago and as such, not the joint of choice for Chicago cons.

"Anyone hauling ass all the way there to see Gomez must have loved him or been pretty tight with him," Halloran said.

After Googling the main number for Menard, Halloran got the prison and asked for the records department.

"Records, Loeffler," answered a bored baritone belonging to Lee Alan Loeffler, a Menard corrections officer nearing retirement and approaching his quitting time of 4 p.m.

"Officer Loeffler, this is Chicago PD Detective Mike Halloran, and I'm looking for all you can give me on visitors to one of your inmates who checked out about a year ago, named Jesus Martinez-Gomez. He shot a federal agent, and we need to catch this asshole now," Halloran said, jamming his sense of urgency to Loeffler.

"Okay, gotcha, detective. Let me check the box (computer). Just a sec," Loeffler said, and began tapping away till he found Gomez's page.

"All right. It looks like he had just one visitor once a month for the past few years. Name of Felipe Lupo," Loeffler reported.

"Got an address for Lupo or a LKA for Gomez?" Halloran asked.

"Yup, one and the same. Got a pen?"

"Shoot," Halloran said.

"Lupo listed his address as 2748 S. Pulaski, in Chicago. No phone listed," Loeffler said.

"Who was his cellmate there? Got that?" Halloran asked.

"Got that and still got him—Jose Fernandez, doing 25 years," Loeffler said.

"Thanks a lot, pal. You been a big help," Halloran said.

"Let's take a ride," Thoma said.

"Seguro."

CHAPTER 21

Gomez wasn't the only one who thought Lupo was a loser. His aunt owned a two-flat in a block of similar apartment buildings that had attic apartments with just one window facing out onto Pulaski.

Maria Tellez's husband, Jorge, had owned the two-flat for 20 years, after saving enough money at the taco restaurant she worked at, and from his job as a CTA bus driver. Theirs was a middle-class immigrant success story.

Maria's late sister, Inez, had died of colon cancer at the age of 36, leaving a beat-up Camry, a 5-year-old pit bull and 12-year-old Luis to her sister. Maria put down the pit bull in the first few days after her sister passed but had no such option with Luis. He was a poor student and dropped out of high school at 15.

Maria, a slightly built seamstress of 42 years, tried to control her teenage nephew but gave up after he threatened her with a gun when she found packets of cocaine hidden in the attic apartment the couple allowed him to occupy rent free. She was not shocked that cold winter evening when Thoma knocked on her front door and announced "Policia." Halloran stood beside her with star in hand.

"Habla ingles?" he asked.

"Yes, I speak enough," Maria replied. "What's this about?"

"Is Luis Lupo here?" Halloran asked.

"I don't know, but I don't think so. He comes and goes the back way, but I haven't heard him today," she said.

"We'd like to take a look at the apartment, if you don't mind," Thoma said.

"What did he do?" Maria asked.

"He may be in some bad kind of trouble, but the sooner we find him and talk to him, the better off he'll be," Halloran told the frightened woman. "How big is the apartment?"

"Just one room, with a sink, a shower and a toilet. He has a bed, a recliner and a big screen TV. That all. I get you key," Maria said and disappeared into a foyer with a holy water font on the wall and a statue of Our Lady of Guadalupe on a small white plastic table by the coatrack. She returned in a minute and handed Halloran the key to the apartment.

With key in hand, Halloran led the way to the rear of the two-flat plus one with Thoma trailing down a narrow dimly lit gangway.

"She's got Our Lady of Guadalupe to pray to for help with her Lupo. Pretty loopy, eh, amiga," Halloran said as they started up the wooden back stairs to the apartment. Thoma grunted as she pulled out her Glock. Halloran already had his Browning pressed against his right thigh.

On the second-floor landing, Thoma paused and whispered.

"What's the play here?" asked Thoma, many years Halloran's junior and light--years behind in street experience.

"We got the key. So, we spread on either side of the door, and I knock. You announce 'police,' and we wait, weapons ready," Halloran whispered. Then he knocked as Thoma shouted at the door.

"Police, Luis! Open the door with your hands in sight, over your head!" Thoma shouted.

Nothing. They waited 30 seconds and tried again. Still no sound or movement.

Standing to the right of the door, Halloran used his left hand to insert the key till he heard the lock click open. He shoved the door open with his left foot and stepped back quickly to the safety of the porch. Still nothing, so they entered.

The bed was unmade, the bathroom dirty and the closet mostly empty.

"Let's check back with Maria," Halloran said. Thoma nodded as they retreated.

Before they knocked again at Maria's door, Halloran said, "you got that CTA shot of our young sprinter who got away at the Daley Washington stop?"

Thoma pulled out her smartphone and with a click, handed Halloran a fuzzy head shot of Victor, still a face without a name, as he vaulted the pay station. Then Thoma sent it to Halloran's phone.

Halloran banged on Maria's back door. She opened the door a crack and then threw it open wide when she saw the same cops.

"No one home," Halloran said. "If you are holding back on us, you're gonna be in a world of trouble, senora."

"I know nothing," Maria protested. Turning to Thoma, she said, "Nada. Nada."

"You know this kid? He's a pal of your guy," Halloran asked, pushing the phone photo at her.

"You can help yourself or hurt yourself," Thoma warned.

"He, I know. But he yust a baby," Maria replied.

"Where's he live? What's his name?" Halloran asked.

"He is Victor. He live on the corner there, down the alley," pointing to the rear of a 12-flat.

"Last name and what apartment?" Thoma demanded.

"I just know Victor, no last name. But he live on the first floor with his mamacita in the apartment closest to the alley," Maria said.

"Let's walk," Halloran said to Thoma, and they started down the alley.

Halfway there, they spotted Victor approaching from the opposite side of the alley. At the same time, the fleet-footed youth spotted them and took off running.

"I'll get the car. You try to catch him," Halloran shouted, and then cut through a gangway to get to the squad.

"Right," Thoma yelled as she took off after Victor.

Back in the squad, Halloran got on the radio, asking for help, giving a brief description of Victor and advising that he was the kid who escaped at the Daley Center.

When he turned onto 28th, Halloran spotted Thoma with her knee in the middle of Victor's back with cuffs in hand as he lay face down on the sidewalk.

Halloran quickly radioed back.

"Take a total disregard on my last message. We got 'em," Halloran said, then walked quickly to Thoma.

"Nice work, partner. Got some speed, right?" Halloran said.

"He slipped on the ice, twice. I didn't," Thoma said.

CHAPTER 22

Since the nation's first Juvenile Court was established in Cook County in 1899, the system had handled kids differently than adults.

No matter how heinous the crime was, if the kid was under the age of 12, he'd never see the inside of an Illinois prison. Victor was street smart, as were Lupo and Gomez. That's why they used "peguenos" like Victor for their dirty work. If a 15-year-old were charged with murder or rape, he could be tried as an adult, but would serve his time in a juvenile facility if convicted.

So, on the way to Area 1 at Wentworth and 51st Street, Victor was all mouth in the back seat of the squad.

"I didn't do nothing, you fuckin' pigs," the 70-pound tough guy yelled from the rear.

"Shut up, kid, and maybe you catch a break," Thoma said, as Halloran eyed the kid in his rearview mirror as he passed the County Jail complex at 26th Street and California Avenue.

Ten minutes later, Halloran and Thoma were hauling Victor through the vast parking lot of Area 1.

"Hey, Pacco, you a tough guy?" yelled a heavily muscled and gang-tattooed African-American youth about 19. "You 'bout to find out how tough you ain't." The loudmouth thug then jumped into a giant black Humvee and disappeared into the 51st Street traffic.

After practically carrying Victor up to the second floor of the detective section, Halloran pushed the boy into an interrogation room, uncuffed his left wrist and then re-cuffed the boy to an O-Ring in the cinderblock wall. Long Formica table, three chairs and the smell of sweat, cigarettes and fear awaited Victor.

"Let's let him stew for a half hour while we check in with the bosses," Halloran said after locking the interrogation room. Thoma nodded as her partner grabbed his cell and quickly dialed Ortiz.

"We got the pequeno sprinter here in a room at Wentworth. What about Lupo? Any sign of him?" Halloran asked.

"We got the narcs, the tac guys and the DEA all looking, but nothing yet. You think the kid'll give him up?" Ortiz asked.

"If I can't scare the truth out of a kid, I oughta hand in my star. Give me and Jane a half hour with him, and I'll call you back," Halloran said.

After 30 minutes, Thoma and Halloran re-entered the interrogation room. Inside, they found a tear-stained, scared-stiff punk, who really wasn't so tough.

"Lemme go. I didn't do nothin'. I want my mamacita," cried Victor.

"Nothing, eh?" Halloran said. "Listen up, kid. You are in such deep shit, you may never again see your sweet mamacita. When you dropped that bag and did a runner, you became an accessory to a kidnapping and the attempted murder of a federal agent, punk. Tell him what happens to someone who is an accessory to the shooting of an FBI agent, Officer Thoma."

"You think you're smart because you got a few slaps on the wrist in Juvy Court?" Thoma asked. "Well, wait till you see the inside of the federal Metropolitan Correctional Center (MCC). As an accessory to the shooting of Agent Ochoa, you're looking at a minimum of 20 years. You will spend the first stretch in a juvenile facility till you're 21, and then the rest of it in a federal prison. And it ain't gonna be close to home. Maybe Colorado."

"And your whole block is going to be swarming with ICE agents. You better pray your madre and her madre have green cards," Halloran warned. "You like men? The MCC residents will love a pretty little boy like you."

At this, Victor broke down into hysterical crying.

"No, please, please, gimme a break. I just run. They give me $100. That's all I did," Victor said, searching Halloran's and Thoma's faces for a sign of mercy. He found none. "Okay, I run between spots with some dope on my skateboard, sometimes…"

"Maybe, just maybe, we can give you a break—a break you don't deserve, you little shit," Thoma said, nodding to Halloran.

"You tell me where I can find Lupo, or better yet, Gomez, and we'll talk to the prosecutor for you," Halloran said.

"I only know where Lupo lives, but so do you," Victor pleaded.

"Listen, you stupid little asshole, enough bullshit. If you're running dope for them, you know where they're cuttin' and countin' house is. Let's have it," Halloran demanded.

"I got no address, but I dropped stuff off for Lupo at a house about a half mile from me. I can show you," Victor pleaded.

At that, Halloran unlocked the cuffs and marched Victor out of the station, Thoma at the kid's side, as he rubbed circulation back into his wrists.

Ten minutes later, Halloran and Thoma pulled up to the house Victor directed them to, a two-story clapboard with crumbling sidewalks and peeling paint.

They parked half a block away at the intersection of 21st Street and Oakley Avenue and pulled Victor out of the back seat.

"You can run home from here," Halloran said, and Victor took off like a scared rabbit, never glancing back.

Halloran called Ortiz and asked for tac unit guys for back-up after explaining Victor's cooperation.

"Sit tight for 10 minutes. I'll get Kassos to set you up. Macel, too," Ortiz said.

"Syl, no feds, just send one tac team. I want to finesse this, not make it an armed confrontation. Okay?" Halloran asked.

"You sure, Mike?" Ortiz asked.

"Sure. I'm looking for fast action, and I think I can handle some Cobra mopes. They ain't looking for heat," Halloran said.

As soon as Halloran spotted the unmarked tac unit Crown Vic pull up to the curb a few car lengths behind, he approached the Cobra building and rang the bell, star in hand and Thoma at his side.

They heard a voice from behind the peephole.

"Yeah, what you want?" came a deep male voice.

"I'm looking to talk to Lupo. Let me talk to the Jefe. This ain't a raid, just a friendly request," Halloran said.

"You wait one minute."

Halloran glanced at Thoma and winked. She shrugged. A minute later, the door cracked with the chain on and a barrel-chested and bearded Latino about 45 looked out and appraised Halloran and Thoma. He had a teardrop tat under his right eye and a snake tat under his left ear.

"Yeah? You got a warrant?" Jefe barked.

"This ain't a bust but a request for some cooperation. But I know a very friendly judge at 26th who will give me a warrant in a second. I just want to speak to one of your guys--Lupo. Not an arrest, just a chat," Halloran said, smiling.

"What you want Lupo for?" Jefe asked.

"There's just one guy asking questions here. Me. I've got good intel he knows a guy who is, let's say, a person of interest. And then we leave you and this stash house alone. Very simple," Halloran said.

"He not here," Jefe responded, glancing at Thoma.

"And he's not at home. We were just there. But I know you got a cellphone number. I'll settle for that," Halloran said.

Jefe stepped back away from the cracked door and scrolled through his cell. "You try 708 201 2626. He'll answer. Give me 30 seconds and I'll text him to talk to you, then you leave. Si?" Jefe asked.

"Gotcha."

And we will get him and his pal, Halloran silently vowed.

.

CHAPTER 23

From his hospital bed, Ochoa was busy working the phone and bugging his boss.

"I think we gotta check with the city to find all the building exits from those underground tunnels and then check the cameras in the buildings to see if we can spot asshole," Ochoa told SAC Macel.

"Juan, you're supposed to be resting, not working this case from the hospital," Macel scolded lightly with a chuckle. "But I know you and I have to say that's a smart idea, but I'll make sure CPD hasn't already done it."

Moments later, Macel checked with Ortiz and found out her troops had been busy trying to track the money, the kidnappers and their supporters. Every possible exit had been checked for cameras, but none yielded shots of Gomez.

"Sounds like Juan is feeling better. Good luck that this piece of shit was a lousy shot," Ortiz said. "Talk later."

Then Ortiz asked Thompson if he had checked with the Illinois Secretary of State (SOS) to see if Lupo had a registered car.

"Yeah, boss. He's got a 2004 black Ford Explorer, license BP2110, expires next March," Thompson shouted back to Ortiz. "I got a copy of his driver's license off the SOS, too, with his pic."

"Send that all to me, text it to Mike and make sure the feds got it, too," Ortiz ordered.

A minute later, Halloran was on the phone dialing Lupo. Went to voicemail.

"Listen, Felipe, or Flip. This is CPD detective Mike Halloran. You better call me immediately—unless you want to be a in a pile of shit you're never gonna crawl out of. Call me at this number. Now." And Halloran hung up.

"Think he'll call, partner?" asked Thoma.

"Fifty-fifty. He's streetwise but stupid. If I don't hear from him in five minutes, I'll leave a stronger message," Halloran said.

"You gonna break the phone if it gets any stronger," Thoma chided.

"I'd rather have this little shit in the back seat or in an interview room, but we gotta work fast," Halloran said.

Just then, his phone buzzed. Unknown number. He connected.

"This you, Felipe?" Halloran asked.

"Yeah, it me, and I ain't looking for any trouble with the man," Lupo said. "What you want?"

"Your pal Gomez is in mucho trouble. He shot an FBI agent, and if we find out you even slipped him a fin to help him, you're looking at the rest of your days in a federal prison, probably Marion. Entiendes, cabron?"

"Yeah, I looking for him, too. He made off with my car, and I don't know where da fuck he is, detective," Lupo said.

"Was it your Ford Explorer that he jacked?" Halloran asked.

"Yeah, I pick him up in the middle of the night at the Wilson L stop. I take him to my pad and I go back to sleep. When I wake, he gone, man. My wheels, too," Lupo said.

"Hold for a second," Halloran said, muting his phone and turning to Thoma. "Call Ortiz and tell her we need an APB (All Points Bulletin) out on Lupo's car. Tell her Gomez has it. And ask her to get it out on ISPERN (Illinois State Police Emergency Radio Network), too."

Halloran flipped back to Lupo.

"Now Felipe, you can help yourself here. I know you're balls-up pals with Gomez and his operation. I'm not interested in your drug dealings. You got any idea where Gomez would be, where he would go?" Halloran asked. "Think carefully before you try to unload any bullshit on me."

"Oh, man, I don't know. We not buddies. I work for him. He very secretive, ya know. I know he sometimes go weekends in Indiana near St. John, and I hear him talking once to Letty about Puerto Vallarta. He from Sinaloa—but he also know Guadalajara. That all I know. I swear," Lupo pleaded.

"Where you at, Flip?" Halloran asked.

"I'm in the city. In my cousin's car, not doing any deals, man," Lupo said.

"Okay. You stay available on this phone, and I won't be dragging your sorry ass in right now as long as you're straight with me," Halloran said.

"I straight. I straight," Lupo said.

Yeah, you not straight? You straight to the joint, Halloran silently vowed.

CHAPTER 24

Shoe leather and video work by the dicks working the kidnapping turned up a recording from a coffee shop across from the Art Institute that showed a man wearing a black ski mask carrying a backpack with a skateboard attached walking across Michigan to a waiting black Ford Explorer. The time on the video showed it was 4 minutes and 35 seconds after the bag was snatched up at the Daley Center.

Back at Ortiz's office, Halloran and Thoma viewed the video standing in back of Ortiz's seat at her desk. Halloran glanced at the family photo on her desk with a smiling Elly.

"Absolutely, 110 percent that's our guy," Thoma said.

"And that puts our guy Lupo in the kidnapping, right?" Halloran asked Ortiz.

"We don't have a clear view of the license plate or their faces, but it's good enough to round Lupo up and empty the state and fed statute books out on him," Ortiz said.

"Yeah, but Lupo don't know that the image is fuzzy. We can work him. Now we gotta bring him in. With the APB on him and the car, we'll get him soon. This asshole isn't smart enough to hole up. Pretty sure he was driving when I spoke to him," Halloran said.

* * * * *

After grabbing his gun and cash at the stash house, Gomez drove the Explorer to a block away from the ex-girlfriend of a fellow gangbanger and abandoned the car on a side street a short walk from her condo in a

6-flat near Grace Street and Pine Grove Avenue. Gomez knew that the rather plump woman in her early 40's always had a crush on him.

He walked to the rear porch and knocked lightly on the kitchen door.

Tessa Sanchez pulled the curtain to the side and peered into the darkness to see Gomez use his cell's flashlight to reveal his smiling face.

"Jesus, Jesus. What're you doing out there?" she asked, as she opened the door to let him in.

"Missed you, mi amor," Gomez said, glancing back at the alley as he closed and quickly bolted the door.

He ordered a pizza and later held his nose as he made love to the lady who would host him for a few days while the heat died down.

* * * * *

Despite the alerts all over the city, state and country with Gomez's and Letty's photos, neither had been caught.

"Okay, what haven't we done? What's the likely run for Gomez, for Letty?" Halloran asked over breakfast at Lou Mitchell's on West Jackson with Thoma and Ortiz.

"My best guess is that Letty has beat a fast track back home. But how did she get there? And where is there? My other guess is that they had the ransom in the van because it wasn't in the apartment. So far, so good?" Ortiz asked.

"I'm with you," Halloran said, finishing off the rest of his Denver omelet. Thoma nodded.

"Further, Gomez is seeing red if she has the ransom, but he knows he's a wanted man, a very wanted man, so is lying low right now. And he's much more street savvy than she is. She's scared shitless, but he's still got an operation to help run, so he's probably still around—somewhere," Ortiz continued.

"Okay, that sounds about right, but we know Lupo is no genius and has fewer resources, so I'm betting he pops up real soon, and he may lead us to Gomez 'cause that footage of Gomez piling into Lupo's

SUV puts him in the kidnap plot and looking at beaucoup fed time," Halloran said.

"Beaucoup? Listen to you," Ortiz jabbed.

"Yeah, my first partner was an ex-Marine who picked it up in Nam. The French had the same luck we did in Southeast Asia. He used to prod me to get things done tout de suite. I thought I'd put too much sugar in his coffee," Halloran said, smiling at his play on words.

"Boss, would it be okay if I made another gentle run at Elly? Different person asking different questions?" Thoma asked hesitantly.

"That's a good thought, detective. Her answering me or Mike in the first hours she was free was traumatic, no doubt. Come over tonight and have a glass of wine with me. Elly will be relaxed now that she's home," Ortiz said.

Halloran caught Thoma's eye and winked.

"Nice. That's a solo. I got other fish to fry," Halloran said.

Just then, Halloran's cell vibrated. It was Roy.

"Halloran," he said.

"Roy. A beat guy in 10 (District) spotted Lupo walking near Ogden and scooped him. No fuss, we got him in the lockup at the district. You want us to take him to the Area or is he good there for now?" Roy asked.

"Tell your guys I'll be there in 15 minutes," Halloran said. Then turning to Ortiz and Thoma, he relayed the not-surprising news.

The partners left Ortiz with her coffee and got in their Crown Vic for a quick trip to the station on Ogden Avenue near Kedzie Avenue.

When they got to the station, they found Lupo sulking in a lockup cell. They quickly took him to an interview room and cuffed him to an I-bolt on the cinderblock wall.

"Flip, you got any idea how much shit you're in?" Halloran asked after he and Thoma sat on the gray folding chairs--perfect matches for the walls.

"Lawyer," Lupo said.

"Thanks for reminding us," Thoma said, and gave him his Miranda rights.

"Of course, you can have a lawyer, your abogado," Halloran said to the heavily tatted-up drug dealer. "But you can listen as long as we're here, right, cabron?"

"Lawyer," Lupo repeated.

"You should know what you're facing and what we got before you fuck things up with a lawyer. You're smart enough to know that, right, amigo?" Halloran continued.

Thoma took the queue.

"Our tac guys and narcs know you and where you operate, but that's small potatoes, chump change, to what the feds can do. We got video of your car picking up Gomez across from the Art Institute just minutes after he grabbed the ransom bag at the Daley Center. That makes you an accessory to the kidnapping, a federal offense. But under RICO (Racketeer Influenced and Corrupt Organization), you're part of the continuing conspiracy that results in the shooting of a federal officer, an FBI agent."

"If your lawyer were here, he'd tell you, you're looking at so much time, you'll be an old man by the time you get out of Marion or wherever they ship dumb fucks like you," she said, nodding slightly to Halloran.

He jumped in.

"Now you can say 'lawyer' all day and all night, you stupid motherfucker, but the cooperation bus will be leaving very soon, entiendes? Your pal Gomez is gonna get caught and he'd give you up in a heartbeat. If you wanna do yourself any good, now's the time," Halloran said, now standing with both hands spread out on the table leaning over where Lupo sat.

"Gimme a minute, will ya. I gotta think," Lupo said, departing from his "lawyer" mantra.

"There's a couple of pissed off FBI agents and an Assistant U.S. Attorney out to make a name for himself on their way here. If we keep this to state charges, we got some room to maneuver with our prosecutor, but that door is closing very, very soon," Halloran said, glaring down at Lupo.

"Okay, okay. But I don't know shit about him other than he's a prick and as violent as a pit bull. Ask your questions," Lupo said.

"Where is he?" Halloran demanded.

"Da fuck would I know? I know he's packing a Glock and he got a shitload of cash from our stash house. Where he went after that—he didn't tell me before he snatched my car," Lupo pleaded.

"Let's start with where his friends hang," Thoma asked.

"He's got no friends. Everyone afraid of him, but no one's a friend," Lupo said.

"How about girlfriends, any whore he frequents?" Thoma asked.

"He a lone wolf, man. And lately he only with Letty. See how that worked out," Lupo said, smirking.

"Where's he from in Mexico?" Halloran asked.

"He from Sinaloa, but he know Mexico City and Guadalajara, and PV, too," Lupo said.

Just then, two FBI agents walked in with their federal prosecutor, who introduced himself to Halloran and Thoma, then Lupo.

"Thanks, detective. We'll take it from here," said Assistant U.S. Attorney Joe Prentiss.

By Prentiss's side stood Juan Ochoa, arm in a sling and a sneer on his face. He nodded to Halloran and mouthed "thanks."

"Gotcha. See you later, Flip," Halloran said, turning to leave with Thoma in the lead.

"What you gonna do for me? I gave you some shit to chase, man," Lupo cried.

"If it's good shit and pays off, it may help you. If it's bad shit, you just made an enemy, Flip," Halloran said.

Back in the squad room, Thoma asked, "Whattya you think?"

"Let's hope he didn't return to Sinaloa, but my bet is he's still around," Halloran said.

* * * * *

In the car on the way back to Area 3, Thoma and Halloran started reviewing where they were with the O'Malley cold case.

"Still waiting for the lab to see if they could get a DNA profile off the barrel flaps," Thoma said.

"Any luck tracking down Lynch's prints from his booking way back then?" Halloran asked.

"That far back, records tells me that those are somewhere in the warehouse—maybe, and he stressed maybe," Thoma said. "We went through a lot of files before we even found the Fitz letter."

"Yeah, maybe a wild goose chase 'cause raising DNA off a print is a long shot, but it is a shot," Halloran said.

"Tried the IDOC (Illinois Department of Corrections) and the County Jail and they laughed at me but said they'd check. Not holding my breath," Thoma said.

"Me neither. Time to grab a swim. First of the week," Halloran said.

After checking in at Area 3, Halloran called it a day and headed home.

As he took his laps in the mostly empty pool, but for an elderly lady clinging to a flotation noodle and softly paddling in the far lane, Halloran turned the case over in his head, again and again.

Mexico? he wondered.

CHAPTER 25

It was dark by the time Thoma arrived outside the Ortiz home and tried in vain to find a parking spot on Dearborn. She parked in a bus stop on Division Street near Butch McGuire's and walked back, nervous and rehearsing her questions.

Her questions would have been asked before, but Elly had just survived a harrowing experience and was still spooked then.

And having a drink with the Chief of D's? Thoma was apprehensive, short of scared. Needlessly.

"Come on in, Jane" welcomed Ortiz. "You know my husband, Joe?" Ortiz asked as she ushered Thoma through the first-floor dining room toward a massive, rehabbed kitchen, all white cabinets and stainless steel appliances.

Joe Ortiz sat at a large oval golden oak table, Elly to his side.

"Thanks for all you've done for us, detective," Joe said. "And this is our daughter, Elly."

Elly also rose and walked toward Thoma, right hand extended.

"Welcome to our home, and also thanks so much for all you did for me with Uncle Mike," Elly said.

Thoma shook the teen's hand and glanced to her boss.

"Okay, we'll let you do what you do so well, Jane. We'll be in the family room watching the news if you need us," Chief Ortiz said.

"Thanks, Chief," Thoma said, and motioned Elly back toward the kitchen table.

Dressed in a blue sweatsuit with Latin School on the back, her dark brunette hair pulled into a tight ponytail, Elly sat next to Thoma, who took the seat at the head of the table.

"I know you've been through this numerous times, Elly, but we thought a fresh interrogator might be useful," said Thoma, then winced at her use of the word "interrogator."

"That's okay, detective. I have two professional interrogators as parents, so nothing you can ask will bother me," Elly said, a laugh escaping as her brown eyes crinkled above a broad smile.

"First off, I wanted to thank you and commend you for having the presence of mind to count off the seconds as they drove to and then down the Drive. Quick thinking," Thoma said.

"Thanks, but besides my parents, I got Uncle Mike, my godfather, preaching awareness since as long as I can remember," Elly said, still smiling.

"Good. Let's talk a minute about remembering. I know you were blindfolded for much of the time, but what did you hear?"

"They didn't talk much and were speaking Spanish. I only know a little bit, so I didn't get anything. And once we were in the apartment, they kept the door closed and I couldn't hear much of anything." Elly continued. "I did hear him call her a 'puta', or whore, several times. I heard him call her 'mia puta,' or my whore. What an asshole. Oh, sorry."

"But when he left the second day, I think, she came in and gave me some water. When she left the room, she left the door partially ajar, and I could hear her on the phone a little. This time I heard her say something like 'puta mia,' not what he said, 'mia puta,'" Elly said. "All the way to Indiana before they dropped me, they hardly said a word. Sorry, detective."

"Did you mention this 'puta' conversation discrepancy to any other detectives?" Thoma asked.

"I don't think so. It didn't seem important at the time," Elly said.

"I don't know if it's important, but we are grasping at anything. If you think of anything else, call me or Mike," she said, handing Elly her card.

At that, Thoma got up and started to leave. Ortiz intercepted her in the foyer.

"Jane, what about that glass of wine I promised you?"

Thoma hesitated. It would be uncomfortable for her schmoozing with the boss, but she didn't want to be rude either.

"Boss, I appreciate the offer, but I'm still on duty, and Elly gave me a bit I want to share with Mike ASAP," Thoma said.

Ortiz's eyes widened and she held up her hands in front of Thoma.

"What 'bit' are you talking about?" Ortiz said, apparently shocked that anything new could come out of her daughter's mouth about the ordeal.

Thoma related the whole flip-flop of "mia puta" and "puta mia."

"Hmmm, had not heard that before. Whattya reckon that means?" asked Ortiz, a second-generation Mexican with passable Spanish.

"Maybe—probably nothing, but I hadn't heard that or read it in any of the supps," Thoma said.

"Well, good work and thanks for coming. Maybe a rain check on that drink when we're not so busy, eh?" Ortiz asked.

"You got it, boss. Good night," Thoma said.

Back at Area 3, Thoma filed a supp on the conversation, focusing on the "puta" discrepancy, and cc'ed Halloran.

Halloran was stopped at a red light when he got the ping of a new email.

Puta mia, mia puta? What the fuck does that mean?

And he filed it in his memory bank for possible future use.

CHAPTER 26

Nearing exhaustion from a long day of cleaning her apartment, Karine Hernandez was headed for her bedroom when she heard a loud knock at the back door.

She pulled the curtain away from the rear door enough to see a Glock pointed at her head.

"Abre la puerta o disparo," whispered Gomez in ordering her to open the door, loud enough for the septuagenarian to hear but not loud enough to alert neighbors.

Hernandez unbolted the door and took the chain off, then opened the door wide for Gomez. She recognized him from his visits to Letty and knew from the neighborhood of his gang affiliation. She was scared that her long life was about to end. She raised her hands and held her breath.

"Relax, mamacita. I not looking to hurt you, but I could," Gomez said, waving the Glock a foot away from her face.

"You heard from Letty or seen her?" Gomez demanded, still holding the gun at his waist.

"No, senor. Not hearing," she said, trembling.

"Where your phone?" Gomez asked. She pointed to a wall phone in the small kitchen, with an old-fashioned circular dial and an aging answering machine adjacent.

"You got cellphone?" he demanded.

"No, senor. Yust dat."

"Lemme see your phone bill," Gomez demanded.

"Okay, okay," the old lady said, and waddled back to her extra bedroom where she kept a desk and a file cabinet.

She rifled through a few files and extracted her last phone bill, dated the middle of the prior month. It showed her incoming and outgoing calls. Just one call to Mexico for five minutes to a number in the Jalisco area.

"Who dis?" he asked, pointing to the Jalisco number.

"Mi prima. Tiene 82 anos. Vive in Guadalajara," she said, saying her 82-year-old cousin lives in Guadalajara.

In Spanish, Gomez told her he'd be back to check her bill in the middle of the month to see her phone traffic. Then he told her if she lost or altered the bill, he would cut off her right thumb.

Hernandez started weeping.

"You be good old lady, you no get hurt," Gomez warned.

This fearful woman was the only other contact Gomez knew for Letty, other than the co-workers at the restaurant.

"Muthufuckuh," he said once outside, frustrated and livid his girlfriend was in the wind with his money, car and diamonds.

"Where you go? Where you at, my little Letty," he whispered into the darkness of the Southwest Side.

CHAPTER 27

Letty knew a lot of people would be looking for her. The cops, the feds, Gomez, but no one knew she'd fled the country. Troubling her, however, was the La Dolce reference she gave to Nuevo Laredo's Roberta Ruiz.

After refreshing for two days in Guadalajara and cashing more dollars into pesos, she caught a bus for the four-hour ride to Puerto Vallarta. There, she applied with a sleazy, leering assistant manager for a job as a waitress at Junior's strip joint, a thinly veiled whorehouse by the marina in PV. Letty figured a shady place like this could lead to huge tips from drunken cruise ship tourists. But when he touched her left breast, she swatted his hand away and marched out, saying over shoulder "Adios, hasta luego, cabron."

Ten minutes later she went into the Scotia Bank near Porfirios's restaurant off the Francisco Medina Ascencion and rented a safe deposit box. She kept 15,000 in pesos and $1,000 in American cash and slipped it into a zippered pocket in her bag. She took the small velour purse with the diamonds in it and shoved it into the deposit box next to the rest of the cash, then closed the box and locked it.

Before emerging from the cubicle near the deposit box, she took a large safety pin from her purse and slipped it through the top hole of the safe deposit key and secured that into the same zippered pocket.

She stepped out into the bright Mexican sunlight and exhaled.

That should do for a while, Letty thought.

CHAPTER 28

Three weeks had flown by since the shootout behind Hamilton's, and Halloran was no closer to finding Gomez—or Letty—than he was that night by the Lawrence Avenue L tracks.

Bulletins were out, border patrol alerted, warrants issued—but no arrests. Lupo was no help, but being monitored before he was snatched up on multiple charges.

"We can get him anytime we want," Halloran explained to Thoma, "but we wanna see if he can lead us to Gomez or the ransom."

"Ya think we should make another run at the landlady to see if she knows anything about Letty's whereabouts?" Thoma asked.

As they sat in the back of Tufano's restaurant in Little Italy, Ochoa, now mostly recovered and still very pissed off, answered Thoma's query instantly.

"You bet. It's better than sitting here with our thumbs up our asses." Ochoa griped.

"My thumbs are twiddling, nowhere near my derriere," Halloran jousted, straight-faced.

"Okay boys let's make a quick trip to Hernandez's place and see if we can shake loose anything today. Can't hurt, right?" Thoma said.

Thoma and Halloran left their personal cars in the valet parking lot and then piled into Ochoa's fed ride, a 2-year-old gray Chevy Impala.

Outside Hernandez's building on Hermitage, Ochoa pulled to the curb and told his partners: "It's my play. I got the Spanish and I got the lead in my shoulder from this asshole. Okay?"

"Lead the way," Halloran said. Thoma nodded.

Ochoa rang the bell, and after 30 seconds with no response, he pounded on the first-floor front door.

A faint "Coming, coming," came from behind the thick black door.

"Federales," Ochoa shouted, and waited. The door cracked open with the chain lock, as Senora Hernandez peaked out to see Ochoa's FBI shield and two CPD stars held high behind him.

"Okay, okay. Si, si," she said as she first closed the door to free the chain and then opened it wide, standing there in a frayed lime-green housecoat.

She stepped aside with the door open for the three to enter.

Ochoa spoke first.

"Has tenido noticias de Leticia ultimamente?" Ochoa asked about her latest contact with Letty.

"No, senor. No en el ultimo mes," she responded, saying not in a month.

Ochoa explained to the elderly landlady that Letty was not in trouble--yet—but if Hernandez heard from her, she was to call him immediately, or she might be in big trouble. He handed her his card, followed by Halloran and Thoma with their cards.

"If you can't get Agent Ochoa, you call us. Entiendes?" Halloran said, confident she understood enough English to get his drift.

Halloran turned to Ochoa and said, "tell her we'll be back to check her phone records each month."

After Ochoa gave her the order about their monthly check, the three retreated to the agent's car.

"I think she gets it," Thoma said. Halloran grunted. And Ochoa added: "No one around here wants the feds snooping around. I'm pretty damn sure she'll call if she's contacted."

* * * * *

As she watched from a drawn curtain in her living room as the three pulled away, she thought to herself:

I tell Gomez and I tell the federales if Leticia calls. That way, I can't lose.

CHAPTER 29

A week later Halloran sat at Area 3 with Thoma as the trail of Gomez and Letty grew colder, so they returned their focus to the murder of Mary Beth O'Malley.

"We gotta wonder if the guy is still alive, right?" mused Halloran in the late afternoon in the nearly empty second-floor detectives' section at Area 3 at Western and Belmont Avenues.

"Yeah, I was just thinking about that letter that Fitz sent to the Pasadena cops and was wondering if our guy ever got caught doing anything else dirty down there, ya know?" Thoma said.

"Good point, and then in the back of my head I was wondering if he did get pinched, was there still a fingerprint on file," Halloran said.

"Let me do it the lazy way, the easy Internet way first," Thoma said.

She Googled the Houston Public Library. Once there, she maneuvered around and found the "Newspapers" file and clicked on it and found the Houston Chronicle archives. Clicking there, she found the search icon and entered "Larry Lynch" and got 23 hits. She narrowed it by adding "arrest" after Lynch's name and got two hits.

She read the first article headlined "Pasadena man arrested in knifing, sexual assault of teen," which was from 1986 and was just four paragraphs.

Thoma read it aloud:

"A Pasadena construction worker was arrested Tuesday in the brutal knifing and attempted sexual assault of a 15-year-old girl on a rural road 10 miles outside town.

"The suspect, Larry Lynch, is accused to accosting the teenager as she walked along the shoulder of Jenkins Road in a farming area. She told police Lynch pulled over and asked her if she had seen his dog. Then he got out of his pickup truck pretending to have a photo of the dog, but instead brandished an 8-inch switchblade.

"The victim told police he dragged her into a ditch by the side of the road and began stabbing her after he tore off her blouse and bra. Suffering more than 40 stab wounds, she pretended to be dead. After her attacker drove away, she walked a half mile to a farmhouse and collapsed after ringing the bell.

"Police arrested Lynch at a construction site after checking their files for similar attacks and found records that showed Lynch had been arrested and served time in Illinois for similar crimes."

"Bingo," Halloran nearly shouted. "What does the second story say? A conviction, I hope."

The second story was from 1988. Thomas read the headline: "Charges dropped against Pasadena man in brutal sexual assault."

Halloran groaned. Thoma swore, "Holy fuck."

Then she read the story:

By Tom Madigan
Harris County prosecutors dropped aggravated sexual assault charges Thursday against a 38-year-old Pasadena man after his alleged victim told them she was unable to positively identify him as her attacker in a 1986 attack on a rural stretch of road outside the Houston suburb.

"We had no choice but to drop charges," said Assistant Harris County District Attorney LouAnn Sims. "She had picked him out of a photo lineup, then out of a live lineup of similarly built men, but after seeing him at the defense table just as the trial was to begin Thursday, she began crying and said she could not positively ID him."

Sims further stated there was no physical evidence to link Lynch to the assault, but the strong similarities to his Chicago convictions and the positive ID led police and prosecutors to charge Lynch.

In those Chicago convictions, Lynch had followed his eight victims at night till they approached an alley, then he would pull into the alley and block their way, records showed. The burly 220-pound construction worker easily subdued his victims and threw them into the passenger side of the front seat, where the door handle had been removed, according to his Chicago convictions.

There were a few more graphs about his criminal past, nothing they didn't know already.

"Okay, now we got two moves," Halloran said. "First, we gotta find out if he's still alive, and that may take some time, given the age of these records. But second and easier, let's check with the cops and prosecutors to see if they have his fingerprints still on file."

"Right, partner. I'll take the tough one and start checking death certificates and death notices and with the Harris County Institute of Forensic Sciences (Coroner). You can call the cops in Pasadena and see what they know. Sound about right to you?" Thoma asked, a sarcastic smile creasing her face.

"Perfect," Halloran said, a two-finger wonder on the keyboard and hardly an Internet whiz. "I'll get to those cops tomorrow first thing, but right now I want to check with the feds to make sure nothing new has popped with our fugitives."

Ochoa answered on the first ring.

"Hey, partner, how's the shoulder?" Halloran asked.

"Getting better every day. Took your advice and started swimming a bit. The SAC has a membership at the Union League Club, so I been going there in the afternoons after the lunch crowd clears. You'd think with a Mac-10, asshole would have done more damage, eh?" Ochoa quipped.

"Glad you're feeling better. Anything new on Letty or Gomez?" Halloran asked.

"Nada. Took another walk down the alleys Gomez used for his getaway, looking to see if he dumped the Mac, but found nothing," Ochoa said.

"Good thinking, but we gotta take another run when all the snow melts, too, right, partner?" Halloran said.

"Absolutely, gotta build the case. Techs got plenty of spent cartridges, but no match on prints or DNA on them. Would be nice to find the gun. Can't figure he was running down Broadway with the machine gun under his arm or on the L," Ochoa said.

"Don't worry, Juan. We're gonna find them and then let your fed prosecutors empty the statute book on them," Halloran said, then disconnected.

Yeah, but where and when, thought Halloran as he drove home.

CHAPTER 30

Worried that Gomez would remember her using La Dolce restaurant for a reference, Letty soon left PV and took a one-hour bus ride to Punta Mita, where a distant cousin from Oaxaca worked as a maid at the St. Regis resort.

The cousin helped her find a room to rent near the beach with an elderly couple from Guatemala who ran the Onda Surf Motel. They soon introduced her to the owner of the Tacos & Papas restaurant, a short walk from the surf, who hired her on the spot as a much-needed waitress.

There, she studied English during the day and waitressed at night, serving low-budget gringo tourists who nonetheless tipped 20 percent or more, especially the men. She felt safe and met her rent and other expenses from her tips, never touching the cash she stashed in the AC vent in her room.

On her fourth Saturday in Punta Mita, she took the 10 a.m. bus into Puerto Vallarta and went shopping for clothes at the La Isla Shopping Center. There, she pulled out her burner phone and called Karine.

"Tia Karine. Estoy a salvo y feliz. Muchas gracias for su ayuda," she said and hung up quickly, thinking it was too brief a call to be traced so she'd be safe. The number would show it came from a Guadalajara number, she knew.

After she heard the message on her machine, Karine Hernandez quickly erased it. But the phone call would show on her monthly bill.

* * * * *

In the middle of the next month, Lupo picked up Gomez at a stash house in Berwyn. They rode mostly in silence to Karine Hernandez's home on Hermitage, arriving an hour after sunset. On Gomez's orders, Lupo circled the block twice and twice went north to south up the alley behind the widow's place.

Pulling on the black ski mask, Gomez crept up to the rear door and rapped on the window twice. In a few minutes, the slow-footed septuagenarian peeked through the window and saw the hooded man wave his Glock toward the door.

Terrified, Hernandez opened the door for Gomez and looked behind him for possible help. The back yard was empty, and no one was in sight.

"You know why I here. Get your phone bill for me—rapidamente," Gomez ordered, pushing the Glock into the woman's ribs and lifting the ski mask.

"Si, si. No problema," she said and hustled down the hallway.

Right on her dresser was the recent bill from AT&T. Gomez snatched it from the terrified woman and quickly took a photo of it with his phone. He didn't want to waste time in her apartment.

"Good—bueno—you keep your thumb," Gomez said, then quickly returned to the rear door and called Lupo.

"Come get me at the back gate," Gomez demanded. He turned to Hernandez.

"Letty call you?" he demanded.

"She just leave message. Say she safe," Hernandez said, shaking.

"Play the message," he demanded.

"I erase. Lo siento," she replied. Gomez raised his pistol as if to hit her but lowered it and murmured "stupid bitch," crumpled the phone bill and tossed it on the floor, then exited the back door.

In seconds, Lupo was there at the alley gate, and Gomez hopped in the back seat. Opening the photos icon, he gazed at the phone number with the Mexico country code of 52 and the city code of 33—

Guadalajara. The call lasted only 10 seconds, but Gomez now knew where Letty was, or so he thought.

CHAPTER 31

That next morning, Halloran grabbed an unmarked gray Crown Vic from the Area 3 parking lot, picked up Ochoa at the Dirksen Building and headed to Karine Hernandez's place.

"Anything new on Gomez?" Halloran asked.

"Everyone's looking, and we're leaning hard on our CIs (confidential informants). We'll get him soon, and your guys are all over it, too, I know," Ochoa said.

Half the cars on Hermitage in front of Hernandez's home were snowed in, the victims of a recent snowfall and the Streets and Sanitation garbage truck plows clearing the street but burying parked cars 10 inches up to their mid-hubcaps.

Several spots had been shoveled out and were marked by lawn furniture in the classic Chicago "dibs" fashion. Halloran pulled halfway into a spot near the corner that had not been dug out, so he left the rear wheels of the Crown Vic free, lest they get stuck in the drift. The rear-wheel-drive Crown Vics were great in a chase but crap in the snow.

"Why don't we just pull into one of the spots with the chairs, Hal?" Ochoa, a native of Orlando, suggested.

"Well, mi amigo from sunny Florida, that would be breaking one of the unwritten rules of Chicago winter etiquette. Gotta respect the working man—or woman—who dug that spot, and I will not break that peace. We're peace officers, right?" Halloran said and pushed open the driver's side door into a drift, just far enough to get out of the squad.

"Still learning, detective," Ochoa laughed.

"This will still be your play 'cause the lady speaks very little English, right?" Halloran said.

"I remember. The bullet hit my shoulder, not my brain, partner," Ochoa said.

"Yeah, sorry, just wanted to make our moves coordinated," Halloran said as they approached Hernandez's front door.

Ochoa knocked three times loudly, then announced, "Policia."

In a few moments, Hernandez cracked the door and then opened it wide when she saw the two law enforcement men.

"Come in, senores, por favor," she said in her mixed-language retort.

"Have you heard from Letty since we were here last?" Halloran asked before Ochoa translated.

"Si, si. Tengo. Vamos," she said and walked back to the bedroom/office.

She smoothed the crumpled bill out before she handed it to Ochoa.

"What happened here?" he asked, holding the bill and looking for the call from Mexico.

"I get angry at Letty. I sorry," she replied.

"Entiendo, senora. It's okay," Ochoa said, examining the bill. Then handing it to Halloran.

"The call came from Guadalajara. I can tell from the area and city codes," Ochoa told Halloran, who took a photo of the bill and handed it back to the widow.

"What did she say?" Ochoa asked.

"She leave message on machine, say she okay," she answered. "Then I erase."

"Muchas gracias," Halloran said, signaling Ochoa he thought that was all that was needed. She walked them to the front door and closed it quickly behind them. They heard the chain slide and a bolt slam into place.

Inside the squad, Halloran spoke first.

"So, how far is Guadalajara from PV? You know?" Halloran asked.

"Couple hundred miles, not too far," Ochoa said.

"Right now, Letty's either an accessory or a witness/vic, depending on how the prosecutors want to play it. But as a cooperating witness— maybe given a deferred sentence-- she would be golden against Gomez. And if we find her, she may lead us to Gomez," Halloran said. "What think, partner?"

"I think what you think," Ochoa replied, then laughed as Halloran backed away from the snowdrift.

*****

With the G and Gomez both gone and seemingly satisfied, Hernandez breathed a sigh of relief and thought to herself:

I didn't lie to anyone, and I don't think I hurt Letty. But God help her. She still in big trouble.

CHAPTER 32

Feeling a bit left out, Thoma beavered away at her computer, fingers flying, while Halloran was out with Ochoa.

Focusing on the O'Malley case, she called the Harris County Clerk, and they were modern enough to have digital records going back to 1984 of all deaths in the county. No Larry Lynches. She then checked with the Clerk on the off chance that he married. Zip again. The Texas cops had told Halloran to be patient, they were looking for Lynch's prints.

But the Department of Motor Vehicles (DMV) had a Larry Lynch whose driver's license had expired three years ago but listed a Houston address. He had the same birthdate, living in a high-rise there. She pulled up the crisscross directory of phones listed at various Houston addresses but could find no listing for Lynch among the scores of names at the high-rise.

Making some progress where little was expected, Thoma was feeling pretty good about herself when Halloran strolled into the second-floor dicks' section at Area 3, known in the media as the Belmont Area to give it a geographic hook.

Both partners had something they were eager—and a little proud—to share. Thoma was all smiles as Halloran plopped down at the adjacent desk. He returned the smile.

"You look pretty chirpy, partner. What's up?" Halloran asked.

She ran through her hits and misses but focused on the address hit.

"So far, it looks like our guy is still alive, Hal," she said.

"Soooo, the opposite of dead? Okay, did you check Legacy?" Halloran asked.

"Legacy? Could you be any more vague?" said a confused Thoma.

"Sure," Halloran smirked and waited a few seconds silently.

Ten feet away, Sgt. Eddie Szymanski chuckled, drawing Thoma's attention. She frowned at Halloran and waited a full 15 seconds more.

"And? What's Legacy?" she asked with an edge.

"Sorry, partner," Halloran repented, with a sly smile. "Legacy.com is a site that carries tons of death notices. I've found a few names of retired cops there, when I wondered what ever happened to–whoever," Halloran said.

"Never heard of it, but I'll check now," she said and quickly logged on to Legacy.com and ran Lynch's name through its database. Again, zip.

"Another box filled. Quick work, Jane. Glad you jumped me on Lynch. Now let me tell you about Letty," he said. Then he went through the revelation of the phone record tracing back to a Guadalajara number.

"And according to Ochoa, that's about a 3-4-hour from PV. I'm going to call Egan to get a UFAP (Unlawful Flight to Avoid Prosecution) warrant, correct?" Halloran asked.

"Good work, and that sounds like a perfect chance to rekindle a moribund romance," Thoma jabbed back at Halloran.

"Strictly professional. I'm hurt you'd be so judgy," Halloran countered. "Moribund? You throwing your master's degree-educated sesquipedalian vocabulary at this ignorant college dropout?"

"Sesquipedalian? Wow!," Thoma replied. "And didn't I hear 'derriere' recently from that dropout?"

"Touche. Yeah, I read books," Halloran responded. "And I don't move my lips when I do. But let me call Egan and see what we can do fast on a warrant."

Halloran got Egan's voicemail and left a message loud enough for Thoma to hear how professional he was, but certainly not "moribund."

"As the senior investigator on this kidnap case, it would be your obligation, your duty, to travel down to sunny Mexico to track down this fugitive. Don't you think, Hal?" Thoma retorted.

"Ahh, yes, my d-u-uty," Halloran said, lapsing into an Irish brogue. "My duty. But it would have to be approved from on high."

"Heh. And you supposin' Ortiz wants anyone but the best on this dangerous assignment catching a 20-something girl in a beautiful Pacific Ocean resort area?" Thoma asked.

"We can hope. And Guadalajara is not a coastal resort.," Halloran deadpanned. "I'm gonna text the Houston records cop, a Sgt. Otis Oliver, to see if he found Lynch's fingerprints."

Thoma jotted Oliver's name down in her phone's "Notes" icon so she could follow if Halloran got too tied up with the kidnap case. Just as she finished typing, Halloran's phone vibrated an alert. It was Egan.

"Afternoon, counselor. I got a problem you can solve," Halloran opened.

"Your problems have been historically kaleidoscopic, detective. What's up?" Egan said from her perch in the First Assistant's office looking south from the 11th floor at 26th and Cal.

Halloran quickly summarized what he and Ochoa had gleaned from the phone bill. Then offered, "I think I may have to return to Mexico, PV and environs, to get young Letty. Will this qualify for hazard duty or at least time and a half?"

"My rosy red Irish ass, it would! No problem with getting the UFAP, but I'm struggling to figure an angle for an accompanying prosecutor—just to make sure no rules are bent or in your case, broken," Egan said.

"Putting in the long hours that I know you do, you surely have some enormous amount of time due coming. At least to get away for a long weekend," Halloran suggested.

"First things first, you silver-tongued rogue. Lemme get on the line with the U.S. Attorney's Office and get the UFAP in the pipeline. The rest? We'll see," Egan said.

Halloran rose from his desk and walked to the end of the mostly empty squad room.

"And don't get me thinking about your rosy Irish ass, you shameless hussy," Halloran joked.

"Enough," said Egan and hung up her land line.

That night, as he swam his laps in his building's pool, Halloran mulled the kidnapping case and his lingering attachment to Egan.

We know where we think Letty is. But does Gomez know? he wondered. *He and Egan got along swimmingly, but did he want to jeopardize that with a proposal? Maybe get a ring just in case the time ever seemed right? Food for thought for another day.*

CHAPTER 33

Entering through the back door of the gang's money-laundering operation, aptly named Lavanderia Loco, Gomez was greeted by Lupo.

"I call that number that Letty called from, but now disconnected," Gomez said. "You think she stay in Guada or head to PV? Eh, cabron?"

"Dunno. Easier to hide in Guada, but easier to make more money in PV. Toss-up, Jefe," Lupo counseled.

"I'm thinking Guada. She can change money, maybe sell some diamonds—easy there. And she can find plenty of places to hole up," Gomez said.

"What? You thinkin' of chasing her down there?" Lupo asked.

"Yeah, muthuhfuck. She ain't comin' back here, is she?" Gomez said. "Long fuckin' drive. Can't exactly hop a plane, ya know? I'm gonna give you 20 g's to get me a used Impala, gray, low mileage--off the books. Answer an online ad and show up with the cash. Tell the guy you don't care about title—you just want wheels, entiendes?

"I gotta find that puta, and when I do, she never gonna be pretty again," Gomez growled.

With that promise, Gomez went to the safe in the basement and took out $20,000 in $100 bills and stuffed it into an envelope.

"You line the deal up on the phone or online. Once you cool, you make the deal," Gomez instructed.

Lupo took the envelope and put it beside his laptop. Then he began searching Craigslist and Facebook Marketplace for the car.

* * * * *

Jose Castillo had worked for 10 years as a prosecutor in Veracruz, then another decade as a defense abogado. In the second job, he made easy money, cash money, and spent little on women or booze. At 47, the bachelor sold his home and moved first to Puerto Vallarta, then to Punta Mita and bought Tacos & Papas.

He built a roomy two-story home behind the restaurant, found a reliable manager and spent his days surfing, reading and attempting a novel. He was relaxing in a rear booth over a Negra Modelo one late afternoon in his restaurant, when a comely young girl walked in and asked in English if he needed a waitress. He always needed a waitress-- the turnover in the wait staff drove Castillo nuts.

"Como se llama, senorita? Castillo asked Letty,

"Violeta Gutierrez. Some call me Letty," Letty said in her improving English. "Do you need a waitress here? I look in here at noon and the place look very busy but only one waitress."

"You got experience?" he asked.

"I work at La Dolce in PV and I work in Chicago at the best Mexican restaurant, Nuevo Laredo," she said, doubting he would check out the restaurants as closely as he was checking out her body with his "elevator eyes".

"Okay, I check you out. Come back tomorrow," he said.

The night manager at La Dolce recalled a Letty who had worked there briefly but could not recall a Violeta.

No problema, thought Castillo. *I don't care where you worked before; you'll be my bride in six months.*

* * * * *

Halloran could tell a Bridgeport guy from an Evanstonian by their accents, and he knew the Brits could nail a Yorkshireman from a Southampton bloke in one sentence. So, he reasoned, could a Spanish linguist nail Letty's accent from that brief interruption on the taped ransom demand? Ochoa thought it likely, so the pair brought the recording to UIC (University of Illinois Chicago) Professor Peter Puente.

"Sounds very much like an accent from Nayarit or Jalisco state to me, with the little she said," Puente said. "Maybe Sayulita or Punta Mita or even San Francisco---a small town north of Puerto Vallarta, not the one where Tony Bennett left his heart."

"Pretty specific, professor," Halloran said. "You sure?"

"Can you tell a New Yorker from a Nebraskan? Same geographic twangs and diphthongs in Spanish that tell the tale," Puente said, smiling at the detective.

"Big help, Peter. Thanks for your time," Ochoa said.

Outside, Halloran turned to his fed partner. "Lunch? Salerno's is close, cheap and has parking—if that concerns you."

"I always drive and park as if Pam Zekman's tailing me," Ochoa said, referring to the veteran Channel 2 investigative reporter.

Over a turkey sub at Salerno's, Halloran told Ochoa his suspected whereabouts for Letty.

"So, we know she gave a PV restaurant, La Dolce, as a former employer, and now Puente is putting her upbringing accent a bit farther north, right?" Halloran asked.

"I'm with ya," Ochoa responded.

"Goodo. Now I'm' thinkin' that if we find Letty, she may lead us to Gomez—if she escaped with the ransom loot, as we suspect. Now we gotta convince the prosecutors to send us down there looking for Gomez ostensibly but really looking for both," Halloran continued.

"Let me reach out to AUSA (Assistant U.S. Attorney) Geri Meckelson for us. She's sharp, cute as hell and knows which judges like her. She'll get us travel approval from her boss and mine and the warrants from a friendly judge. Total package," Ochoa said.

"Terrific. I'll talk to Syl and know she'll make it happen with CPD. I know ASA Egan was already working on the warrant for Gomez. She works well with her fed sisters," Halloran said. "I'm gonna grab a quick swim at home and grab my passport but catch you later."

Once home, he went to his closet and reached to the top shelf in his closet and felt back for his lockbox.

He dialed the combination and the lockbox sprang open. Inside were his prized possessions—his passport, a .38 snub nose, five-round, loaded Smith & Wesson he had found on the street after a gangbanger shootout in Gage Park years ago, and his grandmother's 1.5-carat diamond engagement ring. His "Amma" had willed it to him when he was 23. He'd kept it just in case, but it remained as unused as the snubnose.

"You never know when you're gonna need one of these," he said to himself before he returned the box to its high hiding place, and he went downstairs to swim.

* * * * *

Two hours after passing Tulsa, Gomez started rethinking his destination choice.

Letty knows people in PV, but I don't know if she knows anyone in Guada. So, why should she waste time in Guada with 2 million people she don't know when she may go straight to PV? he now reasoned.

When he reached El Paso, he looked up the local Cobras Jefe and resold the Impala for a few hundred more than he paid for it. As darkness descended, he joined a long line of day laborers shuffling toward the border and Ciudad Juarez. He slipped by easily after flashing the fake Mexican passport he'd bought along with a bogus Indiana driver's license two days earlier at a Little Village backroom operation the gang used frequently.

After spending the night at the Hotel Maria Bonita in Ciudad Juarez, he exchanged $500 American for pesos and took a taxi to the airport to catch the next plane to PV. Unconcerned about warrants and BOLOs there, he used his Indiana DL for his ID and caught a plane leaving at 4 p.m. for the two-hour nonstop flight.

Once there, he bought a used Chevy Malibu for cash after some perfunctory bargaining. Still exhausted by the long trip, Gomez grabbed some fish tacos from a street vendor and then checked in to the Hotel Mio.

The young woman behind the hotel counter asked for his credit card.

"I got no credit card. Here's cash," he growled in English, pushing 3,000 pesos ($150 U.S.) across the counter, exposing his gang tats.

"No problema, senor," she said after recognizing the Latin Cobras tat with the hooded cobra rising.

The next morning, he headed out at 11 a.m. in search of Letty and his loot--cash in his wallet and vengeance on his mind.

"Fuckin' puta," he exhaled as he drove first to La Dolce Vita restaurant on the Malecon overlooking the Bahia Banderas.

CHAPTER 34

Over dinner at Tufano's, their favorite meeting and eating joint in Little Italy, Halloran and Egan exchanged some war stories before zeroing in on the quest for Gomez and Letty.

Halloran did most of the talking—no small victory with the garrulous prosecutor—outlining all they'd gathered about Letty's possible location and the futile search for Gomez. As a member of the FBI Cold Case squad, Halloran had temporary federal credentials, so he would join Ochoa seamlessly on a flight to Puerto Vallarta the next morning.

Ortiz and Macel had compared notes and agreed it was a federal operation, so it would be on the fed dime, Halloran explained.

"So, let me get this straight. You're going on an all-expenses junket to Puerto Vallarta—and I haven't heard any end date—to find a beautiful fugitive on my tax dollars," Egan jabbed, hoisting her glass of the house red.

"Thank God and the CPD I'm here to straighten out your misinterpretation of this trip. An FBI agent and I are off on a perilous pursuit of the man who shot him and kidnapped the Chief of D's daughter and escaped for parts unknown, but we assume he's somewhere in Mexico," Halloran countered.

"Aha. Assume? You know what we lawyers say about that word when we object to 'assuming facts not in evidence?'" Egan said, leaning over to snatch Halloran's bottle of Peroni. Not quick enough to deny a beer connoisseur like Halloran as he beat her to the beer with the quick hands of a former tight end.

"Eh, eh, counselor. You must keep a clear head here. Stick to the red," Halloran said a second before Tina, the highly efficient waitress, arrived with the house special salad.

"So, you are right to be cautious, pessimistic and a potential spoil sport, but Juan and I—and more importantly our bosses—believe Gomez knows at least as much about Letty as we do and is itching to get his hands on the loot and around her neck," Halloran said.

"Letty is bait?" Egan asked, eyebrows raised toward her thick auburn hair.

"Not our choice. Hers, and we would be foolish to think otherwise or not take advantage. She may have covered her tracks carefully, but Juan, the slick FBI sleuth, and yours truly feel confident we can track her down with the help of the PFM (Policias Federales Ministerial), their equivalent of the FBI," Halloran explained.

"I'm familiar. That should make extradition seamless. You catch 'em; we stretch 'em. You know—give them a nice long stretch in prison," Egan smiled.

"You been hanging with the feds too much. That sounds a little like what the defense bar comes up with to allege Spanish Inquisition-like interrogations by letter-of-the-law CPD dicks. I've been known to counterpunch on occasion, but to tie a suspect's hands to one end of a torture wheel and his feet to the other end is an anachronism," Halloran objected with a wry smile.

"Easy, Hal. We're all friends here," Egan laughed.

"How friendly?" he asked.

"Let's see about that after we treat ourselves to some tiramisu," Egan countered.

* * * * *

Ed and Edna Stupanski had been married for 35 years, raised three kids and lived in the same yellow-brick bungalow in Edison Park for the duration of their marriage. That life and that residence ended for Ed, a retired Cook County Sheriff's sergeant, when Ed decided to end Edna's argument with one round from his Glock 45.

Her last words, Ed told detective Thoma were, "You dumb fucking Polack."

"I told what was left of her brains, which were never working properly, 'Smartass Irish bitch.' She had no smart remarks left," Ed said as Thoma clamped her cuffs on him for the short ride to the Jefferson Park District station.

"Open and shut" pretty much described the Stupanski murder, but another open case crossed her mind as she drove to the station.

Gotta figure that Larry Lynch, if still alive, had spent enough time out of the joint working construction and is old enough to have earned a Social Security check. Gonna have to check that out.

After sitting in on Ed Stupanski's recorded confession with an Assistant Public Defender present to protect the rights he waived, Thoma headed back to her desk on the second floor of Area 3.

She called her Social Security Administration (SSA) contact and explained her needs.

"Don't know if he's still alive, but if he is, he may be getting a check. Can you look in your system and see if there's a check going out?" she asked.

She heard some tapping on a keyboard, followed by a pen scratching across paper. "Got a paper and pencil?" SSA asked.

"Shoot," Thoma instructed.

"Larry Lynch, P.O. Box 173, USPO, 1500 Hadley St., Houston, Tx 77002. Got it?" SSA guy asked.

"Got it," Thoma responded. "Any way to know if he's cashing those checks?" Thoma asked.

"Minute," he said. Then he came back. "We show they were cashed as recently as last month. Cashed on the Friday following the second Wednesday—when we issue the checks," he said.

"Big help. Big. Thanks so much," Thoma said. "What bank?"

"Chase, deposited electronically. No branch listed," he said.

"Again, thanks," Thoma said.

"De nada," replied her Hispanic source.

She then checked her "Notes" for the name of the Houston cop in their records section. Sgt. Otis Oliver. Halloran hadn't 'd heard back from him, so she Googled and found the main number at Houston P.D. She dialed it and asked for Records.

A female voice answered "Sgt. Warren."

"Hi Sarge. This is detective Jane Thoma with Chicago P.D. Is Sgt. Oliver working today?" Thoma asked.

"Not today, or any day soon. Otis suffered a stroke last week and is in pretty bad shape. Can't talk and partial paralysis on his right side. Only 59. Can I help you?" Sgt. Maryam Warren asked.

After Thoma explained quickly what Halloran had asked for and why, Warren asked her to hold. In a few minutes, Warren came back on the line.

"From his 'to do' list on his desk, it looks like he sent down a requisition to our morgue—where we keep old records. No sign here that he got an answer. Give me an hour, and I'll check it out. Can I call you back at this number?" she said, looking at the land-line number.

"Yeah, great. But let me give you my cell, too, in case I'm out on a case," Thoma said.

"Is this a hot case?" Warren asked.

"Well, yes and no. It's a cold case and the guy we like for this traces to Houston, but he's old now--74--and we want to get to him soon. No DNA in our files, the case is pre-DNA but we got some old murder scene evidence we got some DNA from. We need to get his fingerprints off the file to check against in case we can raise a DNA profile from the print," she said.

Then Thoma ran through the grisly details of the O'Malley murder, including the lurid oil can stains.

"Jesus, and you think this piece of shit—even at 74—may be in Houston? I'm walking this down myself to get that print card, if it still exists, and will get back to you soonest," Warren said.

"You're the best—cop to cop—really appreciate it," Thoma said, then hung up.

Forty-five minutes later, her cell went off with a 281 area code—Houston.

"Got the card, but you know how iffy raising DNA profiles is from a print?" Warren asked.

"We know, but we got a lady we call 'Wonder Woman' in our state police crime lab. I heard her once say she could raise a DNA profile off the envelope Lincoln used to write the Gettysburg Address on. Can you Fed Ex it to me? I'll send you a check in the mail," Thoma promised.

"Our budget ain't that tight, so I'll eat the charge if it helps get this monster. Jesus, cut her body up. I'll walk it across the street to the Fed Ex office right now, so you should have it tomorrow," Warren averred.

After hanging up on her new best friend, Thoma Google-mapped the Post Office address on Beechnut Street and found it was just a few blocks from I-69 but also close to the Greyhound Bus station in midtown Houston.

Who would have thought a 74-year-old ex-construction worker, ex-con would know how to work a smart phone or tablet? Thoma wondered. *But if he's got a cellphone-- good fuck-- she would need a subpoena to dislodge any information from one of the cell carriers. And which one? But maybe not necessary.*

* * * * *

For the past year, Lynch had been residing in a one-bedroom apartment in central Houston, just a few more memory lapses before he needed to be housed In an assisted living housing complex.

He kept to himself, had few friends, no relatives and spent his days watching soaps and nights watching old movies on A&E. After paying for his room and board with the SSA check, he was left with a few hundred dollars. He was saving the excess for his cremation. He had survived a bout of colon cancer, but his doctor said it was likely to return.

He was raised a Catholic and feared his many, many mortal sins were going to condemn him to an eternity frying in hell.

Or maybe a stretch till his death in an Illinois prison, which was the furthest thing from his mind all these years after he left Illinois.

But it was sure at the front of Thoma's mind and priorities on this Friday evening.

CHAPTER 35

WBBM Newsradio's weather and traffic on his clock radio rousted Halloran just after dawn. He took a quick workout in the pool before catching an Uber to O'Hare for his four-hour flight to PV with Ochoa. Both got there three hours before the flight so they could clear it at the airport with the Transportation Security Administration (TSA) that they were bringing their guns—Ochoa's Glock and Halloran's Browning.

Per Halloran's request, they were both sitting in bulkhead seats in the 737, so he could stretch his legs. Ochoa took the window seat; Halloran the aisle. No one sat between them. Once airborne, Halloran slipped over next to Ochoa.

"Remember Elly talking about how asshole treated Leticia and called her his whore, 'Puta mia'? Well, I've been here before several times and always wanted to check out a more remote area near Punta Mita," Halloran said

"Yeah, go ahead," Ochoa responded.

"Well, first thing I'm doing when we get off the plane and clear customs is call Elly to ask her if she might have heard 'Punta Mita' instead of 'Puta Mia.' That's fractured Spanish anyway; not that Gomez is a scholar. Worth a call and might save us some time. Ya think?" Halloran asked in what was close to a whisper.

"Yeah, absolutely. She made a point of saying she couldn't hear too good," Ochoa replied.

"I think it's an hour or so from PV but something to think about if we get nothing in PV," Halloran said. "Now, my young partner, I'm going to grab about 20 winks to get ready for the hunt."

Back in his seat, he rested his chin on his chest and was out five minutes later. He was awakened by the flight attendant's call to fasten seat belts for landing.

At the gate, they were greeted by PFM agent Pablo Espinosa, a squared-off, mid-30s guy who looked like he could play linebacker for the Bears.

"Bienvenidos, gents. Ochoa and Halloran I presume. Pablo Espinosa," he said as he extended a right hand that had the grip of a boa constrictor. Halloran reached deep into this extended claw and squeezed tight, as did Espinosa. Noticing the extended gripping, Ochoa slapped the Mexican agent on the back and said, "Muchas gracias, amigo," avoiding the perfunctory grip and grin.

The machismo maneuver over, Espinosa instructed the pair of Americans to follow him as he marched through a series of checkpoints to the baggage area.

"We only got these," Halloran said, hoisting his small carry-on. Ochoa followed suit. Outside, they avoided the long lines waiting for the small buses and taxis that squired the gringos to luxurious living in the high-rises that dotted the beaches on the Bahia Banderas.

"I been told you guys are at the Sheraton Buganvilias, so I'll take you there right now," Espinosa said as he opened the tailgate of his SUV.

"Your English sounds pretty American, Pablo. That bilingual bit must come in handy with all the tourists here," Halloran said.

"Yeah, it helps. I was born here but the parents moved to San Diego when I was 4. After I graduated from San Diego State, I went to visit my grandparents in Merida, and, well, found a job and a wife, then kids," he said, shrugging his shoulders as if to say that was enough about him.

Twenty minutes later, they pulled into the Sheraton parking lot, then exited into the 82-degree cloudless sunlight of beautiful Puerto Vallarta, rimmed by the blue/black Sierra Madre mountains.

"I'll give you guys some time to unpack, and here's my card with my cell on it. Just call when you're ready," Espinosa said.

Riding shotgun, Halloran glanced back at Ochoa and raised his eyebrows slightly.

Ochoa nodded, then spoke: "Thanks, but we kinda want to get going. So, give us 15 minutes to check in and then we're good to go."

"Roger that. I'll be here waiting," Espinosa said.

Inside the lobby, Ochoa checked in for both of them, using his fed credit card. Halloran found a quiet spot in the lobby and called Elly. He figured it was about her lunch hour.

"Uncle Mike. I'm in class, but I'll walk out for a minute 'cause I know it must be important if you're calling," Elly whispered, raising her hand and pointing to the classroom door.

"Elly," Halloran continued when she came back on her phone, "do you remember saying how you heard one or both of them at some time saying 'puta mia'? I know you were doing your best to recall exactly but could they possibly have been saying 'Punta Mita'?" Halloran asked.

"I guess, but I heard him calling her his whore a couple times. She was harder to hear but, yeah, she might have said 'Punta Mita' when she was on the phone. I'm just not sure," Elly said.

"Perfect, Elly. Big help. Now get back to class, honey," the godfather instructed, and then disconnected.

* * * * *

At about the same time, a disgruntled, tired and angry Gomez left the La Dolce Vita on the Malecon after learning there was another La Dolce restaurant a few miles north, this one a pizzeria across from the La Isla shopping center.

There, he asked the concierge for the manager and slipped her a 500-peso note.

In a few minutes, manager Miguel Marcos appeared and gave Gomez a quick up and down before asking what he could do for the stranger.

"Just looking for some information on my sister. Our father is dying back in Chicago, and I lose track of her about a year ago. I know she want to see Papa before he die," Gomez said, extending his right hand to shake with Marcos with two 500-peso notes neatly folded.

The manager took the bribe seamlessly, smiling and slipping the notes into his right front pocket. "What is your sister's name, amigo?"

"Leticia. Letty, we call her. She work here once," Gomez replied.

"You in luck my friend. Yust a few weeks ago, I got a call from a Punta Mita restaurant guy asking for a reference for her. I put him on hold a minute and ask around. Couple waitresses vaguely remember her but nothing bad, So, I tell him that," Marcos said.

"Great. What was the name of the restaurant?" Gomez asked.

"Tacos something. Didn't really pay much attention. Sorry," Marcos said.

"Is okay, gracias," Gomez said, then retreated to his car.

* * * * *

After disconnecting with Elly, Halloran approached the hotel concierge.

"You know a restaurant called 'La Dolce?'" Halloran asked.

"Si, I know two. There is the La Dolce Vita along the Malecon in the old part of town, and the La Dolce Pizzeria near La Isla," he responded.

"Which gets the most tourist action?" Halloran asked.

"The one near La Isla," the concierge replied just as Ochoa joined him.

"Let's hit La Dolce near La Isla," Halloran said, as they walked to join their Mexican counterpart.

It was only a five-minute drive for Espinosa in his Land Rover.

When the three armed men exited the huge SUV at the pizzeria, the valet froze.

"No lo muevas!" Espinosa barked not to move the truck. Then the three men quickly found manager Marcos.

In Spanish, Ochoa asked if he knew Letty.

"Popular girl," he said in English, eyeing Halloran.

"Porque?" Ochoa and Espinosa responded in unison.

The bilingual manager replied smoothly in English.

"You the second person in last half-hour asking about Leticia," he said.

Under rapid questioning in two languages, the three were informed of the visit by Gomez and the gist of the conversation.

"How long ago?" Halloran barked.

"Maybe 15-20 minutes ago," Marcos replied.

In nearly lockstep, as if ordered by their commander, the three ran to the waiting Land Rover.

"I call the deputy assigned to Punta now—Pedro Cuellar, a friend of mine-- and get information about restaurants with the name Tacos in it," Espinosa said.

"You drive," commanded Halloran. "Your friend in your contacts?"

"Si, si. look for him under P," Espinosa said, handing his phone to Ochoa.

Ochoa grabbed the cell and put it on speaker so the speeding federale could speak and simultaneously weave through the traffic on the busy highway that led to the airport and to Punta Mita beyond.

The befuddled Pedro managed to blurt out that there was only one restaurant with Tacos in the name in town—Tacos & Papas. He then texted the address to Espinosa's phone. In seconds, Ochoa had punched it into the Land Rover's navigation system.

"Use your siren and lights," Halloran urged from the back seat, leaning forward to see the map appear on the SUV's screen.

"How long till we get there?" Halloran asked, nearly shouting and grabbing Espinosa's right shoulder.

"Usually, it take an hour. I get us there in half that," Espinosa promised as he raced through the traffic near the PV marina.

CHAPTER 36

In 15 minutes, the SUV had passed Bucerias, the last town of substance before Punta Mita. Soon, Halloran spotted Highway 200, also known as Libramiento Punta Mita. As he hit the open highway, Espinosa floored the SUV. Halloran spied the speedometer hitting 150 KPH, or about 90 miles an hour.

As they reached the outskirts of the Punta Mita resort area, the GPS voice started belching out directions shortly after they passed a Pemex. Along the way, they had passed just a few cars and eyeballed the drivers as they passed. No Gomez.

Espinosa slowed a bit in answer to the voice directions to bear right. After they passed the town hospital, Ochoa saw the sign "Tacos & Papas."

There was only one car in front as they skidded to a gravel-spraying stop.

"Pablo, take the rear," Ochoa yelled just before he and Halloran, both hands gripping their semi-automatics burst into the restaurant. An elderly man at the counter raised his hands in surrender. Standing behind the counter was a frightened and shocked Leticia Diaz.

"Letty. We aren't here to hurt you, but Gomez is maybe only minutes away," Ochoa yelled.

"Come with me," Halloran ordered, grabbing her right wrist and yanking her into the kitchen. The chef raised his hands before Ochoa ordered him to leave by the back door.

Marching the frightened, now nearly hysterical and crying waitress out to the rear door, Halloran handed her to Espinosa.

"Cuff her to that doorknob and brace for a possible firefight," Halloran said, then rushed back to the waiting Ochoa.

"We gotta get that truck out of sight if we're gonna get the drop on him," Ochoa said.

First, they had no problem persuading the elderly man at the counter to "vamanos." Once he cleared out, Halloran relieved Pablo of his custody of Letty as he then drove his ostentatious SUV out of sight 200 yards down the road toward the beach, then ran back.

Halloran leaned down next to Letty and spoke slowly and calmly to the weeping girl.

"Letty, what you do in the next few minutes may mean the difference between a life of hell and perhaps a chance to start a good life," Halloran counseled. "Gomez is coming for you, but we are here to protect you. So don't worry. Now I'll take the cuffs off and you come with me."

Letty gasped, choked a bit on her first words, then whispered, "I understand, sir."

As Espinosa returned, Ochoa joined his two comrades as Halloran hatched his plan for all to hear, including Letty.

* * * * *

Gomez knew it would be time-consuming and risky to try to buy a gun, but a lethal knife would serve his purpose just fine, he figured.

So, just a few minutes after he left La Dolce Pizzeria, he turned off Francisco Medina into the sprawling Walmart parking lot.

Inside he wound his way through the massive store till he found the sporting goods section near the pharmacy. There he zeroed in on the hunting and fishing section and spied a Calamus fishing fillet knife with a scabbard for 425 pesos. He broke the plastic seal and unsheathed the nasty locating 9-inch weapon.

"This will scare you, my little Letty, and can scar that pretty face for the rest of yo' life," Gomez said softly to himself, startling a teenage boy nearby.

"No worry, muchacho," Gomez said to the boy.

After waiting in a long line at the auto-checkout, he scanned the knife and paid the freight for the weapon before he walked leisurely to his car.

No hurry, he thought. *I got a nice surprise for that treacherous bitch.*

An hour later, he stopped at the Pemex station not far from the beach and asked the attendant inside if there was a restaurant in town with the name Tacos in it.

"Si, senor. Alli," the overweight but friendly lady behind the counter told the stranger, pointing down the road some 400 yards away.

"Gracias," Gomez grunted before heading back to his car.

* * * * *

In his 30 years as a cop, Halloran had laid out many plans, plots and traps for dumb thugs. Gomez qualified for the latter, so Halloran gathered his two armed pals briefly at the counter. Letty stood by Halloran silently and listened.

"Gotta figure he has no idea we're here and is hoping she'll be alone. So, we surprise asshole. Juan, you hide in the men's john there, but with the door cracked so you can see and hear. I'll be behind the kitchen door but with a view through the window to the inside. And, Letty, listen carefully...

"You'll be standing here behind the counter polishing glasses with your back to the front door as soon as we see a car pull up in front. When he enters the front door and sees you, you move to the kitchen door and I'll yank you back into the safety of the kitchen, got it?" Halloran asked.

Just to make sure, Ochoa went over the plan is Spanish as Letty continued to nod rapidly, her eyes wide, flashing to the parking lot in front and back to Halloran.

"Juan and I will have guns drawn and ready to fire. Pablo, I want you to go wait in your Land Rover till you see him pull into the parking lot. Once you see him enter the front door, you pull in behind him and park, blocking any escape should he bolt," Halloran said. Espinosa nodded gravely, glancing at Ochoa for affirmation. Ochoa winked.

"Facil, amigo," Ochoa assured his new partner. Then he retreated to the men's room. Espinosa fled out the back door, leaving Halloran with Letty.

"Don't worry, Leticia. He won't have a chance to use a gun, and I doubt that he has one; and he won't get close enough to you to use a knife. I want you safe," Halloran said, knowing she would be his best witness if she agreed to a plea deal with the feds.

Halloran then retreated through the kitchen door and whispered back to the frightened girl: "Just wait till you see a car pull into the parking lot, then turn your back to the front door and start with the glasses. You won't get hurt. I promise."

Ten minutes later, Gomez pulled up by the shoulder opposite the Tacos & Papas parking lot and looked up and down the street. It was past lunchtime, and the streets were mostly deserted. Satisfied that everything looked quiet, he slowly turned left into the restaurant parking lot.

Again, he waited a minute before exiting his car after he pulled his baseball cap down low and shoved the sheathed knife into his right back pocket.

As he entered the deserted restaurant, Letty turned and locked eyes with Gomez, hers in abject fear, his in hatred. He pulled the fishing knife from its scabbard and slowly advanced from 20 feet away.

"My little Letty…" Gomez began, sneering.

Halloran reached quickly through the kitchen door with his left hand and yanked Letty back behind him as he emerged from the kitchen with his Browning in his right hand pointed at Gomez, and growled: "On your knees, shithead. You know the drill."

Simultaneously Ochoa burst from the men's room, his Glock aimed at Gomez's midsection and shouted, "On your knees. Now! Then lie flat with your hands behind your neck!" To seal the front, Pablo squealed to a stop behind Gomez's car.

Slowly, Gomez knelt, then lowered himself to the ground and put his hands behind his back as Ochoa rushed up to cuff him.

"Well, well. What have we here? Going fishing, asshole," Ochoa said, taking the nasty-looking knife from Gomez.

"Fuck you!" Gomez shouted, as Ochoa knelt on the back of the man who tried to kill him.

"Fuck me? We'll see who gets fucked, you scumbag," Ochoa grunted, putting his full weight into Gomez's back.

With Gomez cuffed and secure, Halloran checked on Letty, collapsed and weeping on the kitchen floor, where Halloran had tossed her like a rag doll.

"You're okay. Safe," Halloran said, softly lifting her to her feet. "But you're not out of the woods, yet. The rest is up to you."

*****

That evening, after turning over Gomez to the local policia in PV for safekeeping in their lockup, Ochoa and Halloran sat Letty down in Ochoa's hotel room for a lengthy debriefing.

First, Halloran gave her the Miranda rights. She nodded when asked if she understood. Ochoa told her the same in Spanish. Again she nodded.

"Now Letty is the time you can be smart and maybe save something of the rest of your life," Halloran said, looming over her before taking a seat on the bed as she sat at the room's desk.

Ochoa remained standing.

"Start at the beginning of when you met Gomez. Don't lie and don't leave anything out," Ochoa warned the girl, still tear-stained and dressed in her pink waitress uniform.

CHAPTER 37

It took two hours for Letty to go through her terrorizing months with Gomez detailing how he had charmed her with expensive gifts and wining and dining.

When she'd finished, Halloran spoke first after making furtive eye contact with Ochoa to make sure he wasn't stepping on his fed partner's toes.

"Look, Letty. We believe you, but we have only your word for most of this, and it will be up to a federal prosecutor to decide if you are useful or believable. Your part in the kidnapping alone means you could face life in a federal prison. Escaping the scene of the shooting and fleeing to Mexico with the ransom money and diamonds makes you look guilty," Halloran said.

"Por favor, he start shooting. He shoot the policeman. You," pointing to Ochoa. "I scared. So I run, and I keep running till I get here. I didn't know the money and diamonds were in car till I halfway here. But what I suppose to do, turn around and go back while he looking for me. You see the knife. He want to kill me," Letty wept, looking from Halloran to Ochoa and back again.

"Okay, Letty. So, where's the money now, the diamonds?" Ochoa demanded. "That would be the start of getting in front of this," Ochoa said, softening slightly.

"Here. It here in town," she pleaded. "I show you. I give you."

* * * * *

Letty spent an uncomfortable night in the PV women's lockup—just a floor below Gomez. Then at 8 a.m., Ochoa brought her out to Espinosa's waiting SUV for the trip back to Punta to Letty's room where she had her backpack and the safety deposit key safely stashed in the small purse with some of the cash.

"Here," she said and handed the key and the rest of the cash to Ochoa.

"You keep the key. Banks are funny about strangers going into safe deposit boxes. You will have to sign in and then use your key along with the bank's key," Ochoa explained in Spanish.

An hour later, Ochoa escorted Letty into the Scotia Bank near La Isla and into the secured vault, where the banker used his key and she used hers to open the box. Then, the banker motioned for her to use a private viewing room.

Inside the confined room, Letty opened the interior box and emptied out the cash and diamonds as Ochoa gazed at the loot. Then, he put his briefcase on the table and secured the illicit bounty as Letty looked on.

"This is a good start," Ochoa counselled. "How much is gone, spent?"

Letty grimaced, then furrowed her brow in thought.

"Okay, I got maybe 6-7,000 pesos and tal vez $800 in U.S. cash," she said, then rifled through her purse to find the cash.

After an hour sorting through the cash in dollars and pesos, Ochoa figured Letty had spent roughly $1,500 in ransom cash.

Ochoa gathered it all into his briefcase with a combination lock and snapped it shut.

"You're lucky you haven't spent more," Ochoa said. "This amounts to restitution--of sorts--and your lawyer can argue it as such at sentencing."

"Sentencing? What I do wrong? I scared of him. I only use money to survive and get settle here," Letty protested, tears forming in the lids of her large brown eyes.

"Back in Chicago, you will be assigned a federal defender—an abogado-- who can argue for you. I can't promise, but I can say you'd be a good candidate for witness protection, then relocation with a new identity—if you fully cooperate and testify against Gomez," Ochoa explained.

With that said and the remaining loot recovered, Ochoa led Letty out of the bank and hustled her back to the women's lockup.

Two days later, the extradition papers secured and the Mexican authorities anxious to get rid of the fleeing felons, Ochoa turned Letty over to a freshly arrived female FBI agent who took her to the rear of a flight to Chicago O'Hare. In the front of the plane in the bulkhead section just past the First-Class section, Ochoa sat in the middle seat with a handcuffed Gomez seated at the window seat.

"Don't talk, walk or move, shithead," Ochoa said quietly. "Or you can give me an excuse to inflict what your lawyers would call 'excessive force' in restraining you. Comprendes, cabron?"

With his left handcuffed hand, Gomez raised his middle finger as his answer.

"Your IQ? Perfect. You do understand," Ochoa quipped, resisting the temptation to bend the digit back to Gomez's wrist.

The rest of the four-hour flight was indeed silent.

*****

Once Halloran realized his services were no longer needed, he texted Egan.

"Lonely in PV. Want to be sleepless. Can you join?"

Twenty seconds later, his phone vibrated with the name "Egan."

"You got a little lucky there with a beautiful young woman, and now you're hoping to get lucky with a more mature beautiful woman?" Egan teased.

"I've got a lot of unused United Airlines miles and you have an unused condo a few blocks from where I stand, alone, frustrated, forlorn…" Halloran retorted before Egan jumped in.

"But not forgotten, you silver-tongued Irish bullshitter. I just made a reservation for the 9 a.m. flight tomorrow. And I'm supposin' you're thinking about my mother's empty condo at the Grand Venetian?" Egan responded. "Well, you're in luck. We can have it for the next three days. Will the Chief of D's give you a little time due?"

"I think I'm on good paper with Syl—that's Chief of Detectives Sylvia Ortiz to you, Ms. Pushy Prosecutor," Halloran said. "I'll be waiting with the time-share peddlers who know how to take advantage of Yank tourists. Maybe I can pick up a few pointers."

"You're talking about your pointer to a lady of delicate sensitivity? We'll talk more about that tomorrow," Egan countered.

"Pillow talk?" Halloran asked. Then his screen went blank.

Almost immediately after he set it down, it began vibrating again. Caller ID said "Marone." Sun-Times ace reporter Frank Marone. Halloran hesitated a second then connected.

"Frank," Halloran said, leaving dead air.

"Mike, I'm being told you caught Gomez in Puerto Vallarta and some chica, too. True?" Marone said over the traffic noise.

"Frankie lad, your source is—per usual—only about half-right," Halloran said cryptically.

"What has she fucked up?" Marone asked, revealing more about his source than he should—or intended to.

"She? Are you charming the pants off some innocent ingenue at CPD?" Halloran asked, knowing full well Marone would never give up his source.

"You're not the only guy in Chicago with a bit of Irish wit and bullshit to spread to the right source. You know I can't tell you that. But you could tell me where I went wrong," Marone begged, wanting to be accurate.

The two aging Irish-Americans on mostly opposite sides had parried before, with Halloran being as careful as he was helpful.

"You can talk and search at the same time on that smart phone, right, smart guy?" Halloran jibed.

"Yep. Please be my guide," Marone said.

"Well, Google map search Puerto Vallarta and then scroll up north about 60 miles. Whattya see?" Halloran coached.

"Beyond PV I don't see much till I see a little peninsular jutting out west called Punta Mita. Never heard of it," Marone said.

"You have now," Halloran said.

"You saying the pinch went down in tiny Punta Mita?" Marone probed.

"I didn't say that, but I would say that you wouldn't have to worry about printing a correction if you went with that," Halloran continued.

"What about the broad? Who's she?" Marone queried.

"Broad? Who are you? Damon Runyon?" Halloran said.

"Gimme a break--and a bit more. Would I be in trouble if I said a woman was arrested with Gomez?" Marone asked.

"Not with me, you wouldn't. Now if you waited a bit, you might find some good information in an affidavit in the clerk's files at Dirksen about a bit of distaff pulchritude known to be seen with Gomez," Halloran coaxed.

"Jesus, Mike. Pulling teeth much? How old?" Marone zeroed in.

"She became an adult this month. Adios, amigo," Halloran said and disconnected in the middle of another Marone question.

Three days later, he and Egan caught separate flights back to Chicago.

Egan, Thoma, Ortiz? Halloran wondered about Marone's source on his way home. *Doesn't matter,* he decided. But he leaned to Ortiz since she was CPD and been around long enough to play the "source close to the investigation" game.

PART THREE

The Stretch

CHAPTER 38

All seats were filled on the benches in the spacious 25th-floor ceremonial courtroom when the three defendants were marched into the temporary courtroom of U.S. Magistrate Judge Zatwana Brewer for the bond hearing late on a Tuesday.

The TV sketch artists lined the front right row closest to the jury box, print and electronic reporters behind them and an array of court support staff sitting among the score of Assistant U.S. Attorneys and Assistant Federal Public Defenders. Prosecutors to the right and defense attorneys to the left, perhaps arranged many years ago to reflect the attorneys' political leanings.

The marshals brought out Gomez first in his MCC finest orange jumpsuit. The marshals left his cuffs on since there was no jury there to be prejudiced by the sight of a man in iron. He plopped down in a chair next to his attorney, the slick and seasoned Edward Miller III, a familiar denizen of the 26th and California courts but a seldom visitor to the august federal courtrooms. Dressed in his signature sharkskin gray suit with the maroon kerchief in the breast pocket, he nodded to the press as he sat down. No one nodded back but Blair Bhuto, the ditzy Fox TV sketch artist.

Next in the parade was Lupo, still wearing his civilian clothes after being snatched up the night before by the marshals with CPD support at his parents' Little Village home. For the purpose of the bond hearing, he was represented by Assistant Public Defender Suzanne Santogeorgio, a second-year attorney who was looking a bit nervous. He was cuffed walking in, but the cuffs were lifted when he sat at the defense table.

Last up was lonely Letty, looking dazed and red-eyed as she was led in by two beefy lady marshals. No cuffs. She sat down next to her court-appointed counsel, veteran defense attorney Beth O'Hara-Samuels. Samuels whispered to Letty for a minute, asking a few questions, then turned her head back to her paperwork.

"All right. Let's hear the government first," Brewer said in the quickening silence of the courtroom that was used mostly for swearing in new American citizens and new federal judges.

Walking confidently up to the podium was Assistant U.S. Attorney Meckelson, the diminutive head of the office's Fugitive Task Force. Despite her 4'10" height, the comely Meckelson had a way of commanding attention in a crowded courtroom.

"Your Honor, the government asks for no bail for Gomez and Diaz and a substantial bond for their accomplice, Lupo," she said, turning slightly to glance at the defense table. "They are all accused in connection with the kidnapping of the daughter of the Chief of Detectives of the Chicago Police Department, and two are accused in the shooting of FBI Special Agent Juan Ochoa.

"And Gomez and his accomplice, Diaz, fled the country in the aftermath of the shooting and were arrested a few days ago by the FBI and their Mexican partners. Diaz relinquished the remainder of the ransom. Gomez was arrested with a 9-inch fishing fillet knife that the agents believed he was going to use to carve up Diaz for stealing his kidnapping lucre.

"Mr. Lupo is a known gang operator and drug peddler who is complicit in the kidnapping in that he drove the ransom getaway car, and perhaps more. The investigation continues," Meckelson hinted, trusting the judge would take the ongoing investigation into consideration in weighing Lupo's bond.

"Lucre? How biblical of you, Ms. Meckelson," smiled Brewer, looking down from her lofty perch. "Mr. Miller?"

"Your Honor, the government stands before you asking for no bond for a man they shanghaied in Mexico at gunpoint. We ask the court to set a reasonable bond for a man who served nine years in state prison on a conviction that is still on appeal in state court," Miller said, knowing there was scant chance of a bond being set for the man who nearly killed a federal agent and terrorized a teenage hostage.

"I've read the affidavit filed in support of the warrant for Mr. Gomez and the search of his apartment. I'm not impressed by the hyperbole you Invoke with the archaic reference to a suspect 'shanghaied.' You might want to save your eloquence for a trial, eh, Mr. Miller?" Brewer said.

"Bond is set at $5 million and defendant is ordered back to the MCC until that bond is posted or until our next court date," Brewer said, shaking her head slightly at Miller.

"Thank you, Your Honor," Miller said meekly.

"Ms. Santogeorgio?" Brewer inquired of the squarely built young attorney, dressed in a black pantsuit with a white silk blouse.

"Thank you, Your Honor. My client is by far the least culpable in this case. He was nowhere near the shooting and tells me he had no way of knowing what Mr. Gomez was doing when he drove him around the day of the ransom collection. He avers he's the sole support of his aging parents. The defense asks for a reasonable bond," Santogeorgio said, gasping for breath at the end of her obviously rehearsed speech.

"Again, counselor, I have read the FBI affidavit and that says your client was more than an unpaid chauffeur during the ransom run. That plus his lengthy arrest record–bail is set at $1 million," Brewer said.

Lupo raised his palms to his attorney, as if to say "WTF." Santogeorgio sat quickly and whispered something out of the side of her mouth with a sigh.

"Ms. Samuels, have you had a chance to speak with Miss Diaz?" Brewer asked.

"Just briefly. Can I get a continuance till I can speak at length with her, Your Honor?" Samuels asked.

"All right. We will reconvene tomorrow at 10 a.m. Same place. Same players, mostly. Till then, Ms. Diaz will be held at the MCC," Brewer said, and then gaveled the hearing to a close.

CHAPTER 39

Back in the mid-19th century, Beth O'Hara Samuels' great-great-grandmother, Elizabeth Cady Stanton, was a leader in the early women's suffrage movement.

Samuels' mother, Moira O'Hara, went to Georgetown, protested the Vietnam War in marches to the White House and joined the Peace Corps for a two-year stint teaching ESL (English as a Second Language) in the slums of Lima, Peru. After her PC time, she hitchhiked through South America for a half a year, further honing her Spanish skills.

Her dad, Jacob "Jake" Samuels burned his draft card in a demonstration against the Vietnam War in front of the Pentagon, got busted for disorderly, then got a lucky 356 number in the draft lottery. He graduated from Cornell and was accepted at Harvard Law before returning home to Chicago's Hyde Park, a hotbed of protests against the unpopular war. He passed the bar exam without cracking a book or taking a prep course.

At a coffee shop near the University of Chicago campus, he met a young law school student named Moira O'Hara, who soon moved into his tiny one-bedroom on 54th Street near campus. They smoked dope, talked radical politics, worshipped Saul Alinsky and Jane Fonda, and eventually married just before Jimmy Carter was elected and Beth, their only child was born shortly after Moira passed the bar exam.

Over the next quarter century, Beth was indoctrinated into her parents' liberal/progressive/radical politics and philosophy. But after a few years working for the Cook County Public Defender's office, she followed in her mother's footsteps and did two years in the Peace Corps in Colombia, teaching women's health in a rural village 50 miles south of Barranquilla. As she neared the end of her commitment, Beth traveled for two days by bazaar bus to the PC office in Bogota to fill out her application for the U.S. Attorney's office in Chicago.

Months later she was accepted. Upon her return to Chicago, her parents were happy to have her home but not exactly pleased by her new career choice.

"Beth, why would you join an office that is merely a stepping stone for the silk stocking law firms like Jenner, Winston, McDermott and other rich Republican-riddled firms?" asked her mother, her dad nodding along in their four-bedroom condo looking down on South Lake Shore Drive. "Do you want to put people in prison?"

"Mom. Dad. You know I will get great experience there, and they do prosecute white collar crime, political corruption and vicious street gangs that the state either ignores or lacks the resources to go after. You know that," Beth replied, smiling, looking first to her mom and then to her dad.

Dad spoke first.

"We know. We know. It's just so, so…Republican," Jake Samuels stammered.

"At first glance, but you remember how the feds went after former Illinois Republican William Stratton before I was even born," Beth countered.

"Well do I remember. A former federal prosecutor, Bill Barnett, pulled a legal rabbit out of his hat and got Stratton off," Jake recalled.

"We know, honey, and you know it's just so, so…" Moira hesitated, then smiled at her daughter. "Good for your career."

"And you know that every time we elect a Democratic President, we get a Democratic U.S. Attorney," Beth said, and rested her case.

And so, she joined the federal prosecutors' offices at the Dirksen Building and began what turned out to be a stellar 10-year, all-convictions career, with the scalps of Mafia money launderers, crooked City Hall pols and the astounding break-up of the largest drug-dealing gang in the Chicago area and conviction of three of its leaders.

She had offers from all the big firms but chose a 200-lawyer, mid-size firm, Freeman & Patrick, headed up by a former U.S. Attorney, Richard Dennison, with the provision she could be a "panel" attorney for federal cases, which represent indigent defendants for free and only pay the firm a reduced and fixed price for prep and court time.

* * * * *

In one of the windowless interview rooms of the MCC, Samuels took notes on her yellow legal pad as Diaz poured out her heart and her ordeal to the first sympathetic soul she'd encountered since her disastrous relationship began with Gomez. Sitting next to Diaz was an interpreter to aid in the interview, if need be. But Samuels' Spanish was perfect, and Diaz's English was improving daily, so the interpreter sat mostly mute.

"Just so I understand these events, let me concisely paraphrase your experience so I can go to the prosecutor to see what kind of a deal we can make. But first, are you open to relocating and taking on a new identity as part of the witness protection program?" Samuels asked.

"I think so, si, if it keeps me out of prison and helps put Gomez away forever. Si," Letty said, nodding at the attorney.

"Briefly, as to the charges against you, we would argue that: First, you had no idea what Gomez was up to when he drove to the alley carrying a gun; second, that you were scared to death to let the victim go when Gomez left briefly to make a call to line up the ransom; third, that you fled the alley the night of the shooting because you were afraid you were going to be shot; fourth, you fled the country with the ransom, not knowing it had been left behind in the van.

"Finally, you only spent the money you needed to establish yourself in Punta Mita and then turned the rest over to the FBI when asked about it," Samuels summarized.

"Verdad, verdad," Letty said, nodding and looking at the interpreter for confirmation but getting none. That was not part of her role.

"Okay, now I must make my case for a reasonable bond, based on your truthful testimony," Samuels said, patting Letty's hands on the table.

With that, Samuels called for the MCC guard, and off she went two blocks away to her office.

This is just what I've been training for since high school, she thought.

CHAPTER 40

When court resumed before Brewer the next morning, Letty was led into the courtroom by a female marshal and immediately spotted a smiling Samuels at the defense table. Letty was uncuffed and settled in next to her attorney, who whispered to her briefly before court resumed.

"Good morning, counselor. Glad to see you made it," Brewer smiled down at Samuels. Both had worked at the U.S. Attorney's Office, intersecting briefly.

"Good morning, Your Honor. We're ready to proceed," responded Samuels, dressed in her best dark gray Armani suit.

"Prosecution?" Brewer asked.

"Ready, Your Honor," Meckelson said, remaining seated and gathering some papers on the prosecution table.

"As I said yesterday, the government asks for no bail for Diaz. She's accused in connection with the kidnapping of the daughter of the Chief of Detectives of the Chicago Police Department and the shooting of FBI Special Agent Juan Ochoa.

"Co-defendant Gomez and his accomplice, Diaz, fled the country in the aftermath of the shooting, and were arrested by the FBI and their Mexican partners. Once caught there, Diaz relinquished the remainder of the ransom. Gomez was arrested with a 9-inch fishing fillet knife that the agents believed he was going to use to carve up Diaz for stealing the ransom."

Brewer nodded to Samuels.

"Your Honor, my client was an unwilling accomplice to a violent ex-con, armed leader of a notorious street gang. She has never been arrested before and would not be here but for the plotting, threats and actions of defendant Gomez. She fled this country, not to escape the police but to escape Gomez. It wasn't till she was halfway to Mexico that she discovered the cash and diamonds under the passenger seat," Samuels said.

"I ask Your Honor to release her to the custody of her aunt on an I-bond with electronic monitoring. She is surely no threat at 5'2" and 105 pounds and had a spotless record up to this arrest," Samuels pleaded. "Her aunt is the lady in the black dress at the rear of your courtroom."

As Samuels said that all eyes swung to the rear of the room to a visibly embarrassed Karine Hernandez.

"Miss Meckelson?" Brewer said, eyeing the prosecutor.

"Your Honor, all due respect to my worthy opponent, her client could have freed the hostage at some point, she could have surrendered to police after the shootout, and she could have handed over the ransom loot when she discovered that in her car. We repeat our request for no bail for the defendant as a clear risk to flee again," Meckelson said.

Brewer took off her black-rimmed glasses and pinched the bridge of her nose for a minute in thought.

"A moment, Your Honor?" Samuels asked, then quickly retreated to the rear of the courtroom and whispered to Hernandez, who then followed the lawyer through the door and into the corridor.

In Spanish, Samuels asked the elderly woman if she owned her building. She said yes. Then Samuels asked her its value.

"Porque usted pregunta?" Hernandez asked why.

"Would you be willing to put up your home as collateral to ensure Letty returns to court for each hearing?" Samuels said in flawless Spanish.

"It may be worth $250,000, I not sure," Hernandez replied in English. "But I would put it up for Letty. She my only relative. She like daughter, even though I know yust a little time."

"When did you buy the home?" Samuels asked.

"Now it about 26 years," Hernandez replied.

"Let's go back into court," Samuels said.

Back in front of Brewer, Samuels spoke with increasing urgency.

"Your Honor, Ms. Hernandez is willing to put up her $250,000 home as collateral for her niece's return each court date. It's a risky sacrifice, but she loves her niece and trusts her. We ask the court to trust this elderly lady's judgment and my client with the heretofore spotless arrest record," Samuels said.

Again, Brewer paused for a minute in Solomonic thought. She stood straight up from her black leather throne and spoke in a stentorian tone so her voice carried to the rear of the huge courtroom.

"Ms. Hernandez, do you realize if Leticia flees again, you would forfeit your home, which I assume is your most valuable asset? And she must stay at home?" Brewer asked.

Hernandez looked to her left, then her right, seemingly looking for support from the stranger in her row. Then she stood.

"Si, I mean yes, Your Honor, I understand. Letty is good girl. She be with me--it be okay. She come to court again each time," Hernandez said, then quickly sat down.

"Defendant Diez will be put on electronic monitoring and released on a bond secured by Ms. Hernandez's home," Brewer said. "Court adjourned."

Sitting two yards away from Hernandez for the second day was Francisco Eduardo Contreras "Frank E," a lieutenant in the Cobras at a rank equal to Gomez's. He smiled at Hernandez as she filed out of court.

She wondered who he was. Contreras was the Jefe's ears and eyes this day.

CHAPTER 41

Tracing back to her rookie days as a beat cop in the West Side's busy Harrison District (11th), Thoma had asked for and was usually scheduled for the midwatch shift, 7 a.m.-3 p.m.

So, she had kept that routine of early to bed, early to rise that allowed her to have an almost normal life. Dinners, workouts, an occasional date, seeing family—all elusive pastimes for any cop on the overnight (midnight) or the night shift of 3-11.

After visiting her parents in their Edison Park home, she drove back to her Albany Park condo just south of North Park University on Kimball Avenue. Exhausted from a long day of looking through old files and a quick workout at her gym, she had almost fallen asleep at 10:25 p.m. when her cell started vibrating on her nightstand.

She groggily grabbed the phone and checked the caller ID. "Svenson," it read.

"Hi, Karen. What's up?" Thoma asked.

"We got a match. Your Lynch's profile from the print matched the blood on the barrel slat. Nice work," Svenson chirped. "So did the hair from the hairbrush match the victim."

"Nice work, you," Thoma corrected, sitting up in bed now. "No, great work, and thanks for working this up on the same day I dumped it on you."

"I had lunch with my dad at the Union League Club today and mentioned the O'Malley case, and he remembered it well—the head, the legs, the barrels. He was a judge in Civil, and he devoured the newspapers every day. It stuck a rocket up my—let's say—nose," Svenson laughed.

"I'm gonna track down Mike and let him know. He'll want that, and expect a congrats from him, too. He knows how hard you work and how impeccable your work is," Thoma said.

"Stop! Doing my job, which is a lot less dangerous than yours. I put the profile into CODIS, even though your guy's murder predates that index's inception. See if it gets any hits. Good night, detective," Svenson said, and hit the end button on her cell.

Thoma dialed Halloran's cell, hoping a bit that she would land in his voicemail rather than risk waking him up. She got her wish.

"Mike, Jane. We got a hit on Larry Lynch—just got off the phone with Svenson. Great idea on the print. Talk tomorrow," Thoma ended.

As she put her phone down on her nightstand and headed to the bathroom to brush her teeth, she heard her phone vibrate. Picking it up, she saw "Mike" on caller ID.

"We got our guy!" Halloran nearly yelled, who'd just returned from PV with Egan.

"Now we gotta get a warrant and find this fuck," Halloran said. "I'm meeting Egan for breakfast tomorrow at Lou Mitchell's before court—about 7:30. Wanna join?"

"Are you arriving in separate cars?" Thoma asked, giving her partner a licentious overture.

"That would be none of your business, partner. But here, let me put you on Facetime to show you I'm alone in my humble cottage," Halloran said, punching the Facetime icon to take a look at Thoma and for her to satisfy her prurient interest. He scanned the bedroom, focusing on his book "The Gate House," by Nelson DeMille, lying open on an empty bed.

"Okay, okay. Enough. I don't want to be in your bedroom, even if we are partners. So, I'll see you in person tomorrow morning," Thoma said and disconnected, a bit abashed by her impudence.

* * * * *

An hour after Diaz's bond hearing, Frank E. reported back to the Cobras "Jefe Supremo," Hector Hidalgo, at their two-flat just a few blocks west of the County Jail.

"She got released to her aunt on a bracelet leash. What we gonna do about Jesus and his $5 mil bond," Frank E. asked.

"After his unauthorized caper brought the heat of the cops and feds down on us and lost our Mac-10, we gonna do exactly what this dumb fuck deserves. Nada. Let him rot at the MCC," Hidalgo said.

"Perfecto," Frank E. chimed in.

CHAPTER 42

Dressed in a kelly-green Armani suit, Egan arrived at Lou Mitchell's first and took a booth at the rear of the famous breakfast joint popular with politicians, lawyers and cops. She spotted the County Assessor taking a seat about 20 feet away. He spotted Egan and waved. Egan smiled and made a gun of her thumb and index finger and fired at the politician. He smiled and sat down with his deputy and the already seated County Treasurer.

Egan knew the broad, gruesome facts of the O'Malley murder as it was one of Chicago's worst—in a category where "worst" is just awful and not a suitable subject at a dinner party—but she was only vaguely aware of the other crimes Lynch was convicted of and suspected of.

She soon would be. Halloran sat opposite Egan, a distance they both practiced in public.

"Let's wait for Jane before we get into the weeds with the Lynch case," Halloran said moments before Thoma joined them in the booth.

"Nice work on this monster," Egan said as she shook Thoma's hand, cognizant of prying eyes and loose lips. "I know the broad strokes about this shithead. But fill me in on his sheet."

Halloran spoke first, even though Thoma had been the lead for the last several months.

"Well, madam prosecutor, you nailed it when you called him a monster. I assume you know how he walked on the Spyglass murder?"

"Yeah, the only eyewitness faltered on the stand. Bad luck for that prosecutor—and the cops," Egan said.

"Well, Lieutenant Fitzsimmons noticed a few years later that Lynch fit the vague description for a guy who had committed a string of abductions and attempt rapes," Thoma said.

"Eight attempt rapes? What, he couldn't get it up?" Egan asked.

"Sort of," Halloran responded. "He's huge 6'2', 220, but he has a penis the size of a peanut. The victims said he would tear their clothes off and when he couldn't get it in, he'd play with his pigmy pecker to gratify himself."

"Five of the victims positively Id'd him in lineups, and the other three weren't sure because it was dark but said he was the same size, race and had the same MO. He would trail single girls at night, and when they'd approach an alley, he'd pull his car in fast to block them, and grab them then throw them in the front seat of his car, where there was no door handle on the passenger side," Thoma explained, joining Halloran's narrative.

"There's a plethora of supporting evidence, but we'd need to do a little tracking down of witnesses who may well be old and senile or dead, but a few of Mary Beth's contemporaries should still be alive," Halloran said. "Ya think you'll have any trouble getting a warrant for him with what we got so far."

"The dicks would have loved to have DNA back then, eh?" Egan said, more of a statement than a question. "But no, I think when I lay it all out for Judge J. Forbes McCormick, he'll sign away. No one wants this asshole roaming free, even if he is 74."

"Forbes—Judge McCormick to you (nodding at Thoma)--was in my class at the Academy," Halloran said, "but got accepted to John Marshall Law School halfway through and dropped out for law school to be a prosecutor later, then a judge. He speaks our language, and he ain't called Easy Mac for nothing."

"Ah yes, part of the Irish conspiracy in the Cook County judiciary. I see," said Thoma, catching Egan's eye.

"Not a ting wrong wit dat," Egan said in her best Bridgeport accent.

Halloran nodded to Thoma, who then picked up her cellphone and sent Egan and Halloran Svenson's email and attachment to them. Two pings confirmed the arrival.

"Enough. We've got work to do. Now you have to find him," Egan smiled, nodding to Halloran.

"It'll be as easy as catching a coho off a charter boat on the lake," he replied. "Now we'll get that federal UFAP warrant from the feds." And with that, they finished their coffees as Egan headed to 26th Street and the partners headed to Dirksen.

CHAPTER 43

In order to swoop down on and grab Lynch, Halloran and Thoma would need that UFAP warrant. Since they were both sworn in for the joint Cold Case Task Force, it would be easy. But the feds had their channels, so Halloran called ahead to First Assistant U.S. Attorney Muller.

Twenty minutes later, Halloran and Thoma approached the fifth-floor reception window and asked for Muller. They were told by the Latina receptionist named Loretta to wait a minute and to take a seat. It was just approaching 1 p.m., and a steady parade of assistant fed prosecutors started returning from lunch, both the men and women dressed mostly in navy blue suits. A few had dark gray pinstripes on. The partners nodded a smile at each other as they watched the paseo de abogados.

Not for me, mused Halloran, once again thinking the life of a cop is far more interesting than an attorney's.

Muller soon emerged in his crisp white button-down oxford shirt with a dark burgundy tie that screamed Brooks Brothers. He extended his hand and quickly whisked the detectives into the inner sanctum of the U.S. Attorney's Office. Muller's office was next to the much larger office of the U.S. Attorney for the Northern District of Illinois.

Once seated across from each other, Muller pushed an envelope across his desk to Halloran.

"Your UFAP warrant for Lynch and tickets for a morning flight to Houston for you both. It's for a 9:30 a.m. flight, not too early, I hope.

ASA Egan said that would be perfect for you," Muller said, smiling at Halloran.

"Yeah, good. We've worked a lot of cases together, so she would know," said Halloran, no smile crossing his face after Muller's hint at knowledge he did not have.

"This is quite a coup for a case this old. Congrats to you both," said Muller, rising and acknowledging Thoma for the first time but also signaling the meeting was over.

"It was one of the most horrific murders in Chicago history, but we never had enough to charge this asshole. Now we do. Thanks," Halloran said, grasping the envelope and turning to the door. "We know the way."

Back outside on Jackson Street, they paused.

"I'm' going to call Sgt. Warren to see if she can line up an escort for us at that P.O. box," Thoma said.

"Nice," said Halloran. "We may catch this godawful murdering fuckhead at last. Good work, partner."

Also good to show the bosses he wasn't sitting around with his thumb practicing proctology waiting for the Gomez et al trial at the end of next summer, tentatively the last Monday in August.

"Two more items," Thoma said. "First, I want to give Mary Beth's brother, Donald, a call to let him know we got a warrant for Lynch. And second, I want to give a head's up to Warren that Lynch's DNA is now in CODIS, in case she wants to let their Cold Case dicks know it's there to run a CODIS check on any unsolved murders, rapes or attempt rapes that they have DNA on from years back."

Halloran cleared his throat, then smiled at Thoma. "Great idea on the CODIS check, but let's wait on the brother till we have asshole in cuffs, okay?"

"Right. Just a bit anxious to give him some closure after all these years," Thoma said.

"Understood. Now I'm off home to pack and get a quick swim in" Halloran said. Thoma headed back to her Crown Vic to return to Area 3.

On the way to his Jeep parked on Dearborn, he spotted a beggar, dressed in rags, with swollen and cracked lips, one black eye, sitting on the curb by the Monadnock Building on Dearborn. Halloran figured the poor guy had been mugged for the few bucks he might have.

Halloran paused, pulled out his wallet and took out a double sawbuck.

"Get yourself a decent meal inside at Cavanaugh's and use their bathroom to clean up. Now, don't go buying booze with that, okay, old partner?" Halloran said.

"Sure thing, officer," the bum said, smiling to expose half a dozen brown teeth. Even though Halloran was in plain clothes, not his seldom-used uniform, the homeless guy was savvy enough to make him as a cop.

Busted, Halloran thought. *But a higher place in heaven, too.*

CHAPTER 44

After an easy three-hour flight to Houston, Halloran and Thoma caught an Uber to the Best Western on Dallas Street. Sgt. Warren was waiting in the hotel lobby with a glossy 8x10 mug shot from Lynch's last incarceration a quarter century ago.

"It's the latest we got," Warren said. "But it should give us a pretty good idea of what he looks like."

"Yeah. Thanks a lot. He may have shrunk a bit, but he's a big guy –6'2", 220 when he was pinched in Chicago," Thoma said.

The three made plans to be outside the Beechnut Street P.O. the next day at 8:45 a.m., Wednesday, and the second Wednesday of the month, the day Social Security checks issue. They agreed to meet 15 minutes before the post office opened.

After Warren departed, Halloran abandoned Thoma to the government's choice of accommodations to spend his own dime at the nearby Embassy Suites, which had a large outdoor pool.

"It's got a pool," Halloran explained. "Gotcha," responded Thoma.

A swim. A Porterhouse steak on the government dime. A flick on one of the hotel's channels. And bed.

Tomorrow would be a big day, he hoped.

* * * * *

There were two entrances to the Beechnut post office. At 9:01 am., Halloran took one entrance; Warren the other. Thoma stationed herself inside with a copy of the Houston Chronicle to hide behind.

And they waited. And waited. By noon, Warren made a run to a nearby Jimmy John's to grab sandwiches and soft drinks as their vigil was stretching into the afternoon. They ate in shifts.

A fast eater, Halloran consumed his turkey with Swiss, lettuce, tomato and mayo in a few gulps and washed it down with a Sprite. He then borrowed Thomas's Chronicle and sat on a window ledge inside about 75 feet from Lynch's rental box. And waited.

At 3:18 p.m., Thoma spotted an elderly man with a cane making his way slowly to the post office. He was stooped but still above average in height and as thick as an oak tree. She called her partner.

"Our guy, I'm betting. I'll approach after he opens his box," Halloran whispered into his phone to alert Warren. He nodded to Thoma. She raised her head slightly and patted her hip where her Glock was holstered. They expected no resistance but were wary nonetheless of a man so large and with so violent a sheet. Warren puffed on a Salem as she stood outside, looking at her cell.

Lynch opened the small P.O. box and withdrew one envelope, barely glancing at it as he folded it in two and stuffed it into his right back pocket, then turned to see Halloran standing just to his rear left.

"Larry Lynch?" Halloran asked just as Thoma approached from the right rear.

"Who's asking?" Lynch said, glaring at Halloran, then eyeing Thoma closing in to his right.

"Detective Mike Halloran, Chicago police, assigned to the joint federal/state Cold Case squad, and the lady coming up on your right is Jane Thoma, also a Chicago detective, and we've got a warrant for your arrest," Halloran said, nodding to Warren who was hustling into the lobby.

"You got no jurisdiction here, you dumb Mick flatfoot," Lynch snarled, then tried to brush by Thoma. Before he even made contact with her, Warren moved in, handcuffs in one hand and the UFAP warrant in the other.

"This says otherwise, dumbfuck," Warren said, pushing the warrant into Lynch's face. "Seems just about right to me that two female coppers bust you for the murder of an innocent young girl. Turn around and put your hands behind your back. You have a weapon?"

"I've no weapon and nothing to say to youse low-life pigs," Lynch spat.

At that, Halloran grabbed Lynch by the shoulders and spun him into the wall of P.O. boxes. He held Lynch's right wrist for Warren to cuff it, and then the left.

The few afternoon customers stared as the three cops marched Lynch out to Warren's waiting squad car. Thoma pushed his head down as he was shoved into the rear seat behind shotgun. Halloran got in from the left rear and joined Lynch while Thoma sat front passenger side next to Warren.

Fifteen minutes later, they were all crowded into an interrogation room at a nearby police station.

"You have the right to remain silent..." began Warren as the old man gave her the stink eye.

"I know my fucking rights, you dumb cunt," Lynch yelled. Warren finished the warning and nodded to Halloran.

"Well, shithead, you using the 'C' word certainly sets a tone," Halloran said. "Now tell me exactly how you cut off the head, arms and legs of Mary Beth O'Malley."

"Fuck you. Mary who? Never heard uh her. She some skank you found dead in an alley?" Lynch snarled.

"If you were to read the affidavit we filed to get that warrant, you'd learn that we extracted a DNA sample off the flaps you made on one of the 55-gallon drums you used to seal that girl's body parts before you dumped them in Montrose Harbor. Now back then we had no such things as DNA profiles, but Larry...you cut yourself and bled onto that barrel flap.

"Then a few months ago we extracted a sample profile from the fingerprint card used to book you way back when they arrested you in 1986 in nearby Pasadena, when you tried to kill another young girl—a girl who was so traumatized by you, she couldn't testify," Halloran said.

"You got shit, you stupid dick," Lynch said. "Now I want my lawyer—you know, the one the cunt here told me I had a right to."

With that request, Warren nodded to her Chicago counterparts and left the room to fetch a public defender. Thoma started texting Donald O'Malley to inform him they had just arrested his sister's killer.

Halloran headed outside, ostensibly for a breath of fresh air. For years, Halloran had worked big cases, "heater" cases, press cases. Perhaps the only reporter he truly trusted was the Sun-Times' Marone, the veteran police reporter who always had his phone on.

Looking at his cell 's contact list, he found "FM," which could be anyone. He hit the call, or "phone" icon and heard it ring three times.

"Hey, Mike. Long time. Thought you'd forgotten about me after the Gomez bust," Marone chided after spotting Halloran's caller ID.

"Feds clusterfuck. You know that game. But I got a good one. Pull the clips on the gruesome murder in 1978 of Mary Beth O'Malley. Got a DNA hit on that with one major mephitic moron named Larry Lynch, age 74. Pinched him in Houston today. Check the affidavit filed in the M-files at Dirksen. It'll lay It out for you," Halloran guided.

"Who else knows?" asked Marone, always Looking for the exclusive on a huge story.

"You're my guy, Frankie boy," Halloran said, and disconnected.

In the morning, the honor boxes in front of the Cultural Center on Michigan Avenue showed a stark difference. The Sun-Times screamed: "Old man charged in sensational 1978 murder of North Side teen." The Trib yawned: "Guv weighs budget cuts."

Two days later, after a perfunctory extradition hearing, a cuffed and more subdued Lynch was in the last row of a 737 bound for Chicago, flanked by Halloran and Thoma.

A media mob of mics and pencil pushers staked out O'Hare gate K-28. Halloran was braced and wordlessly steered Lynch through the moving throng till he and Thoma got to the lower-level arrival gates.

As he jumped into the back seat of a waiting CPD Crown Vic with Lynch by his side, he asked Thoma:

"You like the limelight?"

CHAPTER 45

Assistant Public Defender Marcia Tully was an 8th grader at St. Ignatius when she overheard her parents whispering about the murder of Mary Beth O'Malley.

Her dad, the Honorable James Tully, had made his daughter sit by his side in bond court several times after she turned 12. He and his wife, CPD Lieutenant Sarah Connors, didn't just believe in preaching tough love, they practiced it with each of their six children. The day after Marcia heard the whispering, her parents sat the family down at the dinner table to outline exactly what happened to Mary Beth, who lived only a few miles away.

Now a seasoned APD, Marcia drew the short straw and was deemed by her boss as most qualified to step up to defend Larry Lynch. She held her breath and her nose when she interviewed the vile Lynch in the lockup behind Bond Court at 26th Street.

"I won't bullshit you, Mr. Lynch," Tully told the shackled Lynch. "The prosecutors say they got the DNA from the 55-gallon drums and yours from your arrest card. They tell me it's 14-quadrillion-to-one match. With that and your sheet, there's no way anything I say can get you bond. You understand?"

"So, you call me 'Mister' out of respect for my age but not for the crime I'm accused of, bitch?" Lynch spat out at his lawyer.

"Look, you syphilitic asshole. It's my job to defend you, regardless of what I think of you. But since it's just us girls here," she whispered through the bars, "I remember this murder well. And though I was against the death penalty, I kinda wish it was still around for a degenerate sick prick like you."

"I could not give less of a fuck. I got colon cancer and maybe a year left, they told me. Let's get this over with," Lynch said.

"Good idea. See you in court in a few minutes," Tully said, and pirouetted out the door to the courtroom. The courtroom of the Honorable Jack Kupper was jammed with the usual suspects--TV sketch artists, reporters, scores of cops and the morbidly curious.

"State of Illinois versus Larry Lynch," the judge's clerk called out. "Is the state ready?"

Standing her full 5'10" and decked out in a jet black Armani suit with her signature 3-inch heels, Egan answered "State is ready." Then nodded to Tully.

"Ready, Your Honor," Tully announced.

"State?" queried Kupper.

"Your Honor, standing before you is the man who committed what can arguably be called the most horrific murder in Chicago annals. He killed and dismembered a 16-year-old child, we know not what order he inflicted his debased horror on Mary Beth O'Malley, but we do know it was he who killed her nearly a half century ago, chopping up her body into pieces to fit in two 55-gallon drums he dumped in the pre-dawn hours in Montrose Harbor.

"He did almost nine years for other sexual attacks on innocent young women. The State asks for no bond for this killer," Egan said, then sat down at the prosecution table, nodding to Tully.

"Defense?" asked the judge.

"Defense accedes to the court's wisdom," Tully said without standing or looking up from her notes.

"Defendant is hereby remanded pending trial," Kupper said. "Next case."

"That the best you can do, you sorry bitch?" Lynch stage whispered as the courtroom quickly emptied.

"For you, yep," Tully said, gathered her files and walked wordlessly out of court and past a throng of reporters she had no interest in speaking to.

Egan followed and did step up to the wall of mics in the spacious courthouse lobby at 26th and Cal.

"I'm not a betting woman, but I would wager that the geniuses in Springfield who abolished the death penalty may not have had Larry Lynch in mind when they did away with the ultimate justice," Egan said, then smiled for the cameras before marching off to the elevator bank.

There, she encountered a smirking/smiling Halloran, holding the door to an empty elevator.

"Bravo, madam prosecutor. Got time for a quick bite at Thai Noodles?" Halloran asked.

"You might not believe this, but this one is so vile, I lost my appetite. But how about dinner tomorrow night?" Egan asked.

"The pleasure would be all mine," Halloran smiled.

"Yeah, we'll see about that. Tufano's at 7?" Egan asked as the elevator door opened on the 11th floor.

"Meet ya there," Halloran concluded as he continued up to the Investigations Bureau on the 14th floor.

There, he joined Thoma, who quickly cornered him with a "follow me."

CHAPTER 46

On their way to the parking lot east of the courthouse, Thoma broke the silence as they hustled through the slicing March rain to their Crown Vic.

"This is the first good rain since the last snowfall. I wanna check that alley behind Hamilton's for that gun Gomez used on Juan. I'm betting he tossed it into a snowbank, and it just might reappear with the rain melting the snow," Thoma suggested.

"Good thinking, partner. Really good," Halloran gushed uncharacteristically.

"Well, thanks but don't treat it like it's a once-in-a-millennium event," Thoma said as she slid into the driver's seat.

Halloran replied from shotgun.

"Jeez, Jane. That was a sincere compliment. I wish I'd thought of it but of course will claim partial credit if we find it," Halloran laughed, then gently punched his partner in the right shoulder.

Half an hour later, parkas on and hoods up, Thoma and Halloran began their search along the L tracks wall some 20 feet north of where Gomez opened fire. Halloran took the west side of the alley, Thoma the east, as they slowly walked south through the rain and slush.

"Got something," Thoma yelled after just a few dozen feet. She held up a casing from a Mac-10, Gomez's weapon of choice.

"Bag that, Jane. I'd compliment you but you'd probably miss the sincerity in all this muck," Halloran joked "Plus, the techs already recovered a dozen or so casings that night at the scene."

"You mean 'bag that,' like in an evidence envelope? That'd never have occurred to me," Thoma fired back.

An hour later, they reached the end of the alley at Rosemont.

"Okay, I doubt he carried it across the street, but maybe we come back tomorrow morning and check that block before it ends just short of Granville," Halloran said.

"Just a sec," Thoma said, and motioned with a nod across the street to a homeless man who had just entered the alley south of Rosemont with a shopping cart. He began opening a dumpster and peered inside.

Thoma marched across the street, Halloran following, and approached the vagrant.

"Hello, my friend. How ya doin'?" Thoma asked.

The man, about 55, was dressed in oversized and beat-up Reeboks and a tattered peacoat with frayed cuffs, with straggly gray hair past his ears.

"I ain't done nuthin," the man responded as Thoma and Halloran both flashed their stars.

"No one said you did, friend. But I want to ask you a little favor—a lucrative favor if done right," Thoma said.

The man let the dumpster lid down with a swoosh but with a stench of spoiled meat that reached the two cops.

Thoma held out a $20 bill.

"This is yours for doing us a favor of keeping your eyes open for something we think is buried in the snow drifts here in this alley but also may be in the block behind us," Thoma said. Halloran saw where his partner was going and reached into his wallet and pulled out a $50 bill.

"And this if you deliver," Halloran joined in. He also held out his card.

"Not too long ago, an FBI agent was shot in the alley behind Hamilton's, and we believe the shooter dumped the gun in the snow as he fled. Are you in this alley every day?" Thoma asked.

"Bums like me gotta eat," he said. "So, yeah. Most days."

"What's your name?" Halloran asked.

"Eddie McGhee," he said, smiling with his dirty, nicotine-stained teeth.

"Here's my card, and my partner's" Thoma said, grabbing Halloran's card and handing it to Eddie in a fluid sweep.

"If you see it, don't touch it. Just call us ASAP," Halloran said.

"Call you? With what? My latest Apple? Got no phone," Eddie said, shrugging his shoulders.

"I'll give you a burner phone to use to call me only," Halloran said, then turned to go back to the Crown Vic. There he fetched said phone from his briefcase and returned to Eddie and Thoma at the mouth of the alley.

"You know how to use this?" Halloran asked, as he held it out just beyond Eddie's grasp.

"I wasn't always a drunken bum. Yeah, I can handle this," Eddie sullenly responded.

"I've punched in my number so all you have to do is call it back. If this works out and you find the gun, you get the phone as a bonus," Halloran promised.

"Gotcha," Eddie responded.

"Okay. Don't fuck this up," Thoma said.

At that, the partners turned and headed back to the squad.

"We'll alert Juan and the beat guys, too, of course. And we'll make a few runs when we have time, but Eddie's up and down those alleys every day. And now he has an incentive to stay sober," Halloran said, as Thoma pulled into traffic heading back to Area 3.

"Maybe better than rehab," Thoma said, turning to wink at her partner.

"We'll see. We'll see. But it would be great to match that gun with maybe asshole's prints and the slug that was lodged in Juan's vest. Right? And maybe a DNA match," Halloran replied.

"Goddamn right," Thoma said.

CHAPTER 47

Growing up fatherless on the mean streets of Uptown in the late-'50s and mid-'60s, Reggie Roberts met a lot of strange men his mother, Ismelda, would bring home for half-hour "visits" in their one-bedroom apartment in the Malden Street walk-up.

Several clients of "Easy Izzy," as she was known on the streets, were gangbangers who taught Reggie how to hustle to make a buck. That could mean running drugs or simply waiting until the 4 o'clock joints emptied out to follow a staggering drunk to "piss alley" and roll him for whatever he had left after a night of hard drinking.

Reggie caught his first beef as a juvenile for just such a strong-armed robbery when he was 15 and spent a couple months in the Juvenile Detention Center, also euphemistically called the "Audy Home" by the cops and prosecutors.

Izzy was doubtlessly guessing wildly when she told Reggie he got his size—6'2" at 15 and girth (225 pounds)—from his "day daddy," who she claimed once played on the Chicago Bears' taxi squad before he was fatally shot by an off duty female cop he tried to mug in an alley not far from Mother's on Division Street.

By the time he was 45, he had already spent half of his life behind bars—Cook County Jail, Stateville, Menard, Pontiac. When he tried to rob a 7-Eleven in Morton Grove, he got a bit careless in suburbia and assumed Rumanna, the Pakistani woman behind the counter, was alone at 10:30 p.m.

Syed Muhammed had just finished drying his hands in his immaculately clean men's bathroom when he clearly heard, "This is a stickup. Empty the cash register into a bag, and don't do anything stupid."

As he exited the men's bathroom, Syed emptied his Glock 45 at the back of the gunman as his wife hit the floor. Six shots found home in Roberts' body—three in the back, two in the ass, and one in his right thigh, narrowly missing his femoral artery.

He survived and was convicted of armed robbery, agg assault and a host of other charges that amounted to Class X felonies that earned him a 30-year sentence. Halfway through his stay at Stateville, the Illinois Appellate Defender's office got his conviction overturned for an error in jury instructions. He was granted a new trial and sent back to his home away from home—Cook County Jail.

In his first visit with his appellate attorney, Priscilla Printon-Patel, Roberts watched as she opened her attaché case to withdraw some legal papers and spied a nice array of Cross pens lined up on the inside of the case. He filed that away for future reference and then listened passively as PPP explained the legal genius behind the successful appeal.

The case had been reversed and remanded for a new trial after he had served more than 18 years at Stateville, whose only redeeming charm was its proximity to Chicago, about an hour away.

Two weeks later, Roberts swabbed his butt crack with Vasoline before his next visit with Triple P. Ten minutes after she arrived, she pulled out some papers and launched into her legal spiel. When her cell went off, she walked to the corner with her back turned to whisper to her caller. Roberts reached quickly into the attaché case and snatched a silver Cross pen.

Quickly he lowered his pants and shoved the pen up his butt. When PPP finished her call and turned back to her client, he ventured:

"Can we make this a conjugal visit?" he asked, proffering his manhood to the aging spinster.

"Guard!" she shrieked and ran for the exit door.

Minutes later, when the guard's wand sounded a warning when it passed near Roberts' hips, the professional inmate offered "hip replacement. Gets me every time." The guard shrugged and passed Roberts back into Division 1, where the 35-and-older inmates were housed.

As the senior top dog on his tier, Roberts was always looking for another weapon. That night he removed the ballpoint filler and slowly and silently ground the pen's tip on the concrete floor till it was sharp, the kind easily hidden and perfect for inserting into an enemy's ribs. And there were always enemies.

*****

Division 1 was built in the late 1920s, the first building adjacent to the new courthouse at 26th and Cal in what was to become a sprawling complex that by the early 1990s had housed more than 10,000 inmates in a series of buildings that stretched to 31st Street.

Lynch had spent more than a year awaiting trial at a young age before he was convicted in the sexual assault cases and sent to Stateville. He'd also later spent some time in the Harris County Jail in Texas before the rape and attempt murder charges were dropped after the victim balked at testifying at trial.

So, when he first ventured into the Division 1 tier for the older inmates, Lynch had little trouble picking the top dog as Roberts laser-locked his eyes with the new addition. They were about the same size but Lynch had 15 years on Roberts.

Roberts smiled and used his right index finger to move from his left earlobe to his right; Lynch raised his right hand with the swastika at the lower end of his right middle finger to push up his glasses and return the "fuck you" salute from Roberts.

A silent war had been declared.

CHAPTER 48

Even though Halloran had told his fed partner Ochoa about the deal he made with Eddie, Juan made a run down those alleys every day he could when the temperature rose to 32 or above. But he still had his cases, old and new, to tend to.

On a rainy but warm Wednesday in late March, Juan had to testify before a federal grand jury. But as luck would have it for the usually luckless Eddie as he made his rounds down the alleys this day, he spotted what looked like a black pipe sticking out of the shrinking snowdrifts. Coming closer, he dug down a few inches and saw the snub nose muzzle of the Mac-10 inching out of the snow. He pulled out the burner from his frayed backpack and dialed the only number on the phone.

"Detective, I think I've found that weapon. It has a short muzzle showing and the rest is still buried in snow," Eddie explained.

"Where are you?" Halloran barked.

"Uh, I'm just about 50 yards past Rosemont going south into the alley," Eddie replied.

"Stay right there and don't touch anything. We'll be right there," Halloran said. He then called Ochoa but got his voicemail. He next called his old partner, Syl.

"Syl, Mike. I think we found the Mac-10 that asshole used on agent Ochoa. Can you get the feds out there?" Halloran asked from his desk at Area 3, a good 25-minute ride away, and gave her Eddie's whereabouts to relay to the FBI tech guys.

Next, he signed out a free Crown Vic to head off to reward Eddie for a job well done. His promised Grant in addition to the Jackson Thoma had delivered.

By the time Halloran arrived, a small army of fed techies were chipping away at the snowdrift as Eddie struggled to explain his find.

"This is one of my best CI's. Mike Halloran, CPD Area 3 and Agent Ochoa's partner," Halloran said as he flashed his star at the agent who appeared to be in charge.

"Gotcha. Good work," said the agent who remained nameless.

Halloran pulled the $50 from his wallet and slapped his promised Grant into the right hand of a grinning Eddie.

"Thanks, detective," Eddie said.

"No, thank you, Eddie. Nice work," Halloran said, slapping Eddie on the back.

*****

On Sept. 28, 2013, jury selection for Gomez began right where his bond was set, in the largest courtroom at Dirksen, the walnut-paneled ceremonial one on the 25th floor. A huge crowd was expected.

The case had been randomly assigned to the Honorable Palmer Ogden Fields, a blue-blood patrician whose lineage stretched back more than a century to the pre-Chicago Fire days after the Civil War. With his pure white hair, square jaw, thick black eyebrows over steely blue eyes, he exuded power, authority and a no-nonsense demeanor impossible for even the most flippant and cocky lawyer to miss—or mess with.

"Gentlemen and ladies, this is a case that strikes at the very heart of a peaceful community, which is something we all would agree is a primary goal of a civilized society. The defendant is accused of the attempted murder of a federal officer, FBI Agent Juan Ochoa.

"My first question to all of you," Fields said in his deep baritone, staring out into the panel of prospective jurors seated silent and expectant before him, "is--are any of you related to anyone in law enforcement? If so, please raise your hands." A mid-50s white lady in the second row raised her left hand at the same time a young black man in the last row thrust up his right hand.

Without asking if they could be fair in weighing the evidence, Fields thanked them for doing their civic duty and appearing per their summons and then sent them home.

In five hours, Fields had whittled the panel in half with his penetrating questions. A little more than half of the survivors sat in the jurors' box and the four chairs adjacent reserved for the alternates. The judge asked the defense first, then the prosecution, if they wished to exercise any of their peremptory challenges to the 16 prospects seated before them.

Gomez's lead attorney leaned over to his two associate counselors and whispered briefly. After a few minutes, Miller III, the slick, seasoned and—as widely considered by the press to be sleazy--lawyer, stood up in his shiny gray suit, and said, "'Defense would join your honor in thanking Juror Number 33 for her service." He smiled and nodded respectfully to the judge.

Fields rose a foot from his black leather throne and glared at Miller for 5 full seconds silently, as if he might have been counting off to control his temper.

"Mister Miller, I want to make made myself crystal clear. I will NOT tolerate any theatrics in my courtroom. You are NOT JOINING me in anything that transpires in MY courtroom. This is your challenge alone. Do we understand each other?"

"Yes, Your Honor," Miller said softly, lowering himself to his seat a few seconds before Fields also resumed seating,

"Juror Number 33, you are excused. I thank you," the judge said, emphasizing the word "I."

Number 33 had related during questioning that she was a retired court reporter, someone who had plenty of experience listening to pompous and theatrical attorneys defending those accused of some of the vilest crimes imaginable. Miller knew his blend of bravado and bullshit was unlikely to fly with such a seasoned court participant. And with her background, she might likely have been chosen as the jury's foreperson.

The prosecution in the person of Meckelson excused Juror Number 10, a clerk in the law library at the University of Chicago School of Law, a mecca for those who leaned downwind of Karl Marx.

Over the next three days of tedious questioning, a jury of five men and seven women was chosen, with four alternates.

There were three white men, a Latino and an African-American—one an electrician, one a CTA bus driver, one the owner of a small Portage Park taco/burrito restaurant, an accountant and a grad student at DePaul University.

The women were four white, one second generation Haitian, and two Latinas. There were two housewives (self-described), a waitress, a retired Catholic grammar school principal, a computer programmer, a crossing guard and clerk at a Target in Uptown.

"Ladies and gentlemen, you're about to perform one of the highest callings for American citizens—jury duty. This case has received considerable media attention. But I admonish you—No Googling, no YouTube scrolling, no newspaper research and during the trial, no radio or TV.

"It's late on a Friday afternoon, so enjoy your weekend and I will see you Monday at 9:30 a.m. sharp. No TV!" Fields admonished again and then swept off the bench and through the door behind his clerk to the plush chambers federal judges enjoy.

CHAPTER 49

Proco Morel knew his way around the MCC. The guards called him a "frequent flier," but the inmates called him "Jefe."

He wanted to visit Gomez himself to get a read on his junior lieutenant's state of mind. In other words, he wanted to vet him as a possible "flipper," a guy who would cut a deal with the feds to leverage a cushy deal in a nice prison, some called Club Meds.

One of his trusted "mixers," Horatio Baez, dropped him off in front of the pawnbroker joint on Clark, just a baseball toss from the MCC and just south of the Loop's Brown Line L tracks.

Once inside the MCC after a thorough search, Morel was led to the visitors' room, where awaited his once-trusted junior Jefe, Gomez. "Once-trusted" because Gomez had been trusted with huge sums of money and highly valuable quantities of coke and fentanyl at the gang's stash/mixing house in Little Village. But trust was ephemeral, Morel knew.

"Oi, cabron. Que tal?" offered Morel.

"All good, amigo, considerin'," Gomez replied.

Then in coded language-- a mixture of Spanish and English-- they began an elaborate and cryptic banter, feeling each other out like a pair of light heavyweights circling in the first round with some feints and jabs.

"You case creeping up to trial, friend. You feel okay 'bout you lawyer, you outlook? Any movement on things," Morel parried, opening the door to where Gomez might feel he could maneuver.

"Ya know how they be? Fulla shit. My lawyer say they feds want to talk, but what 'talk' mean is they hope I give 'em' sumptin. I tell her I'm a good listener, but I know it all be shit they want about the gang. I tell her I listen as long as they gonna make my stay here a bit better. I hear the prosecutors once got putas in here for the top Gangster D," Gomez said, deadpan.

Morel nodded, mindful of the feds listening in and recording every word. "You smart boy, amigo. I know you'll figure things out."

Gomez grunted and cast a wary glance at the guard 20 feet away texting on his phone. Gomez interpreted Morel's remark as a veiled warning not to do anything stupid, like agree to cooperate to bring down the Cobras or Morel. Like Gomez, Morel wasn't giving away much.

The two had worked closely over the last few decades, and Morel knew Gomez had made no deals to shorten his sentence before in state court. But Gomez now was facing up to 30 years with the Class X felony he faced in state court---and what could be a de facto life sentence from a federal judge not likely to cut a break for a dangerous felon who used the gang's machine gun to cut down an FBI agent.

The visit lasted 30 minutes, with the remainder of the conversation dealing with bars, restaurants and "putas" they both knew well. It ended with another subtle, multilayered farewell from both.

"Be good. Stay safe," Morel said. Innocuous enough for the federal eavesdroppers, but Gomez interpreted it thus:

"Don't be stupid and start giving up your gang or me for a deal. Or maybe you won't be so safe in here or in prison. The gang has long tentacles."

Gomez nodded and fist-bumped the glass partition, Morel slowly raised his right hand and fist-bumped back but then raised his index finger, pointed and winked. Gomez nodded but didn't smile. He didn't take the raised finger as a friendly wave but rather saw it as a warning.

What da fuck that finger mean? You threatening me? Gomez pondered the pointed finger as he walked back to his cell.

"How it go in there, Jefe?" Hernandez asked as his boss settled into the back of the Lexus.

'It went," Morel replied, not too satisfied by Gomez's "listener" response.

CHAPTER 50

First up was the main witness and victim. Juan Ochoa wore his three-piece, dark blue, pin-striped suit with his red and white silk tie over a crisp white oxford button-down.

When called by Meckelson, he strode confidently to the witness stand to the left of the judge but within clear sight of the expectant jury.

"Can you state your name and profession for the jury, Agent Ochoa?" Meckelson asked, "and then give the jury a brief synopsis of your education and assignments?"

Ochoa sat up straight as a crutch and briefly made eye contact with the bus driver before listing an enviable list of credentials and awards. When he paused, Miller jumped up with a cute "we are well aware of the agent's background and arrest record, so can we move on?"

"I decide when WE have heard enough, not you Mr. Miller. Sit down now and wait your turn," lectured Fields.

A chastened Miller sat down quickly and leaned over to whisper to Gomez, who closed his eyes briefly and grunted, pulling back from Miller.

"All right, Agent Ochoa, thank you. Can you please tell the jury how you became involved in this case?" Meckelson asked.

"Surely. It was in January of 2011 when Mike Halloran, a CPD-- Chicago Police Department--detective, and my partner in the joint federal and state Cold Case Task Force, got an urgent call from his old partner and now Chief of Detectives Sylvia Ortiz that her daughter had been kidnapped. Mike and I were sifting through old evidence boxes but he ran out of the warehouse like his hair was on fire," Ochoa said.

"I understand. At what point did your boss get you involved in this case?" Meckelson asked.

"Almost immediately. My boss, Special Agent in Charge John Macel, had been alerted since kidnapping is a federal crime and he told me to join Detective Halloran forthwith. Which I did," Ochoa said.

"Did 'forthwith' merit a 'hair on fire' departure for you, too, Agent?" Meckelson asked, smiling but avoiding eye contact with a jury that seemed to enjoy the banter.

"Objection, Your Honor, the prosecution is leading the witness." Miller barked.

"Overruled. Ms. Meckelson is asking the agent to relate what he experienced early on in this case. It's called direct examination. You will get your chance," Fields admonished with a raised voice and right eyebrow.

"Yes, Your Honor," Miller said, glancing at the jury but finding no joy there. Gomez slowly shook his lowered head.

Meckelson nodded to Ochoa, who quickly resumed his narrative.

Already prepped, Ochoa moved smoothly to the events on the night he was shot.

"Our investigation traced the kidnappers to a garden apartment on Hood in the Edgewater neighborhood. Mike and I and a team of other agents and police staked it out, front and rear. That was just shortly after the victim made it home. We waited till after 1 a.m., but then Mike and I called it a day and left it to the overnight guys," Ochoa continued.

"Mike left a few minutes before me, but as I was heading out just a few blocks from the apartment on Hood, I spotted the suspects' van. And he spotted me. I caught up to them in an alley by the L tracks in the 6300 block of Broadway when they—the driver ran into a snow pile, and I pulled in front to cut them off," he continued.

"And did you see a female riding shotgun? Did she have a weapon? Fire at you?" Meckelson asked.

"Can't be sure if she had a weapon because after the bullets started flying, she backed out of the snowbank and took off," Ochoa said.

"Okay, Agent, but let's back up to what happened when you exited your vehicle?" Meckelson asked.

"I jumped out low, pulling my weapon, but he was using a machine-handgun, and I fired a couple rounds over the top of the car door before I was hit in my vest. That stunned me, then a second round hit me in my shoulder. My Glock fell out of my hand—after I was hit," the Agent explained.

"What happened next, Agent?" Meckelson continued.

"Well, it's a little foggy. I was on the ground, and I could hear sirens closing in. I saw Gomez run by. In what seemed an eternity I was pressing my hand up against the wound and it was flowing pretty good. Then Mike was there, kneeling beside me, telling me I was okay. Just 'a nick,' I think he said. Easy for him to say but reassuring," Ochoa said, a slight smile creasing his tense face.

"And that 'Mike' would be CPD Detective Mike Halloran. Correct?"

"Correct."

"Agent Ochoa, do you see that gunman in court?" Meckelson asked.

"Yes, ma'am. He's sitting right there next to his lawyer, with the smirk on his face, dressed in a dark blue suit," Ochoa said, pointing to Gomez, who stood despite a futile attempt to stop him by Miller.

"Thank you, agent. Moving forward, you came to learn that Gomez escaped, but you and Halloran, Detective Halloran, also ascertained in the process of your investigation that Letty Diaz had fled to Mexico, presumably with the ransom cash and diamonds. Is that correct?" Meckelson asked.

"Objection, Your Honor. Counsel is leading the witness," Miller shouted.

"Maybe so, but witness and prosecutor are also saving the judge and jury time getting to the essence of this crime. I see Detective Halloran on the witness list. He'll undoubtedly have more to say on this later."

"Thank you, Your Honor. What happened in Mexico, agent?" Meckelson encouraged.

"Well, we had pretty good intel that she'd worked or said she worked as a waitress in Puerto Vallarta, so we first headed there, Mike and me.

At the restaurant we learned she had used the restaurant for a reference to get a job waitressing in a taco joint in Punta Mita, about an hour north of PV.

"So, with the local federal police we hightailed it to Punta Mita. But we also soon learned that Gomez was also in the area, hunting Letty." Ochoa continued. "So, we set a trap."

"Thank you, agent. We will be hearing the details of that trap from your partner, who will be called later in this trial, but now, we thank you for your service and your testimony. Counselor?" she said, turning to Miller.

"Thank you. Just a few questions, Your Honor. Was it dark in that alley when this shooting occurred?"

"Yes," Ochoa responded cautiously.

"And when you got out of your car, things happened pretty fast—in seconds?" Miller asked.

"That's correct," Ochoa said, jaws tightening.

"So, just so I, and the jury, understand. It's dark. You leaped from your car and took cover, bullets flying. You're wounded and lying on the ground as the driver roars off and the gunman runs past you as you lay bleeding and in pain? And yet you think you can positively identify my client as your assailant?" Miller asked, turning to the jury with an incredulous shrug.

"Yes, counselor, I can. I'd been looking for this man for days, with his photo inculcated in my memory, and he was driving the same car as was used in the kidnapping. It was him," Ochoa emphasized, pointing again to Gomez.

"Well, some may believe your incredible observations skills and the 'inculcated' image in your mind, but others may find it a stretch. We'll let the jury decide how extraordinary your memory is of events that happened in seconds in the dark," Miller said. "I have no further questions of this witness."

"Redirect, Madam prosecutor?" Fields asked.

"No, Your Honor, and as we are nearing 5 p.m., would this be a good time to adjourn until tomorrow?" Meckelson suggested.

"Capital idea. Ladies and gentlemen of the jury, till tomorrow at 9:30 a.m.—no TV," admonished Fields, "but a Netflix movie won't hurt."

CHAPTER 51

While some media wags covering the trial expected Elly to be the next witness, Meckelson knew better.

For starters, she wanted Halloran on the stand to tie up the narrative and knew he would need no prepping for his time with Miller; Halloran had slapped him down from the stand before in prior jousts with the oleaginous lawyer.

Practice, that's what lawyers do. Cops perform, Halloran thought.

"No sweat, Geri," Halloran assured the prosecutor after court adjourned following Ochoa's testimony. "I got this."

* * * * *

Wearing his herringbone brown tweed sportcoat, a neatly pressed powder blue button-down shirt, and a maroon polka dot tie, Halloran marched through the gates separating the court from the visitors and circled the witness stand before sitting to Fields' left. He nodded to the judge, who reciprocated.

Without prompting Halloran stood and raised his right hand as the clerk swore him in.

"Good morning, Detective. Can you tell the court your name and spell it and relate how many years you've been a police officer?" Meckelson asked perfunctorily.

"Yes, ma'am. My name is Michael Halloran—that's H-A-L-L-O-R-A-N. And I've been a police officer for 26 and a half years, 20 as a detective," with the last tidbit aimed at the jury, deadpanned.

"Thank you, and can you tell us how you became involved in this case?" Meckelson asked.

"Surely. I was working a cold case at the West Side warehouse with my partners when my cell went off and saw it was Chief of D's Ortiz," Halloran explained in taciturn style.

"And was that unusual?" Meckelson asked.

"Well, yes and no. Yes, unusual for a dick like me to get a workday call from the chief, but no because she was my partner for several years before she started climbing the ranks," Halloran continued.

"And when you answered, did you quickly learn the reason for this unexpected call," she asked.

"I did. She summoned me to Police Headquarters—her daughter Elly had been kidnapped," Halloran continued.

"And did that news have special import to you?" Meckelson urged.

"It did. I've known Elly from the day I held her head steady as the priest poured holy water over her forehead as she screamed bloody murder. I'm her godfather—proud to say," aiming the last three words at the younger Hispanic woman in the jury box.

"What happened next?" Meckelson asked.

"I jumped in the Crown Vic and broke every traffic law on the books to get to HQ. There, I then learned more and saw the photo that the defendant sent to Sylvia Ortiz," he continued.

"Objection. Testifying to facts not in evidence, Your Honor," Miller nearly jumped out of his chair next to Gomez.

"Sustained. I assume we'll put some meat on the bones, Ms. Meckelson?" Fields asked.

"Yes, Your Honor, we will. Detective, you saw a photo of Elly with her mouth taped shut. Is that correct?" Meckelson asked.

"Objection. Leading!" shrieked Miller, still standing, feet spread wide in victory after the judge's first agreement.

"Overruled. Continue, Detective," Fields said, not bothering to look at Miller with his ruling.

"Well, by the time I got there, all the CPD brass and the FBI were already there, and Syl, uh, Chief Ortiz, outlined the plan the brain trust there had already launched. I added a few thoughts," Halloran said.

"Well, we had very little to go on, and though we all lost some shoe leather in the next couple days, we wound up just waiting to hear the ransom demand—which came a few days later from a burner phone," Halloran continued.

"A phone not registered to anyone," Halloran said mostly to the jury.

"And what did that demand say?" Meckelson asked.

"He demanded 60k in cash and a quarter million in diamonds-- 1- and 2-carat size--and instructions of where the drop would be," Halloran told the jury.

"And the plan by the FBI and CPD was what?" Meckelson asked.

"The plan approved by Chief Ortiz and her husband was to get the money and diamonds, take a verification photo of the ransom for the kidnappers, then work with the FBI to snare the kidnappers when they grabbed the loot," Halloran continued.

"And then what happened?" Meckelson asked.'

"Best-laid plans, eh? Well, the drop spot was under the basement-level escalators at 69 W. Washington, which has a long hallway leading north to the bottom of the Daley Center. We were all set up when this skinny kid, maybe 14-15, picks up the gym bag and walks calmly to the security check at the basement level of the Daley Center, then drops the bag near one of the access doors to the basement subfloors," Halloran testified.

"Then what happened?" Meckelson prompted.

"Then the kid walks for about 10 yards into the main corridor slowly. At about the same time, those undercover cops near the bag drop suddenly see the small door open, a hand reaches out and grabs the bag, slamming the door behind him and chain-locking it," Halloran said.

"Then the kid starts sprinting like a bat out of hell. Well, most of the cops and agents began chasing, but this kid must run a 10-flat 100-yard dash and leaps over the turnstile at the Blue Line and catches a southbound train before the doors close.

"Meanwhile, our guys tried to open the door where the drop was made, but they needed a chain snipper, and we weren't prepared with one. So maybe 7-8 minutes elapsed while we located maintenance and got the chain cut open. But by this time, ass---our bad guy was long gone. The subterranean tunnels are a labyrinth. We lost him," he concluded.

As Halloran paused, the school principal slowly shook her head, while the grad student next to her merely rolled his eyes in disbelief.

"Detective, can we assume the 'bad guy' got away with the bag containing the ransom?" Meckelson asked.

"Yeah, and so did his young sprinter, though we got a blurry overhead photo of him exiting the L stop near UIC," Halloran said.

"Was this a shocking development, detective?" Meckelson said, stating the obvious rather than let the defense later lampoon the joint local/federal effort.

"Let's say it was not law enforcement's finest moment. Hell, yes, we were embarrassed and pissed—frustrated," Halloran said, looking at the grad student, who looked sympathetic now.

"At what point did Gomez become a suspect?" Meckelson asked.

"Well, we looked for motive first, then opportunity. We looked for ex-cons who'd been released in the last year that had been prosecuted by Joe Ortiz or arrested by his wife, Syl, Chief Ortiz. Gomez was on a short list, and the rest had alibis, were out of state or were back in the joint. Gomez stood out at the top of a very short list," Halloran continued.

"Anything else?" Meckelson asked.

"Things moved pretty fast. Then after a few days Elly was released and she gave us the tat ID, and we were pretty sure we had our guy," Halloran said.

"Okay, let's move on to the night Agent Ochoa was shot. You two had just parted after a long vigil at the kidnap site when you got a call from your federal partner. Right?" Meckelson asked.

"Leading. Objection," Miller rose from his chair.

"Yes, but it moves the narrative. Overruled," Fields sighed.

"Correct, Juan called me when he spotted Gomez's van just after I parked my car in my garage, maybe a mile away. I told him not to engage, but he was in full pursuit mode. I ran back to my car and raced to the alley. I found Juan shot in the shoulder just before more cops and the paramedics arrived. I told him it wasn't life-threatening," Halloran continued.

"Just a nick, you said?" Meckelson asked.

"Yeah, might have. But I was focused then on finding the shooter. I ran like hell down the alley but found nothing. Without wheels, he figured to be headed to the Granville L station. At the end of the alley, I ordered a young uniform with a squad to take me—fast—to the Argyle station. There I vaulted the turnstile and raced up the stairs in time to catch a southbound train. I went car to car but found nothing, nobody but a few bums and a drunken kid.

"At Lawrence, I got off. Went downstairs and cursed the night. Couldn't believe we lost him," Halloran said.

"But not forever, correct Detective?" Meckelson asked.

"Correct, counselor. We traced his girlfriend, who drove the van away from the shooting that night, to Punta Mita, north of Puerto Vallarta in Mexico, and found her waitressing in a taco joint. But the local cops got intel that Gomez was right behind us. So, Juan hid inside the john, I was in the kitchen near Letty, the girlfriend—if you want to call her that—and waited," Halloran continued.

The bus driver leaned forward as did the waitress. They felt the climax was near. They were right.

Halloran continued, warming to his narrative.

"Within about 10 minutes, in walks Gomez, some sort of knife in hand, and he spots Letty by the kitchen door. At that point, I pull her back into the kitchen, my gun in the other hand, and Juan comes up behind, his gun raised and pointed at Gomez, and we tell this, this…suspect to kneel, then lie flat, and we cuff him. And, there he is," Halloran said, pointing his index finger like a gun at a grinning Gomez.

"Yeah, smile now, shithead—sorry, Your Honor, ladies and gentlemen of the jury—it just slipped out," Halloran shrugged, somewhat unconvincingly.

"Good to apologize, bad choice of language. And several months later, did you recover the Mac-10 used to wound Agent Ochoa?" Meckelson asked.

"Yes. One of my CI's – confidential informants—discovered the machine gun about a block from where Agent Ochoa was shot. The FBI recovered it and took it to their lab on the West Side. Ballistics tests there showed it was the gun that shot Juan."

"Thank you, Detective. Your witness, counselor," Meckelson said, sitting back down with her legal pad in hand, a pad she never once glanced at during her examination of Halloran. More of a prop.

"Let's break for lunch," Fields said. "Back at 1:30."

CHAPTER 52

After glancing around to make sure there were no jurors there, Halloran grabbed a rear table at Cavanaugh's, kitty-corner from Dirksen, and ordered a cheeseburger from the waitress before he was seated. No Lagunitas IPA today, he resolved.

He devoured the burger in less than 10 minutes, then took off through the lobby of the historic Monadnock Building, admiring the architecture, the black wrought iron banisters, and feeling like he was visiting another century. He exited on Van Buren Street under the L tracks, turned west and walked slowly to and then up Clark Street on his way back.

Don't have to rehearse anything for this empty suit, Halloran thought. *I've handled far better mouthpieces than this mope.*

After Halloran retook the stand, Fields reminded him that he was still under oath. It was the same reminder every judge makes to a witness when he resumes his seat, but it always rankled Halloran, just a bit. He was ready for Miller as he nodded slightly to the jury and sat back in the witness box adjacent to the judge.

He watched as Miller advanced in his tiny and shiny Ferragamo loafers with the gold buckles.

"Thank you, Ms. Meckelson," Miller said. "Detective Halloran, how many complaints have you had sustained against you for excessive force in your career?"

Game on.

"I don't have an exact count on the number of complaints, but I can tell you that in more than a quarter century on the job sweeping bad guys off the street, I've incurred many complaints as an active street cop and detective. None sustained. Not one," Halloran said.

"That would be none sustained by CPD's own Internal Affairs Department. Correct?" Miller asked.

"It's a 'division,' not a 'department,' but mostly correct, and also none sustained by successor hybrid review operations with civilian members, with some of your fellow travelers on board," Halloran said.

"I see, and have you been sued in civil court for some of your, perhaps overzealous, arrest tactics?" Miller asked.

"Objection, Your Honor, defense counsel has wandered way off the reservation from direct exam."

"Sustained. Stick to asking about the direct testimony, or risk the wrath of this court," Fields warned.

Like water off a duck's back, the judge's rebuke had no visual effect on Miller.

"So, officer, did you see my client, Mr. Gomez, shoot Agent Ochoa?" Miller asked.

"I did not. He might not be alive if I'd been there to protect my partner," Halloran sneered.

"Is that a threat, ex post facto, detective?" Miller queried.

"No, that's my opinion—and duty," Halloran retorted, and locked eyes with the bus driver, ignoring Miller. The juror nodded his head ever so slightly.

"Did you see my client abduct Elly, your goddaughter?" Miller persisted.

"Same answer. If I had been, your client might be pushing up daisies now instead of sitting there in a new suit smirking at these proceedings," Halloran responded.

"Oh, quite the temper! Glad you never had the pleasure of cuffing me, or worse," Miller said.

"Enough, Counselor. The court does not appreciate, nor will it tolerate, your attempts to get a rise out of Detective Halloran, a respected and veteran CPD detective," Fields said. "Do you have any other questions pertinent to his direct testimony?"

"Uh, no, Your Honor," Miller said, shrinking down from his diminutive 5'6" even further as he stood at the defense table.

"Redirect?"

"No thanks, Your Honor," Meckelson said.

"You're excused, detective," Fields said, then watched as Halloran walked back toward the gallery but feinting a slight move toward Miller before he reached the gate.

Miller flinched then shrieked.

"Did you see that, Your Honor?" Miller whined. "He made a threatening move toward me."

"What I saw was a once great tight end with a slight limp left from his glory days," Fields smiled and nodded to the back of his last witness.

How in the fuck did he know I played tight end, Halloran wondered as he entered the 25th floor hallway and headed to the elevators.

CHAPTER 53

"You'll do fine, my darling daughter. Just tell your story as best you remember it, and I bet you remember it as well as you did the route they took after they grabbed you," comforted Syl, holding Elly's left hand at their kitchen table after breakfast.

"Yes, honey, you'll make us proud, but we're already as proud as can be of you," added Joe, standing at the sink, washing his morning coffee cup.

"You're sure Uncle Mike will be there?" Elly asked, ashen with tears welling up in her brown eyes.

"Yes, he already testified yesterday so he can be in court, and the way he batted that defense attorney around, that poor schmuck will still be talking to himself," Syl said, laughing to lighten the moment for her teenager.

"Did he hit the guy?" exclaimed Elly, eyes now wide and looking from mother to father.

"Ha. All but," laughed Joe.

Twenty minutes later, Joe dropped his wife and youngest child at the Adams Street side of the Dirksen Building before heading to paid parking a block away.

Standing by the security checkpoint was Halloran, who greeted his goddaughter with a big hug.

"After what you've been through, this'll be a walk in the park, honey," Halloran assured Elly. "Miss Meckelson will do the direct, asking you questions you know the answers to by heart. And don't worry about the shyster, the worst question will be can you positively identify him, and you can't. But you can talk about the cobra tat."

"Thanks, Uncle Mike. You'll be in court? I know you will. I'll be looking at you," Elly said.

"That's my girl," Halloran said as Joe joined wife, daughter and good buddy in the elevator up to the 25th floor.

Dressed in black slacks, a light blue Eileen Fisher linen blouse, and black pumps, Elly strode confidently to the witness stand and raised her right hand to tell the truth when so instructed by the clerk.

After Meckelson asked a few rudimentary questions establishing Elly's identity and background, the prosecutor asked Elly to relate the events of the evening of her abduction.

"I was on my way home from school, the Latin School, and was halfway between Clark and Dearborn on Schiller when I was grabbed from behind, and a man showed me a gun and told me not to scream," Elly said, her voice quavering a bit, as she looked to Halloran in the second row of the gallery. He winked and nodded slightly.

"Then what happened?" Meckelson asked.

"He told the girl at the wheel to come back and tape me up. After that, she got back in the driver's seat and started driving east on Schiller. The man still held me tight as we drove onto what I figured was the Outer Drive, going north. After a minute or two, he told me he was going to take his hand off my mouth to tape it shut, and if I screamed, he was going to slice my face open," Elly said, now tears welling up but not falling.

"And then?" Meckelson asked.

"I was scared, real scared, but I remembered what my parents told me—don't resist a gunman--and memorize details. So, I started counting as soon as we got on the Drive. After a few minutes, we slowed and stopped. She rolled her window down for a second—I could feel the cold air, even though I couldn't see. He told her to toss the phone.

"And after about eight minutes, we slowed and turned off hard right, and then went for a bit before turning left onto an east-west street," she continued, glancing at the jury, where she found several sets of sympathetic eyes.

"Go ahead, Elly, tell your story," Meckelson encouraged.

"Well, we made a few stops, which I figured were stop signs, and then heard the L passing overhead just before we came to a complete stop at what I figured was a stoplight. Then another stop briefly before we turned left and then quickly right into what I figured was an alley, then after a few more seconds we stopped. Then after about an hour we went into a basement apartment," she continued.

"Were you mistreated or injured?" Meckelson asked.

"No, but—uh—" she hesitated.

"But what, Elly?" Meckelson asked softly.

"Well, at one point after he fed me, he had his hand on my shoulder, then started coming down with his hand toward my breast...but the girl yelled at him in Spanish 'Don't molest her' and he stopped, but then a few seconds later I heard him slap her and yell at her—she seemed nice," Elly continued.

"What next, Elly," Meckelson said, moving away from the teen's kind words for one of her kidnappers.

"It was the third night, I think, that they brought me back to the van and headed to what I learned was an area near St. John, Indiana, and they let me go after calling my mom. I was in the middle of a field and made it about a mile away to a farmhouse, where a wonderful farmer named Elmer helped me, let me call home and then drove me all the way home," Elly concluded, again fighting back tears, staring at her parents holding hands next to Halloran.

"Finally, Elly, one last important question and I'll be through. Do you see that man who kidnapped you in court?" Meckelson asked.

"I think so, he had a tat on his hand like the defendant, but I can't be sure. I never saw his face. I'm sorry," Elly said, a tear now coursing down the right cheek.

"That's okay, Elly. Thank you for reliving your ordeal for the jury. We have other witnesses who can bury Mr. Gomez," Meckelson said.

"Objection, Your Honor. She can't predict what other witnesses will say. And 'BURY?'" screamed Miller.

"Sustained. Ms. Meckelson call your witnesses to testify; don't try to do it for them. The jury will disregard the prosecutor's last remark about other witnesses. Your witness, Mr. Miller," Fields said.

"Thank you, Your Honor. Just a few questions, if you please. Can you positively identify Mr. Gomez as the man who abducted you?" Miller asked.

"Objection, Your Honor. Asked and answered," Meckelson said, rising from her chair with hands outstretched to the judge.

"I'll allow it. Not asked in precisely those words. Overruled. Witness can answer," Fields said, nodding down to Elly.

"Not positively, but I'm pretty sure he's the guy," Elly said.

"The jury will disregard the second part of the witness's answer about being 'pretty sure,'" Fields instructed.

"And finally, Ms. Ortiz, were you injured during your captivity?" Miller asked.

"I was handled roughly but not to the point I'd call it an injury," she said.

"I have no further questions, Your Honor," Miller said from his seat.

As she walked past the jury box, she noticed the retired principal dabbing her right eye with a tissue.

CHAPTER 54

It had been a horrible time in and out of America for Letty Diaz. And now it was about to get possibly worse, she knew. Beaten, jailed in two countries and terrified on countless occasions by Gomez and the police, and scared to death at various border crossings, it was her turn on the stand to testify—in a language she was still learning.

Her attorney, Samuels, had struck a deal with the prosecution for a reduced charge with deferred sentencing based on her full and honest testimony against Gomez.

"You have a compelling story to tell, just remember not to fudge—or try to help Gomez—with your testimony. That can only hurt you, and you've some powerful people who know the full story and can help you after you testify," Samuels promised.

"Remember you have testified before the grand jury, and any deviation from that could hurt you. Right now, Meckelson has got you on one count of wire fraud for when you paused to toss Elly's phone out the window at Fullerton. But you lie or change your story to help Gomez, and they will throw that deal out," the lawyer warned.

"I understand. I tell the truth," Letty promised.

* * * * *

After her testimony and safely back at home, Elly asked her mom to step into her bedroom. Joe was at work; they were alone in the Dearborn mansion.

"Mom, I answered all the questions from the police and the FBI, but I held back a part of my ordeal—just too embarrassed but it may be important at some point—I don't know. Can I tell you?" Elly asked, sitting on her twin bed with the pink duvet.

"Honey, you can tell me anything. I gave birth to you, breast-fed you, wiped your butt till you were toilet-trained. Digame, mi hermosa hija," Syl told her daughter gently.

Suddenly, Elly laughed softly.

"Funny you should talk about wiping my butt. That is exactly what Letty did for me. I was there for three days, so, yeah, I had to poop—several times. And each time, Letty would clean me up; Gomez wouldn't take the tape off me. She treated me like I was her child. I think she might've saved my life..." Elly started crying. Her mom joined her on the bed and wrapped her arms around her distraught daughter.

"It's all right, baby. It's all over now," Syl said, patting her daughter's back.

Elly sat up straight and pulled away from her mother.

"No, mom. It's not. Letty still has to testify and then she'll get sentenced. She's as much a victim as I was. She shouldn't have to go to prison," Elly pleaded.

"Your dad and I and Uncle Mike are working on that, honey. You worry about your next b-ball game," Syl patted her daughter on the hand. "Now homework."

* * * * *

That night, Halloran stopped by the Ortiz home, and the three old friends began plotting.

The Ortizes knew exactly what Letty had done for their daughter and were going to help. And Halloran had friends in important places in Mexico; he knew the whole story and knew full well that Gomez had terrorized this young woman, almost a teen herself, into helping in his plot.

Yet, Meckelson had charged Letty with one count of wire fraud. With a five-year sentence and a $250,000 fine hanging over her head, Letty was determined to tell "nothing but the truth, so help her, God."

"So, I got a good feeling from talking to Geri, but she's playing her cards close to her chest till Letty testifies. But that doesn't mean we can't start planning to help this child, who helped keep Elly safe and who didn't do anything worse than fall for shitface's bullshit when she arrived here," Syl said.

Most times when it came to interacting with the feds, Joe left the details to his wife. But this was an extraordinary circumstance, and Joe, the highly successful lawyer responsible for their sweet life, had been making his own plans. But he deferred to the godfather.

"I know you think I only travel to PV, but for years, I used to travel to Isla Mujeres, a little spit of land about a 20-minute ferry ride off Cancun. On my second day on my first trip, after booking a real shithole online, I went exploring and on the rim of the downtown, I found an aptly named hotel called Hotel Secreto.

'There I met an American named Stan who owned the Secreto and had married a beautiful local mujer who also owned a little hotel nearby. Long story short, they married, had kids, and he built the Secreto, a boutique, nine-unit escape with an infinity pool, a great breakfast, and a view of the crashing waves about 100 yards away from my balcony," Halloran paused.

Syl said, "And...?"

"And I stayed there a half dozen times, and me and Stan hit it off. He was a former cop from Houston who came for a short vacation and found love and a job he liked better than chasing Texas banditos. I called him yesterday and asked if he could use an experienced waitress, bilingual and beautiful," Halloran continued.

"And?" Joe asked before his wife could.

"Letty's got a job waiting with a great family and no known ties to her former life on the other side of the country. I think she'll be safe there forever, with shithead looking at what will be a life sentence," Halloran continued.

"My turn," Joe said. "Mike and I been talking, and we're going to buy a little two-unit townhouse in a condo complex there for Letty, then rent it to her at a very reasonable price. An investment for us and the second unit a place for Mike to visit when he feels the urge to get away."

"You guys!" Syl said. "Plotting behind my back. How much?"

"We have invested the settlement wisely, and Mike lives like a pauper, so together, it's gonna work. We may make a tidy profit at the same time we help the girl who helped our girl," Joe said.

"Well, okay, but it's going to be my duty to check this out as soon as the trial is over and things settle," Syl admonished the two conspirators. "Maybe just me and Elly."

CHAPTER 55

Samuels looked her client over carefully in the small interview room adjacent to Fields' courtroom. Letty was dressed just as instructed and provided: a mid-calf navy blue dress, a flowered, off-white peasant blouse and dark blue flats.

"Now don't be afraid to smile if the testimony merits it. Remember, you are charged, and the jury will hear that, but your testimony will paint you as a victim, almost as much as Elly was. The jury will see who's at the defendant's table—him, not you," the veteran defense attorney said just before court was to resume for the morning.

"I tell the truth. I no lie," nodding her head, the black ponytail swaying.

Just then, the bailiff poked his nose in and said, "Show time. You're up," pointing to Letty.

Wide-eyed, Letty entered the enormous chamber and the first person she saw was Gomez, scowling. Two rows back, she spotted Elly with her parents, Halloran and Ochoa. Elly smiled and nodded to the terrified witness. Letty grimaced and slightly nodded a smile. Most of the jury caught the subtle interplay. Here was the star witness.

"The witness will please raise her right hand and repeat after me," Fields' clerk began.

After taking the oath, Letty settled warily into the black leather chair in the walnut-wooded box.

Meckelson asked Letty to identify herself, "and please spell your first and last names."

Letty began in a whisper but was quickly interrupted by Meckelson.

"Please speak up," the prosecutor urged.

Fields joined in with avuncular fashion, smiling down at the witness.

"Pretend you're speaking to the last person in the last row, and it'll be fine," Fields said gently.

"Yes, sir—er, Your Honor," Letty said, voice rising.

"Now Leticia, you understand that you have been charged in this case, but sentencing has been deferred and will largely depend on your truthful testimony, your attorney has explained. Correct?" Meckelson asked.

"Si—I mean, yes ma'am," she said, searching the gallery for her attorney. Samuels nodded and smiled from the second row right. It seemed to calm Letty, as her shoulders slumped into a more natural position on the stand.

"Please tell the jury how long you have been in the United States, rather, when did you first arrive here and how?" the prosecutor asked.

"I came here first time about two year ago. A coyote took me. Cost me 24,000 pesos—about 1,200 Amayrikan dollar," Letty said.

"Coyote? Tell the jury what that is, please," Meckelson prompted.

"Coyotes be bad men that take your money and get you cross the Rio Grande into U.S.A.," Letty said.

"And eventually you made your way to Chicago. Is that right?" Meckelson asked.

"Yes, ma'am," Letty responded, now catching the eye of Halloran, who winked with a slight nod. It helped; Letty was beginning to relax slightly and snuck a peek at the jury box before the next question.

"And so, as I understand it, your aunt helped you get a job here at a famous Mexican restaurant, which is not on trial, based on your experience waitressing in Mexico. So far, so good?" Meckelson asked.

"I sorry. No understand 'so far good'" Letty looked around, now getting a bit worried she would falter on the stand. Or worse, lie.

"Miss Diaz, the prosecutor wants to know if she is correct in saying that is how you got a job here. Okay?" Fields helped, again smiling down at the rattled witness.

"Yes, yes. She correct," she told the judge, then turned to Meckelson and said, "Yes, you right, correct."

"And was it there at the restaurant that you met defendant Gomez?" Meckelson asked, having circled behind the defense table and now theatrically pointing to the back of Gomez.

"Yes, is true," Letty said in a strong voice.

"Now, according to your grand jury testimony, Gomez ingratiated himself—was very nice—to you in the first month or so of your relationship, taking you to nice restaurants, buying you some nice clothes. Is that correct?" Meckelson asked.

"Si, si. I sorry. Yes, yes. Is true," she said.

"And at some point, he asked you to sign up for an apartment in the 1300 block of North Dearborn, you told the grand jury. Did he tell you why he needed you to sign?" Meckelson asked.

"He no say why. And when I ask why, he slap me in the back of my head and say, 'My business not your business.' It first time he hit me," Letty said, "but not the last."

"Objection, Your Honor. Is this still grand jury testimony, Ms. Prosecutor?" Miller thundered.

"Mr. Miller. You will wait for my ruling and address me, not the prosecutor. Understand? I don't think federal court differs in that capacity from state court, right, Mr. Defense Attorney?" Fields jabbed his right index finger at Miller.

"Sorry, Your Honor," Miller said quietly and sat back down.

"Now—overruled," Fields said, without explanation.

"And was it sometime later that Gomez coerced—persuaded—you to get a second place in a basement apartment on Hood, further north?" Meckelson asked.

"Yes, ma'am," Letty said, keeping her response short as suggested by her attorney.

"And did he explain this to you?" Meckelson asked.

"No, and I not ask," Letty said, catching the eye of the bus driver but seeing no reaction.

"And when did the purpose of this second apartment become clear?" Meckelson asked.

"Objection, Your Honor. Foundation?" Miller said, just to disrupt Meckelson's flow.

"Sustained. Ms. Meckelson?"

Just showing a hint of annoyance, Meckelson led Letty through the who, what, where, why, how and when to lay the foundation of how the Hood apartment was rented. Miller knew the prosecution could easily do just that but used the objection to throw off the rhythm of the direct examination.

"Ladies and gentlemen, this might be a good time for our morning break. Take 20 minutes to stretch, but remember not to discuss the case," Fields said and whisked back to the inner sanctum of his chambers.

As the courtroom cleared, Jane Thoma came rushing in and grabbed her partner.

"We gotta talk," and walked straight out to the corridor. Halloran followed, curious and just a tad annoyed when he wanted to give a snarky comment to Elly about Miller.

With Halloran's right elbow in hand, Thoma guided him a dozen steps from the exiting courtroom crowd.

"Lynch got shanked at breakfast today at County. He's in the infirmary, but they may take him to Stroger (Hospital)," Thoma whispered rapidly.

"Holy shit. Is he gonna make it? We can only hope for the best," Halloran's standard reply when scumbags like Lynch are wounded.

"Too early to tell, but I figured you'd wanna know ASAP," Thoma said, still clutching her partner's arm.

"Not much we can do, but thanks for the head's-up. Now, I gotta hit the head," Halloran told his partner.

"Geez, TMI, Hal," Thoma said, and retreated to the elevators.

As Halloran washed his hands in the john, Miller walked in and up to the urinal, giving Halloran the stink eye.

"Nice work in there, counselor. Foundation? Classic," Halloran said, and chuckled as he went back to court.

CHAPTER 56

When the jury filed back in, the principal smiled at Letty, apparently feeling it was not inappropriate since Letty wasn't on trial.

But Letty still looked scared as court resumed and was easing her anxiety by twisting a handkerchief in her hands. Samuels pulled out a handkerchief and shoved it into her purse, signaling Letty to stop. Bad look to be showing her nerves, her attorney's earlier advice resounding in her ears.

"Miss Diaz, you are still under oath. Proceed Ms. Meckelson," Fields said.

"Thank you, Your Honor. Do you need me to repeat my question, Ms. Diaz?" Meckelson asked.

"No, I remember. When did I know why a second apartment? He told me when we pull in that alley he gotta collect a drug debt. He show me gun. I know it bad when he grab this little girl and pull her in back of van. Then he order me around. He got gun. Girl scared. I scared crazy. So, I drive like he order. Then he tell me pull over and he hand me phone to throw. I throw. Now I really, really scared," Letty continued, now sans handkerchief.

"The jury has heard from Ms. Ortiz herself, so let's focus on what you did in that apartment, shall we?" Meckelson said.

"Objection!" Miller cried.

"It's all part of the same criminal pattern, Your Honor," Meckelson responded.

"Overruled. Continue, Ms. Meckelson," the judge audibly sighed.

"He feed her. He let her go toilet, but he keep her hands taped. I help her. Once, I catch him with his hand on her shoulder after she eat, and he start moving he hand down. I yell him to stop. He stop but he slap me down then," Letty continued.

"Is it not true that at one point he left you alone in the apartment with our victim when he went to make his ransom demand on the burner phone?" Meckelson asked. "Why didn't you run, or let her go? You had the chance, didn't you?" Meckelson asked, glancing at the jury for reaction. Her questioning looked like it was getting mixed reviews.

"Yes, is true. Is true. But I scared. He got gun. He got car. I not knowing where I am. Where he is. I fraid he come back. If he catch me letting her go, he beat me, maybe cut my face. Maybe kill me. Maybe kill her. I no know. I, I… I sorry, Elly," and she burst into tears. Elly stood up, tears pouring down her face, and ran from the courtroom, Syl in quick pursuit. Then Joe.

"Time for a short break," Fields said as his clerk handed Letty a box of tissues.

Five minutes later, Fields asked Letty if she was okay to continue.

"I okay now, judge, sir. So sorry," Letty said, her face florid but eyes now dry.

"And let's move on to the release. Did you and Gomez dump the victim in a field in Indiana and then go spend some of the ransom money at a fancy Rush Street bistro?" Meckelson asked.

"Is true. Is his idea. Now I his captive. He has gun tucked in his back pocket. The money, the jewels, he lock in car under my seat," Letty continued hesitantly.

"Okay, now you head back to the Hood apartment. What happened next?" Meckelson asked.

"Real bad happen next," Letty continued. "He driving and he see polices near apartment, so he turn and race away, but once polices see us, he start chasing. Jesus driving real fast and turn into alley, make many turns. Then stick in snow," she continued.

"He grab his gun and jump from car at same time police guy jump from his car. Jesus begin shooting—rat a tat-tat, so many bullets. He hiding and shooting, tell me to drive, turn around. I get out of snow, but then I see chance and drive away and keep driving long time," Letty said.

"And then?" Meckelson urged.

"Then, I drive and drive and drive. Take nap at rest stop but then keep driving...all the way to El Paso. Then I grab stuff and park van in front of church parking lot and walk across border," she continued, till Meckelson interrupted.

"By stuff, you mean the ransom money and diamonds?" Meckelson asked.

"Si, yes. I have no money, no clothes, so I need money," Letty nearly whispered, lowering her head to stare at her hands folded in her lap.

"And would it be accurate to say you spent less than $1,500?" Meckelson asked.

"Si, yes, I pretty sure," Letty said, again searching the jurors for their reaction. And found none.

"So, after your arrest in Mexico, you turned over the remainder of those dollars and the diamonds to Officer Halloran and Agent Ochoa. Is that true," Meckelson asked.

"Si, si, Miss Meckelson. You have it all I gave to you," Letty responded.

"Well, not I, but it is being held as evidence and will be returned to the Ortiz family after the trial," Meckelson said, smiling at the grad student juror as if they were sharing a joke.

"Nothing further, Your Honor."

"Thank you, madam prosecutor. And I believe it's time for lunch. See everyone back at 1:30," Fields said.

CHAPTER 57

As Egan and Halloran sat down for lunch at the nearby Italian Village restaurant, the detective's cell buzzed for attention, still on silent from the court setting. He glanced down and saw it was Thoma.

"Hey, Jane. Direct with Letty went smoothly," Halloran began before Thoma jumped in.

"Great, but got some good news and bad news out of the jail. They shipped Lynch to Stroger Hospital, where they did a full exam after he was admitted. The slash in the back over his right kidney was deep but stitched up well at the jail. But they found that the cancer had spread from the colon to the liver," Thoma reported.

"He's in intensive care with a DNR (Do Not Resuscitate) he signed. They think he's circling the drain," Thoma said.

"Think we'd better get over there now and see if this shitbag wants to make a deathbed confession," Halloran said. He turned to Egan. "Sorry, but I got to run to Stroger to see if we can get him to talk."

"Sounds like you better head out. I'll pick up my own check," Egan said. "You think he's gonna kick soon?"

"In God's hands, and He ain't smilin'" Halloran deadpanned.

Fifteen minutes later, Halloran met up with Thoma outside the ICU unit, headed up by Dr. Janie Toohey, standing next to Thoma. They spoke briefly in hushed tones.

"I'm giving you 20 minutes. He doesn't have long left," Toohey said.

"It'll either be a quick no or a slightly longer yes," Halloran said.

Lynch was wired up with an intravenous feed and an oxygen mask. His slitted eyes opened slightly when the two detectives entered and flanked either side of the hospital bed.

Halloran took the lead.

"Okay, Larry. We're here to give you the opportunity to do the right thing as your dirtbag life is circling the drain. Lynch sounds Irish and so I'm guessing you did the sacraments in grammar school. Well, now you're ready for Extreme Unction, but you can clear your conscience and get a slim chance that the door to the heavenly gates is not posting the 'No Vacancy' sign when you kick and appear to old St. Pete," Halloran said.

Thoma winced a bit but remained silent. She stared at the supine suspect. He moved his right hand slightly. His middle finger rose to give Halloran his answer.

"Perfect," Halloran said. "Now with the sands of your life dripping to the bottom of your hourglass, at least you are consistently a lame shit. I'll tell the nurse you're not interested in seeing a priest," Halloran said, nodding to the door as a sign to his partner that it was time to exit.

As they approached the door, Lynch mumbled something through the mask with the second syllable that sounded something like "you". The first syllable was not "luck."

As they exited into the hallway, they heard alarms shrieking from Lynch's room as two nurses sprinted by the two detectives.

"What a shame," Halloran said. "But his life has been a series of shames."

"Maybe save the taxpayers the cost of incarceration and a trial," Thoma said.

"Yup. Woulda been nice to get that confession for Mary Beth's brother—that is if he even cares," Halloran said, and slipped behind the wheel of the Crown Vic.

An hour later, Halloran checked Lynch's condition from his cell on the way home.

A text from Toohey read: "Patient Larry Lynch: Deceased."

Live by the sword; die by the sword, thought Halloran, *or helped by the shank.*

CHAPTER 58

Court buffs who were mostly retired old men were the first to fill the second row behind the defense table. Reporters grabbed whatever slots were open and flipped open their notebooks as Letty walked back up to the witness stand, still a "deer in the headlights" look about her.

Miller rose slowly from his chair next to Gomez. He half-turned to the gallery and spotted Becky Thompson from Channel 7 and winked at her. She quickly got mesmerized by the blank pages in her notebook. Miller thought the media loved him; he was so wrong.

"So, Ms. Diaz, when you returned to Mexico, did the border guards there ask you what you were doing in the U.S.?" he began.

"I think so. I say 'tourism,'" she practically whispered.

"Tourism? Is that what you call entering into this country illegally, participating in a kidnapping and returning home with a small fortune in cash and diamonds?" Miller said, walking to within a few feet of Letty but eyeing the jury.

"No. No. Not what I say..." Letty blurted before Meckelson jumped to her feet.

"Objection, Your Honor. The witness is not on trial and this jury doesn't need counsel twisting her words to his own purpose," Meckelson said, pointing to Miller, whose smile slightly dampened.

"Overruled, for now. Defense counsel can delve into areas brought up on direct, but tread lightly, Mr. Miller. This is the witness's second language she is grappling with and doesn't need you as her interpreter."

"So, just so I understand fully, you're asking this jury to believe you were a victim, not a kidnapper, who went along to get along and enjoyed good food and a fortune and hotfooted it to Mexico the first chance you got. Verdad?" Miller said, throwing in one of the hundred Spanish words he knew.

"Hotfoot. I no understand," Letty said, looking to Fields for help.

"That is Mr. Miller's unique way of saying you left the country," Fields explained.

"Si, yes. I leave. And si, I a victim too, I fooled by him," she said, pointing at Gomez, who stared into space as if bored by her testimony.

"Moving on...So, Ms. Diaz, from your testimony it appears you lied by sneaking into this country, you lied to get the Dearborn apartment, and then lied to get back into Mexico with the stolen loot in your possession? Am I missing a lie?" Miller asked, rolling his eyes theatrically to the ceiling of the huge courtroom.

"I no lie to get into this country. No one ask me anything as I got to other side of Rio Grande," she protested.

"I see. You didn't lie because you weren't caught, but the rest of those times, you lied. Correct?" Miller plowed on.

"Si, yes. I lie because I scared of him," she said, pointing to Gomez. "I fraid he cut me or kill me, so I do what he say."

"Yes, yes. But we have only your word that he was coercing you. And you admit you lied repeatedly and on both sides of the border. Why didn't you just pull out of that alley after the shootout and head for the closest police station and tell them your story?" Miller prodded. He had the jury's attention now on this key and critical question.

"He got gun. He could kill me with his hands. He has a gang to help 'im. I scared, so I ran. I know it look bad if I walk into police's station, will they believe me? I not think of it as I drive away. I think Mexico only safe place for me. So, I run," she said, tears welling up in her eyes. She gazed at the jury. A few nodded to her. A bad sign for Miller.

"As she is an admitted liar, I see no reason to further try this court's or this jury's patience or tolerance for whoppers," Miller said, then turned abruptly from Letty to return to his seat, patting Gomez on the shoulder and whispering something to him.

"Your concern for this court's patience is ill placed, Mr. Miller. I decide that. Ms. Meckelson? Redirect?" Fields asked.

"Thank you, Your Honor. Now Letty, did I or any member of the U.S. Attorney's Office promise you anything in return for your truthful testimony?" the prosecutor asked.

"No, no. My lawyer explain me. She say just tell truth," Letty gulped as she gazed toward O'Hara-Samuels, who nodded to her client.

"Mr. Miller?"

"Nothing further."

"You are dismissed, Ms. Diaz," Fields said.

"Thank you, Your Honor," Letty said, and looked for reaction from the jury. The principal smiled.

"Miss Meckelson, your next witness." Fields said.

"The prosecution would now like to read a stipulation agreed to by both sides," she said from a sitting position.

"Please proceed. The jury will hear a statement of facts agreed to by both the defense and prosecution," the judge told the jury.

For the first three years as an AUSA, Michael Powers Gorham handled bank robberies, child porn, and mail and wire fraud cases that were likely to be pleaded down to misdemeanors. Then a child porn case turned out to be mailed to a retired Circuit Court judge from Lake County, Illinois. That got some ink. So, when it came to choosing a second chair to push the evidence cart for Meckelson and take notes in court, Gorham was deemed ready.

The handsome, square jawed Gorham stepped up to the podium with his one sheet of paper and nodded to the jury box first, then thanked the judge.

Gorham read from a single sheet of paper in a strong, confident voice after he reached the podium.

"If called upon to testify, FBI Lab Technician Oliver Streeter would testify that he extracted fingerprints from the Mac-10 recovered in the snow a block from the shooting scene. And the fingerprints on several cartridges and on the magazine from that gun matched the fingerprints of the defendant on file with the Chicago Police Department.

"Moreover, Illinois State Police Crime Lab DNA Expert Karen Svenson would testify that an oily print from one of the .45 cartridges contained a DNA profile that matched the DNA profile for defendant Gomez," Gorham concluded.

"With that, the prosecution rests," Meckelson said, standing after Gorham finished.

"Mr. Miller?" Fields asked.

"At this late hour, I would ask for time to confer with my client before we resume tomorrow morning," Miller said.

As the court adjourned, the first spectator to leave was the quick-footed Victor on his way to report back to Morel. Outside, he practically bumped into Lupo, who was on his way to chat with Gomez at the MCC. They walked away from each other wordlessly.

CHAPTER 59

Mindful of the feds listening in, Lupo started slowly with Gomez.

"You okay in here, amigo?" Lupo asked.

That drew a disdainful snort from the man in shackles.

"Like a day on a Cancun beach with a Modelo and a horny chica. What you think, estupido?" Gomez whispered in a raspy voice.

"Jefe Proco wanted me to ask, make sure you okay," Lupo said.

"I need yo' tell Jefe I holdin' the line here and add that he need to crank up the support for me in here," Gomez said, cupping his right hand up to his face, showing the gang sign of a cobra about to strike.

"We done here, Meester P," Gomez said, his not too subtle code for a pig, to summon the guard.

Hours later, Lupo reported back to Proco Morel, word for word the message Gomez wanted sent to his boss.

"You understan', cabron?" Jefe asked.

"Uh, he want you help somehow?" Lupo asked.

"I teach you sumptin, estupido. He say 'line' mean he want meth or coke to snort, and when he say 'add,' it mean he wants it in an Adderall cap. So, you go downstairs and get me an Adderall cap, some crank, some bit of fen. Yo' understand?" Jefe asked, patting the 9 mm Staccato by his side. "I mix myself."

"Si. Si. Ahora," Lupo said, then hustled off to the mixing room. In 20 minutes he returned with the mixes Morel had ordered.

"Allight, you go now. I take care uh this," Morel said, dismissing Lupo with a wave of his hand, which then returned to the semi-automatic on his table.

"But first you find Victor and send him in to see me. I need his report."

Victor, now just a few months short of his 18th birthday, was waiting down the hall when Lupo walked out. Lupo just thumbed the teen toward the entrance to Jefe's inner sanctum.

The fleet-footed teen had moved up in the gang after his vital role in the kidnapping and the dismissal by the cops as not a key player worth their time or the courts'. He walked in gingerly and nearly bowed to Proco.

"How's it looking in there?" asked Morel, who wanted a fresh set of eyes and ears monitoring the trial. An older underling like Lupo would try to spin the tale, Morel reasoned, whereas the kid would soak in every detail and regurgitate it to his Jefe.

"Well, I don't think the judge likes Jesus' lawyer. He's always getting overruled, and gets a little verbal spanking, too. The jury seemed to like Letty, who cried a lot," Victor began.

"What Gomez doing when she cry?" Morel asked.

"Not much. He like to smirk sometimes at her. Smirk the right word? Like a fake smile," Victor asked.

"Smirk is the right word, but not the smart move for Gomez. Where the trial at now?" Morel asked.

"I ask one of the old men who come every day to watch, and he say now is time for defense witnesses, and he was betting Gomez would want to testify, but his lawyer will argue against that, the viejo say," Victor reported.

"He just estupido enough to think he outsmart the feds. Show how crazy nuts he is. How did the Ortiz girl do?" Morel asked.

"She was very convincing but couldn't ID Gomez, except by a tat she saw. But Letty testified what she did with the girl—took care of her. Letty say Gomez slapped her around a lot," Victor said.

"Our Jesus has wrong first name. Should be Lucifer the Loser," laughed Morel.

"Lucifer?" Victor asked.

"Never mind. Good work, pequeno. I have more use for you down the highway—road," Morel said, then told the teen to come back in an hour for the pill for Gomez.

* * * * *

At about the same time in the attorney conference room attached to the ceremonial courtroom, Gomez and Miller clashed.

"What you mean, I can't testify?" shouted Gomez.

"It's not that you CANNOT, it's that you absolutely SHOULD not. You got a sheet as long as Ashland Avenue. You got tats all over. You got three victims—including a very sympathetic Letty—who testified against you. You get on the stand and that smart prosecutor gonna rip you another asshole—fitting for your record," Miller responded.

"And the judge and jury already think you're a shitbird. Getting on the stand and letting the other side go through your past arrests and convictions will earn you a certain conviction with an additional 20 years for lying on the stand, which you surely would do," Miller continued.

"You got some major cajones calling me a shitbird, you sleazeball. If we were on the street, it'd be me cutting you a new asshole, you dumb fuck," Gomez lashed back.

"Well, look around, stupid. We're not on the street where you know the rules; but here in court where I know the rules and the consequences, and I'm telling you it would be a very, very foolish move for you to take the stand. Let my closing argument paint Letty as the greedy little mastermind of this, and you might get one juror, or two, to vote NG (not guilty) and thus, a hung jury, although I wouldn't bet on it. But it is your only viable bet," Miller lectured.

Gomez went silent. Held his breath for half a minute, then said: "Okay, okay. You da legal genius. I keep my mouth shut and ass in the chair."

The U.S. marshal assigned to guard Gomez rapped on the door after hearing the raised voices.

"You okay in there, counselor?" he asked through the closed door.

"We're good, thanks," Miller said, raising his voice to be heard through the thick oak door.

"Good?" Gomez snorted. "Far fuckin' from it."

CHAPTER 60

Donald O'Malley never moved from his parents' modest bungalow home on Fargo Avenue despite the constant reminders that his sister once lived in the vacant bedroom adjacent to what was once his parents' bedroom.

He graduated from Lane Tech, went a year to Wright Junior College, then got a job with Streets & Sanitation, courtesy of a family friend with some minor clout at City Hall. He seldom dated and lived a mostly solitary life, occasionally going to a Cubs or Bears home game—by himself.

He nodded to his neighbors and would stop and chat if one stopped him. To the neighbors, it seemed he never recovered from the devastation that his sister's murder had wrought on his family. They respected his privacy.

He was at home when the front doorbell rang and he spied a large plainclothes cop holding his star up to the peephole.

"Officer, what can I do for you?" O'Malley said, swinging the front door open.

"Donald O'Malley? I'm Detective Mike Halloran, and I have some news concerning your sister's killer," Halloran said, then followed O'Malley into the kitchen.

"Coffee, officer? It's a fresh pot," O'Malley said, his slippers still on with a faded flannel plaid shirt over his pajama bottoms.

"No, thanks very much. My partner, Jane Thoma, contacted you after we arrested Larry Lynch. But several days ago, he was shanked—stabbed—at the jail, and yesterday he died, probably because of the wound but perhaps because of his cancer. No matter. The scumbag who killed your sister is dead and probably headed for Potter's Field in an unmarked grave," Halloran said.

O'Malley sat down on the kitchen chair his parents probably bought when he was in grammar school.

"He have any relatives?" O'Malley asked.

"None living, and if it's any consolation to you, he had a string of horseshit construction jobs, no friends and lived in an SRO (single room occupancy) in a rundown section of Houston when we grabbed him. The world is better off without the likes of Larry Lynch," Halloran practically spit out.

"Amen," O'Malley said, glancing up at the image of the same plaque of Jesus that had adorned the family kitchen wall when Mary Beth was still alive.

Halloran remained standing.

"This is a half century late perhaps, but I am sorry for your loss," Halloran said, extending his right hand to the still-seated O'Malley. "We Irish often say, 'It's sorry for your troubles I am' but that doesn't even come close to describing your family's horrific tragedy. This will, I hope, put some closure on this for you," Halloran said, in a voice amping down to a near whisper.

"Yes, yes. Thanks for coming in person. And thanks for your diligence and your service," O'Malley said, shaking lightly, then letting go of Halloran's hand.

"I can let myself out, Mr. O'Malley," Halloran said and began exiting.

"Yes, yes. Okay," O'Malley said in a voice barely audible.

The public thinks going after bad guys is the toughest part of this job; telling the family is the worst. The worst.

CHAPTER 61

Becky Thompson was holding forth in the Dirksen press room as the media waited for the defense case to unfold.

"No way shitbag will testify. Too much baggage. Meckelson'll crucify him," she predicted.

Just then one of the elderly court buffs poked his head into the press room and announced: "Looks like they may start a bit early." The buffs often knew the cases and the inner workings of the building better than the beat guys for the Trib and Sun-Times. Sam, a retired IRS investigator, was the news bearer this day—and welcome.

Off the phalanx of the Fourth Estate marched to catch the elevator up to 25. There. in the courtroom, waited Fields.

"All right, ladies and gentlemen," he said as the jury filed in. "Please be seated. Mr. Miller? Are you ready?" the jurist asked.

"After consulting with my client, he's decided against testifying," Miller said, looking for any reaction from the jury. Their faces remained expressionless.

"Mr. Gomez, is it your choice not to testify?" Fields asked.

Gomez stood. "Yes, Your Honor." Then he sat.

"Your first witness, Mr. Miller?" Fields asked.

"The defense rests," Miller replied, launching murmurs through the gallery.

"Okay, closing arguments tomorrow at 10 a.m.," Fields ordered, then reminded the jury--no discussions about the case among themselves or with others and no TV, radio or newspapers.

* * * * *

Standing in the living room of his one-bedroom condo at Sandburg Village, Gorham went over his closing for the 12th time, this time before his girlfriend, Julia, the nurse. After finishing the 20-minute speech, he looked to Julia.

"Perfect, though I don't know the facts, I would only suggest you move around a bit more and leave your notes in your hand more as a prop than a crutch. And Mike, this time not one 'you know.' You are ready, honey," she said, beaming.

The following morning, it was Meckelson who pushed the cart into court as a confident Gorham marched in, holding just his legal writing pad. The ex-linebacker's biceps strained beneath his dark blue, pinstriped suit.

The two prosecutors sat down with the FBI agent assigned to the case not named Ochoa. She was Catherine G. Moran, a wily 12-year vet who ran half-marathons when she wasn't chasing her two toddlers or bad guys.

None spoke as they waited for Fields. Nor did they move or speak as the marshals led Gomez in and seated him next to Miller.

The gallery was packed, more than usual, with the press, the buffs, the curious, and a contingent of young federal prosecutors s anxious to watch, learn and later emulate when it was their turn. The Federal Defender's young attorneys also had a half dozen grouped in the last row, whispering in anticipation.

As Fields entered from the door next to his bench, the murmurs ceased.

"Good morning. Please bring in the jury," Fields ordered.

Seconds later, the jury filed in, the principal in the lead, followed by the bus driver, with the grad student trailing last. After they were all seated, Fields spoke:

"Good morning, ladies and gentlemen. We are now starting closing arguments. First, we will hear from the prosecution, then the defense and finally the rebuttal from the prosecution, since they bear the burden of proof beyond a reasonable doubt. The lawyers will emphasize what they believe the evidence shows, but you are the final evaluator of the truth of what you have heard. Mr. Gorham, I believe you're the leadoff hitter," Fields said, smiling at his metaphor.

Gorham stood and grabbed his legal pad.

"Thank you, Your Honor. On behalf of the prosecution, I'd like to thank the jurors for their attention and the time they have given our justice system away from families, friends and jobs," he said, then cleared his throat before resuming as he reached the podium.

"What we have here is a simple case of revenge, greed and contempt for the law. Jesus Martinez-Gomez stewed in his own vitriol for years after being sent to prison by the victim's father, Joe Ortiz. Then, from the prison library or perhaps from the prison grapevine at Stateville, he learned that Joe Ortiz had won a large settlement in a personal injury case he handled. So, Gomez started plotting," Gorham continued.

"Objection, Your Honor. Learned counsel cannot possibly know what my client was thinking and we heard no testimony about library visits," Miller thundered, standing and pounding his tiny fist into the defense table.

"True enough, Mr. Miller. But this is argument, and the prosecution can extrapolate a theory based on what evidence was presented. Overruled. And take it easy on the furniture in my courtroom," Fields scolded. Several jurors held hands to face to cover their smiles at the judge's gentle joust.

Undisturbed by Miller's theatrics, though expected and lame, Gorham walked up to the far corner of the jury box, closest to the gallery.

"You heard from young Elly Ortiz how she was snatched up just a football field length from her home on a chilly evening. The defendant was wearing a ski mask that covered his face, so Elly was unable to positively identify Gomez but for a tattoo common to all in the Latin Cobras. But then you heard in great detail from Gomez's girlfriend at the time, Letty Diaz, who linked the defendant unequivocally to the capture and kidnapping caper, masterminded by a slick ex-con she barely knew.

"You also heard from Agent Ochoa, who saw the man who shot and nearly killed him in that alley behind Hamilton's. Detective Halloran painted a clear path from that alley to a small taco restaurant in Punta Mita. Letty Diaz filled in many of the gaps law enforcement had to show conclusively that Gomez was a violent, avaricious ex-con responsible for the kidnapping," Gorham continued.

"As if the testimony wasn't sufficient to send Gomez away for a long, long time, we have a DNA match, his prints on the Mac-10 and on the shell casings recovered at the site of Agent Ochoa's attempted assassination..." Gorham said but was then shouted down by an objecting Miller.

"Assassination? Assassination? Who's Agent Ochoa—the president of the United States or the puppet president of some banana republic?" shrieked Miller.

"Sustained. Mr. Gorham, attempted murder might be a better choice of words and a bit less inflammatory. Continue, a bit more temperately," Fields cautioned.

"Yes, Your Honor. And finally, we have him armed with a knife while invading that restaurant intent on doing Letty Diaz in after forcing her at knifepoint to relinquish diamonds and cash. Fortunately, Agent Ochoa and Detective Halloran were a step ahead of him.

"This is not a 'whodunit' you might watch on TV. It's a 'he did it.' You have heard overwhelming evidence of the guilt of this evil, habitual thug. So," as Gorham walked slowly past a riveted jury, "you can only return one verdict. Guilty."

He turned slowly and walked back to the prosecution table but glanced into the gallery for a second in time to see Halloran nod and Thoma rub her nose with her right thumb, a cryptic thumbs-up for the young prosecutor.

Halloran leaned over to Ochoa. "Succinct, powerful and covered the bases." Ochoa added, "Meckelson will put the nails in asshole's coffin."

Fields looked to Miller. "Your turn, Mr. Miller."

CHAPTER 62

Miller strutted up to the jury box, smiling.

"I want to thank each of you for your kind attention. This will be the last you hear from me. But I want to draw your attention to what you may have missed a bit from Mr. Gorham's summation about a certain Letty Diaz, mentioned almost as an aside. That was purposeful, ladies and gentlemen, for there will be no canonization of Ms. Diaz, a major player—the major player in this kidnapping caper, if you will.

"You saw her crocodile tears as she minimized her involvement in this case. But let's look at it through another lens—the lens of nuance that seeks a truthful picture. We know who rented the apartment to spy on the Ortiz family to get details of Elly's habits. We know she rented the Hood Avenue flat. We know she went out celebrating on Rush Street after she had the ransom.

"Further, we know she never—ever—called the police. Not when my client allegedly left to make a phone call. And certainly not after she escaped that alley with a quarter million in diamonds and 60 Gs in cash. She seduced my client and persuaded him to pull this off, and then when she had the chance, the first chance, she absconded with the lucre to an obscure little village in Nayarit, Mexico," Miller said.

"Objection, Your Honor. How did counsel ever make that fanciful leap? Not based on the evidence," challenged Meckelson.

"Overruled. It's argument, and we all heard what Ms. Diaz said she did and didn't do," Fields said.

"Thank you, Your Honor. I'm not going to try to put a halo over Mr. Gomez's head. He has done time and paid his price, but this was not his plot. It was hers--Letty Diaz's get-rich scheme to realize her perverted version of the American Dream. She used her sex --and cunning to con a con—not easy to do," Miller said.

"We know she's a government witness and the better the story, the lighter she hopes her punishment will be. She told some whoppers up there, but don't fall for her version. You will decide the culpability of Mr. Gomez, but trust Judge Fields, an honorable and experienced jurist, to do right by Diaz," Miller concluded.

"That's enough buttering up, Mr. Miller. 'Honorable'? I hope so, that's why you and opposing counsel and everyone else addresses me as 'Your Honor.' Are you finished?" Fields asked, glaring down at Miller.

"Yes, Your Honor—sir," Miller stammered before he sat down to a scowling Gomez.

"Good time for lunch. See you all back here for Ms. Meckelson's rebuttal at 1:30 p.m.," Fields said.

The gallery emptied, except for Victor, who waited for the courtroom to empty. When he was alone, he walked up to the defense table and sat in Gomez's chair. He looked around. No one in the room, save him. So, he rolled up his sweater sleeve to take off the duct tape holding Morel's special pill for Gomez. Looking around one final time, he reached under the defense table and taped the pill to the table's underside, right where Gomez always sat. Then he left. The hallway was empty as he made his way to the elevator and the posh cafeteria below.

*****

An hour and a half later, it was Meckelson's turn to tie a bow on her case.

Dressed in a dark green St. John's suit, white linen blouse, her highest heels and a red silk scarf, Meckelson strode to the podium and stepped up on the 3-inch platform the court provided for the tiny prosecutor. Tiny but fierce.

"Defense would have you blame a young woman-- barely of age--for masterminding a caper Gomez had been plotting for ages. Mr. Miller would have you picture a Bonnie and Clyde duo. In reality, it's more of a Shirley Temple and Clod. Puhleeeezzzz. Your common sense will pull you away from that nonsense.

"Yes, she faces sentencing in this case and consideration for leniency based on her truthful testimony. Judge Fields and my office will be the judge of her candor. But you good folks should concentrate on the avalanche of evidence that points to this man," Meckelson said, pointing her right index finger like a weapon at Gomez, who looked back into the gallery.

"Don't look back there for help, Mr. Gomez. None there. And none on this side of the gate. The testimony of Elly Ortiz, Agent Ochoa, Letty Diaz and Detective Halloran has constructed a roadmap Google would envy that leads straight to you. You jurors will hear about 'reasonable doubt' when Judge Fields instructs you after I finish.

"There is no reasonable doubt here. No doubt whatsoever. And I have no doubt you good people will render a just verdict. I ask for a guilty on all counts," Meckelson said, then walked the length of the jury box making eye contact with each juror. "All counts."

Ochoa almost clapped. Halloran nodded to Meckelson. Thoma gave a quick smile.

"All right. The lawyers and I will take some time now to go over jury instructions. It may take some time, so you may have the rest of the day off, and return tomorrow at 10 a.m.," Fields said. The press was already leaving, eager to file their stories and grateful for an early exit.

Halloran, Thoma and Ochoa rose as one and headed for the elevators.

"Now we wait," Halloran said, as the elevator doors closed behind the three. "Cavanaugh's?"

"You betcha," said Thoma.

CHAPTER 63

After Fields delivered the jury instructions the next day, he let the alternates go home but admonished them to stay available in case one of the jurors had to be excused for some reason.

Just before the jurors left, Victor caught Gomez's attention, then put his right hand forward, palm up, then withdrew it into a loosely held fist, nodding slightly to the defendant. Gomez blinked twice, then glanced at the two marshals who were whispering to one of Fields' comely law clerks. Gomez reached under the table and felt the tape with his right hand, stripped it off the bottom and then folded his hands beneath his armpits, securing the taped pill under his left armpit. No one paid any attention to his slight movement.

Moments later, the jurors filed silently out of court. It was just 10:50 a.m.

Inside the jurors' deliberation room, the bus driver launched the discussion.

"I think Miss Mikucki should be the foreman. She has probably the highest level combined of education and dealing with adversity," LeShaun Johnson said.

The accountant quickly seconded the suggestion.

"I know numbers, but she knows life," offered J. K. Toomey, a South Sider from Mount Greenwood.

"Well, thank you, I guess. But this will be a duty rather than an honor. So, I accept. I would think the first order of business is to order lunch," she said, then the 60-something-year-old educator smiled.

"Just joking. Principals have senses of humor, but let's get right to it. I'll pass around these pens and post-its, and you can all anonymously vote G for guilty, NG for not guilty, and U for unsure."

Everyone nodded agreement as the pens and paper circulated around the long oblong-shaped walnut table.

When the folded notes were passed back to Mikucki, she read them silently, then announced in a firm voice:

"Eleven G's, one U, and no NG's," she said. "It's a start. Let's hear from the unsure first."

The grad student opined first. "I just wonder how Elly spent so much time with the defendant and could not give a positive ID."

"She was blindfolded, she testified, and Letty backed that up, and his DNA was on the Mac-10, and the gun was discovered along the path that Halloran chased him," Mikucki said.

"Don't forget Ochoa also identified him," the bus driver added. Several other jurors said, "That's right."

Before lunch was ordered, one of the marshals knocked on the door to interrupt the jurors.

"His Honor wants you all to return to court. You can leave your notebooks and pens here," the marshal said.

The bus driver muttered softly, "What the fuck?" before joining his fellow jurors as they followed the marshal back to court.

* * * * *

Sitting at a table for four at the Greek Islands Restaurant on Halsted, Halloran had just ordered moussaka when his phone buzzed an alert from "GM," that read "Fields just summoned all parties and the jury back to court. No reason given." He held it up so Ochoa and Thoma could read Meckelson's text.

"Fucking A? They just went back," Thoma said.

"Usually, the judge would say the reason, like 'the jury has a question.' Right?" Ochoa joined in

"Let's head to Dirksen," Halloran said.

"Little strange, eh?" said Ochoa to the more experienced Halloran. "Yup," Halloran summarized as he drove quickly east on Jackson, over the Kennedy bridge.

At Dearborn, he turned left, and then left again to park illegally on Adams. The three marched in quickly and flashed their credentials before heading to the elevator.

They met Miller at the elevator door, then rode silently up 25 floors, all eager to learn the reason for the extraordinary summons.

* * * * *

Judge Fields was not wearing his robe. He was only wearing his blue dress shirt, suit slacks and his signature red bowtie and maroon suspenders. He faced the jury box and explained.

"There's been an unfortunate development. The defendant somehow got ahold of some drugs apparently laced with a highly toxic level of fentanyl that he took shortly after he arrived back in his cell at the MCC. There he convulsed and lapsed unconscious within minutes. He was rushed to Northwestern's ER but efforts to revive him were unsuccessful, and he was pronounced dead shortly after 12 p.m.

"So, any verdict you were about to reach is now a moot point," Fields told the jury. "His guilt was not proven under the law while you still deliberated. The U.S. Marshal, the MCC and the FBI under the guidance of the U.S. Attorney's Office are all investigating. But as to you good people, I want to thank you for your service and for paying close attention to all the evidence.

"This is not the conclusion anyone involved was seeking, but it is just that: A conclusion. Thank you again, and you can go home and resume your lives. You are free now to discuss the case, but you are also free to refuse to discuss the case with the media. Your choice. The marshals will escort you out once you have gathered your belongings," Fields said, then stood and returned to his quarters.

CHAPTER 64

In the corridor outside the courtroom, Meckelson asked the whole support team to join her in her office's conference room. Once gathered, she began in a soft voice after Halloran, Ochoa, Thoma and Gorham followed her in. Egan was already there waiting.

"Anyone have a guess how this happened?" Meckelson asked.

"My bet is the gang wanted to silence him before he could try to cut a deal before sentencing. It was crystal clear he was going down," Ochoa said.

"The Cobras didn't want asshole running his mouth to you or to us at CPD. And I have a sneaking suspicion how they got to him," Halloran said. "I'm sure you noticed our fleet future felon, young Victor, sitting in the rear seats for much of the trial. Right?"

"Sure, a kid that age stuck out like a sore thumb, but he could never get close to Gomez. The marshals kept a close eye on Gomez, and the courtroom was packed every day," Ochoa said.

Then five minutes later they all adjourned their meeting to gather in SAC Macel's office.

"I don't expect any of you who worked this case to feel sorry for this scumbag defendant, but we can't even hint that we are going to give this less than the full court press to find out how he got this fatal dose. Clear?" Macel said, meeting the eyes of each party. None blinked.

Halloran broke the momentary silence of the still-stunned group.

"Sir, I have an idea that somehow that kid Victor, the courier of the ransom in the halls of the Daley Center, may have had a hand in this, but I stress the word 'may'. I just saw him in court during the trial and thought it strange. Then he was sitting alone when the court emptied before Geri's close," Halloran said.

Macel raised his right palm.

"Thank you, Detective. But we will handle it from here. It's clearly federal, so you, Thoma and Egan can leave this mess to us," Macel said, nodding to the conference room door.

"Thank you, Agent Macel. You have all our numbers in case you want one of us," Egan said, then stood and headed to the door. Halloran and Thoma followed.

They walked wordlessly to the elevator beyond the security window. Inside the elevator alone as the doors closed, Thoma practically yelled, "What in the holy fuck?"

"Jane, it's clearly federal, and I get the heebie-jeebies in that building. So, color me a happy guy," Halloran said.

As the elevator door opened on the ground floor, Egan smiled.

"What a shame. We can all be proud of the work we did, and you can bet, Mike, that Chief Ortiz won't be in mourning," Egan said.

"True that. I got to go to 35th Street and tell Syl myself. Jane, I don't think I'll need you."

"Roger that, Hal. Less time at HQ for me, the better," Thoma said.

Egan marched off to her Crown Vic on Dearborn to head to 26th Street. From her car, she texted Halloran.

"Tufano's at 7?"

Halloran had just started the car when he saw the text.

He answered with a thumbs up.

Then Ortiz called. She beat him to the punch.

"Mike, I just heard. How in the whole fucked-up world did this happen?" Ortiz asked.

"I got my money on our little Victor somehow slipping a fent-laced pill to him. How? Up to the feds, Macel made that clear," Halloran answered.

"Well, it couldn't happen to a worse piece of shit. And no doubt we will be crossing paths with young Victor soon—that is, if the feds don't nail him with this. Great work by the whole team. Can you stop by for dinner tonight to celebrate?" Ortiz asked.

"Grant me a rain check, Syl. Okay?"

"Don't be a stranger and get back to me next week to set a date. Elly wants to hug you. Joe, too," laughed Ortiz.

Back home, he flipped the keys to George the garage attendant and told him he'd be back for it at 6:30 p.m. Inside the massive building overlooking the north end of the Outer Drive, he was pleased to find a mostly empty pool, per usual except for a grampa playing in the shallow end with a granddaughter. Halloran quickly changed into his suit and swam for 20 minutes in the far left lane, contemplating the successful case and his upcoming date with his favorite prosecutor.

Refreshed, he threw on khakis, a white button-down oxford shirt and a blue blazer before grabbing his strong box to extract a surprise for Egan. Driving out of the garage onto Sheridan, he slipped a disc in with a collection of favorites, leading with Aliotta Haynes Jeremiah's Lake Shore Drive.

"There ain't no road just like it, anywhere I found, heading south on Lake Shore Drive, heading into town," Halloran joined in as he entered the Drive off Bryn Mawr bound for Tufano's.

"Just you and your mind and Lake Shore Drive..." Halloran sang softly as he lapsed into deep thought as he whisked by the Wilson Avenue exit.

CHAPTER 65

After turning over the keys to the Jeep to the valet in front of Tufano's at the obscure Vernon Park Place locale in Little Italy, Halloran was greeted inside by manager Joe.

"Hey, Mike. Been awhile. Gonna be alone or joining someone?' Joe asked.

"I'm early. Got a place in back kind of quiet? ASA Egan will be joining me," Halloran said.

Joe nodded as he raised his right index finger in the direction of veteran waitress Tina.

"Mike, how ya doin'?" Tina asked.

"Sneakin' by," Halloran replied with a quote Marlon Brando used in "One-Eyed Jacks" back in the day.

"Gotta be a bit sneaky to catch the bad guys, eh?" she replied as she walked Halloran to a table for four in the southwest corner of the restaurant, just in front of the large partitioned private dining room reserved for special occasions, like police and prosecutor retirements.

As he followed Tina, he nodded to a few young beat cops in uniforms that revealed they were 12th District guys. He then spied retired CPD Superintendent Frank Klein dining alone late and their eyes locked. Halloran stepped off Tina's path to walk over to the retired boss to pay his respects.

Klein was a cop's cop who worked his way up from a beat Patrolman to Superintendent. Along that career path, he'd been Halloran's boss when they both worked at the busy Area 4 on the West Side.

Not standing but putting aside his tiramisu, Klein extended his hand as Halloran approached.

"Mike, good to see you. Catch any bad guys today?" he asked.

"They catch themselves, boss. You know that. But a few largemouth bass have landed in my net in recent weeks," Halloran replied, giving the stout, sitting boss a firm shake.

"I read about the Lynch case. Great work. I remember hearing about that when I was a teenager," Klein said. "But I won't keep you. Always good to see you."

At that tacit dismissal, Halloran nodded before replying "Same here, boss."

After ordering a Peroni from Tina, he was left with his thoughts, and his mind started playing an old Cole Porter song's lyrics. "And though, I'm not a great romancer, I'm sure that she's bound..." and then the lovely Mary Kay Egan waltzed in and plopped down opposite the detective, dressed in a white Irish knit sweater, Levis and black pumps.

"Penny for your thoughts, Officer Halloran," Egan asked, her blue eyes twinkling atop a broad sparkling smile.

"Well, my thoughts don't come that cheap, counselor, but I have been doing a bit of thinking lately," he said, his meaty right hand reaching across the table to grasp Egan's left hand. She immediately sensed the mood had shifted as her smile faded from wide to pensive.

"Is everything all right, Mike" she asked, slightly squeezing Halloran's hand.

He glanced around for a second to make sure no one was left within hearing distance.

They locked eyes for a moment before Halloran spoke.

"Mary Kay, we've known each other for a long time now. Had some great times together, like the same vacation spots, agree on the important things. So, I'm wondering..." he paused, stood up, reached to his rear pocket and withdrew a small red velvet box, and then dropped to one knee, the good one.

"I love you, Mary Kay, and would be honored if you would make an honest man of me and be my wife, till death do us part," Halloran said, opening the red box to reveal his grandmother's diamond ring.

"Oh, Mike, my sweet, sentimental soulmate, I thought you'd never ask," Egan said, dropping to her knees to give the nervous detective a huge hug and a prolonged kiss.

At this, Tina, Joe, the two uniforms, all began clapping. Klein was in the corridor between the bar and the restaurant and turned to see what all the clapping was about. He then joined in the small reverie and shouted:

"Perfect."

Halloran and Egan stood as one.

"Let's see if it fits," Halloran said, slipping the heirloom on to Egan's left ring finger. It was a little tight but Egan licked her finger and forced it down.

"Would you mind if we went to tell my mother about this after dinner? She'll be thrilled that you've snatched me from the jaws of spinsterhood," laughed Egan.

"Of course," Halloran replied, still clutching Egan's left hand as they sat down amid the still lingering applause.

* * * * *

At 82, Bridget Fergus Egan walked with a cane, but that and her pure white hair were the only signs of aging.

She heard the doorbell ring at her neat off-white stucco bungalow near the corner of 105th Street and Bell Avenue and wondered who might be disturbing her peace at this late hour.

When she opened the door, she spotted her middle child, Mary Catherine, holding hands with an enormous man she'd heard about over the years. Though she came over from Galway at the age of 9, she still had a bit of a brogue and clung to the old ways.

"Ye are welcome," the widow said, and swung wide the solid oak front door.

Egan dropped Halloran's hand and swept in for a quick hug, then stepped back and held her engagement ring a foot under her mother's still-sharp eyes.

"We're engaged," Egan gushed.

The old lady stepped aside from her daughter and took three cane-aided steps to wrap her arms around Halloran. Never a hugger, Halloran nevertheless reached down to deliver a gentle embrace to his future mother-in-law.

"I love your daughter and will take good care of her," Halloran promised.

"Stand side by side," she ordered.

Halloran's 6'5" positioned himself to the right of the 5'10" Egan.

"Foirfe (perfect)," the octogenarian approved in her native Irish, then in English. "God bless."

-30-

EPILOGUE

A month after the sudden conclusion to the Gomez trial, Halloran was back at his post at Area 3 when his phone vibrated to signal a text.

"Can you come see me at HQ tomorrow morning?" Syl texted succinctly.

Halloran responded. "What time?"

"10 a.m." Ortiz answered.

The next morning, Halloran sat in the waiting area outside his old partner's inner office. Ortiz soon emerged and waved Halloran in.

"Morning. What's up?" Halloran asked.

"A lot. Take a seat, Hal. The new mayor is going to name me superintendent tomorrow at an 11 a.m. City Hall press conference. And I'm going to need a new Chief of D's. You," Ortiz said, locking eyes with her old partner and longtime friend.

"Now just listen," she ordered quickly. "It's an incredible waste of talent and smarts to leave you out on the street looking into old cases. There is no one whom I trust more or believe can make the Detective Division the best in the nation but you. You'd be sitting where I'm sitting, and Mike, you're too old to be chasing bad guys down dark alleys."

"Geez, Syl. You know how I feel about ordering guys around..." Halloran began.

"Mike, I need you, and you are perfect for this. Your deputy can handle the paperwork and issue the orders. And speaking of orders, this will be my first order," Ortiz said with finality.

The next day, Halloran stood uncomfortably in uniform behind the mayor as she introduced Ortiz as the next superintendent.

Politics being what it is in Chicago, Ortiz persuaded Halloran to take as his deputy an African-American lieutenant from the Rogers Park District, a highly decorated 20-year vet who survived a shootout with the Gangster Disciples. They knew each other only by reputation. She handled the paperwork and politics, and Halloran inserted himself into cases that interested him.

* * * * *

While out on bond awaiting sentencing, Lupo took his ill-gotten gains and escaped to Zihuatenejo to open a bar he called El Mercado Abierto, "the open market" in English, which is what the Cobras ran on the West Side.

The DEA and CPD concluded Operation Abierto six months later and completed a sweep of the Cobra's West Side safe/operations houses. They snatched up Victor, by then an adult in the eyes of the federal government, as he was between pickups, laden with coke and cash. He sang like a canary and told the feds just where they could find Lupo. He was arrested in Mexico on a UFAP warrant a few days later and was looking at more than 20 years in a fed joint.

Victor would testify against him and Morel and receive a deferred sentence, a new identity, and a new home on the West Coast.

The remnants of the now-leaderless Cobras split up Little Village corners and depended on making their side deals with the Gangster Disciples to continue to pour poison onto the streets of Chicago and nearby suburbs.

* * * * *

Egan was appointed to fill a vacancy on the First District Appellate Court of Illinois. A month into her new post, her fertility doctor informed her that one of the eggs she had frozen at age 29 had been impregnated by one of Halloran's swimmers.

On March 17, "little" Patrick Egan Halloran was born at Northwestern Medicine Prentice Women's Hospital, a very healthy 10 pounds, 2 ounces stretched over 23 inches. Mother and child were healthy, and the ecstatic dad predicted they had just produced the next generation tight end for Notre Dame and the Bears. Mom said her son had a great name to run for a judgeship.

The End

ACKNOWLEDGMENTS

This sequel book sprang from my years as the press guy for the Cook County State's Attorney's office, but much of it traces to my 28 years as a reporter in Chicago, chasing cops, fires, thugs and any witness who would stand still for a few questions in person or on the phone.

So many thanks to the hardworking prosecutors and police I dealt with and who trusted me to interpret their work to a skeptical press and for stories I used for this book. They will hopefully understand certain liberties with the law I took to facilitate the narrative.

Specifically, I would like to thank Assistant U.S. Attorney Sheri Mecklenburg, John Kupper, former media adviser to the Cook County State's Attorney's Office, retired Chicago Police Chief of Detectives Eugene Roy and former Chicago Tribune ace copy editor Ross Werland for his editing skill.

Lastly but most importantly, I want to thank my family for their patience and encouragement through the years of stopping and starting novels. Not surprisingly, as they and these novels grew old together, my children, Katie and Mike, found time to guide me legally and electronically as they forged admirable careers as attorneys. And, of course, my wife, Janice, who held my hand throughout and caught numerous errors.

ABOUT THE AUTHOR

John Gorman started his journalism career in 1972 at the storied City News Bureau of Chicago after serving in the Peace Corps in India. He joined the Chicago Tribune in 1974. He spent half of his 26 years at the Tribune as a reporter covering courts, cops and catastrophes and was twice a runner-up for the Pulitzer Prize. He was the first reporter at the scene of John Gacy's home in 1978 after the police began finding bodies buried in his crawl space. As an Assistant City Editor for 13 years, he oversaw the city desk, herding, helping and harassing reporters. Later, he spent nearly a decade as the Communications Director for the Cook County State's Attorney's office. Prior to starting his journalism career, he drove a taxi in Chicago, bartended in Australia, South Africa, and various gin mills in Chicago and traveled through Europe before returning to the U.S. in 1971. He was an All-City basketball player at Loyola Academy and played Division I ball for Xavier University in Cincinnati. His previous novel "Death Before Life" received glowing reviews on Amazon. "Snatch & Catch" is his second *Mike Halloran Detective Novel*. He lives in Hinsdale with his wife, Janice.

Milton Keynes UK
Ingram Content Group UK Ltd.
UKHW020812080824
446708UK00026BA/351